'Choose the marriage-bed or the King of Death!'
Such is the ultimatum from King Iasos to his wilful
daughter. But Atalanta was raised among the beasts
of the wildwood, swift and savage, and has no
intention of being any man's wife: for she has
vowed herself to chastity and to the goddess
Artemis.

Suitors from every kingdom of Greece are gathering
to compete for the hand of Atalanta, among them
Meleager, rash young prince of Kalydon, who has
pledged himself to hunting the sacred boar of
Artemis.

And all the while the gods are trying to find a way
to end human strife and bloodshed, and Hercules
is given the task of organising the very first Olympic
Games.

By the same author

Asgard
Krishna
Jormundgand
Dragon

OLYMPIAD

Nigel Frith

UNWIN
PAPERBACKS

LONDON SYDNEY WELLINGTON

First published by Unwin® Paperbacks, an imprint of
Unwin Hyman Limited, 1988

UNWIN HYMAN LIMITED
15–17 Broadwick Street, London W1V 1FP

Allen & Unwin Australia Pty Ltd
8 Napier Street, North Sydney, NSW 2060, Australia

Unwin Paperbacks with Port Nicholson Press
60 Cambridge Terrace, Wellington, New Zealand

British Library Cataloguing in Publication Data

Frith, Nigel
  Olympiad.
I. Title
823′.914[F]   PR6056.R58
ISBN 0–04–440155–8

Set in 10 on 11 point Times by Grove Graphics
and printed in Great Britain by Cox & Wyman Ltd, Reading

To Robert Booth

Contents

Preface

The epic is an old and sacred form, and it is good that in our age and among the readers of fantasy it can live again as a popular tradition after ten centuries of sleep. One of the techniques of Homer's epics is that of *celestial machinery*, whereby the gods are revealed influencing and directing human affairs. In the epics of *Pangaia*, this technique has been applied to the question of the origins of the modern world.

Oxford 1988

Characters

All the characters in the book are from ancient Greek myth and legend. The story is set in the year of the first Olympiad: 776 BC

Gods

Zeus	the sky-god
Hera	his wife, goddess of marriage
Artemis	virgin goddess of the hunt
Apollo	her brother, god of the sun
Athene	goddess of wisdom
Hermes	messenger-god

Mortals

Meleager	prince of Kalydon
Atalanta	princess of Tegea
'Rhexenor'	a lovely youth
Heracles	the strong-man hero

Other Gods

Demeter	mother-goddess of crops
Aphrodite	goddess of love
Ares	god of war
Hephaestus	the smith-god
Dionysus	god of wine
Poseidon	god of ocean
Lacona	a lake-nymph

Other Mortals

Oeneus	King of Kalydon in Aetolia
Althaea	Queen of Kalydon
Plexippus ⎱ Toxeus ⎰	her brothers, priests of Artemis
Iasos	King of Tegea in Arcadia
Clymene	Queen of Tegea
Dryas	a shrewd hero of Thrace
Acastus	an impulsive hero of Iolcos
Lelex	a lecherous hero of Sparta
Caeneus	an ambivalent hero of Magnesia
Peleus	a doughty hero of Phthia
Ancaeus	a misogynist hero of Arcadia
Damon	an Arcadian shepherd
Thyrsis	another
(Augeias	King of Elis, deposed by Heracles)
Oenomaus	King of Elis, posed by Heracles
Myrtilus	his charioteer
Hippodamia	his daughter
Pelops	her suitor, a fierce hero of Lydia
Trophonius	a one-handed griper from Lebadeia
Koroebus	first victor in the Olympics, a cook from Elis
Nestor	a canny hero of Pylus
Eurytion	another hero of Phthia
Castor ⎱ Polydeuces ⎰	illustrious hero-twins of Sparta
The Delphic Oracle	

THRACE

Bosphorus

Mt Pangaeus

PAEONIA

Hellespont
Troy

Lemnos
Lesbos

IONIA

Mt Olympus

THESSALY

LYDIA

EPIRUS

PHTHIA

Chios

AEGEAN SEA

AETOLIA
Kalydon

Delphi
Lebadeia

BOEOTIA

ATTICA
Athens

Patrae
Mt Erymanthos
Elis
Corinth

ELIS

Mycenae

CYCLADES
Naxos

ARCADIA

Olympia
Pisa

Rhodes

Pylos

Tegea

Melos

Sparta

Thera

IONIAN SEA

CRETE
Mt Ida

OLYMPIAD

PART ONE

Meleager's Hunt

Chapter One

Of untamable Atalanta this tale tells, and of Meleager, the rash-brained hunter, that together in the rivermeads of Alpheus came to compete at the sacred Games of Olympia, at the running and the leaping in the days when the world was young, the year of the first world-uniting Olympics.

For Meleager was seeking a company of hunters from among the princes gathered at the race-track, since far off in his father's kingdom there stormed a shaggy menace, and men he needed to catch the tusky monster. But by the woods of silvery Elis, stalking the dappled game, he fell into the path of the fair virago, unpursuable Atalanta, she whose lovely legs could outstrip any men daring to strip against her.

But first the beast Meleager hunted: what was the savage bane, and how did it come to ravage Aetolia? A giant wild boar was that foe, a furious Titan pig, bristling with mane and armed with man-goring tusks. Sent by Artemis, the animal-goddess, it ransacked the farms and vineyards, serving the furious virgin of the wildwood. But Prince Meleager would not suffer its bitter depredations: he alone of the city sought to hunt it, and so one winter dawn in secret he ordered his men prepare: together they would hunt the bristly killer.

Now while the winter's dark was still sunk deep on the city of Kalydon, and in the palace all were a-bed and slumbering, amidst the stables by the agora the servants prepared for the chase, and warriors eagerly sharpened their hunting-lances. Yet as they worked and prepared themselves, their leader was not there, Meleager, the son of King Oeneus. But to the stables there came in haste Meleager's groom a-running, and one of the hunters called to him and stopped him.

And the hunter cried, 'Ho, lad of the stable, where is your master, boy? It is near the dawn. He should be here to lead us! This prince of yours has mad-brained schemes, and rouses us all to his tasks, but then when the moment comes, he is still snoring! Will you go and wake him, or shall I blow my hunting-horn? If we do not stir ourselves, dawn and the king will catch us!' And at these words the groom stopped appalled and pulled a face of horror, and ran from the stables towards the palace.

But the prince Meleager was still asleep, high in his room off the gallery, where some sounds of the hunt were heard in the darkness. And thus from beneath his prickly blanket lifting up his head, he roused at last with turbulent mind half dreaming. Then hearing suddenly the snorting of horses, he leapt up from his bed, and naked flung across his shoulders a cloak. And fastening it with a golden pin, and pulling the russet wool about him, he looked out from his door across to the city square.

And thus he thought, 'It is near dawn. The hunters are all a-work! Here have I snored like a sluggard! I must to them quickly before the king or my mother, Althaea, awakes, or there will be much trouble brewed by our horses.' And frowning with haste he ran softly down the stairway and into the palace courtyard, where his groom came leading his Thessalian mare. And Meleager leapt on the mare bareback, and clapped her belly with his heels, and her hoofs cast up sparks as they flew into the agora.

'Now, men,' he yelled, impatiently addressing the milling hunt, 'we cannot trot and chatter here all day. Before the sun is up we must hit the hills, and seek in the forest vales for tracks of this snouted monster. I claim the first blow, and the right with my sword of hacking off its head. We shall bear it back stuck on a clutch of spears. Bring the scouts to me, and the peasants who saw the monster last. Though it be to Hell, I shall lead the way!' And Meleager yanked his horse round, the mare snorting in fear, and he rode off to consult with his leaders.

Now high in the sky above great Greece, buoyant upon

the night, in the starry parts of heaven where fly the Greek deities — for ever above immortal Hellas do the immortals wing, watching earth and guiding the steps of men — the virgin Artemis saw this hunt, and Meleager leading his men, and she raged, as they went to the stables to get the rest.

And thus did she cry, 'Wretched prince! Arrogant Meleager, you, you have set these grooms a-working! Well are you known as a youth ungoverned, always braving and scheming, trying high deeds with your swaggering cronies! You imagine to hunt what is sacred to the gods! Untaught boy, foolhardy! Only death will you reap at this enterprise! For this I swear: he who first strikes and kills my sacred Boar: he will not live to see the day ended!' And the goddess like a shaft of lightning flickered down from the heavens, and swooped upon the land of the prince Meleager.

Now the cold was deep and bitter in the slopes of Aetolia, and the frost was on the balconies of Kalydon, as the virgin of the scarlet arrows fell from under the stars, and sought among the slumbering ones of the city. She glided by the stables and square where the men prepared, but all their secret workings she ignored. Instead she came to where two uncles of Meleager had their quarters, priests of her temple: Plexippus and Toxeus. And they lay in their separate homes, snoring in gorgeous sleep. But the goddess whispered in their slumbers.

'Ho, Plexippus, hey, Toxeus! Priests of my temple, will you snore ever at your hearthside? Your deity has been insulted, granddaughter of Titans, Artemis of the hunt, who has plagued your country! I tell you expect greater plagues, if your nephew has his will. Ay, Meleager, the rash-brained: he is hunting this morning! He seeks to kill the Boar-Giant, sacred beast of penance. Penance enough will follow, if he succeeds!' So spoke the goddess, and the priests arose both troubled, and hurried to do her bidding.

But when the goddess had whispered these words, like a white owl, crescent-horned, she looped from the window and up to the temple-top, and here did she peer below, and

5

study with swivelling head the frosty roofs and curling smoke of the city. The clatter of waking hoofs leaving the stables she heard, and the panting of eager dogs, quick-scented, and then there came hunters with spears, their horns slung over their shoulders, as the day lapped still the mudbanks of the night.

Yet glimmering through the colonnades, as the sky grew grey above, with murmuring voices there came a line of torches, and Oeneus, the king, with ribbon-bound brow, and ringleted beard, came forth staring with dismay. Behind him marched the priests of Artemis, Plexippus and Toxeus, bristling with religious indignation. And the king's party came one way, as Meleager trotted forth the other, and the two confronted each other between the buildings.

'My son,' then said King Oeneus sadly, 'wherefore this benighted flight? Do you seek to steal secretly from the palace? Your uncles here, the sons of Thestius, they have roused me at dawn. Surely their fears cannot be true? Do you seek to try strength with the divine beast of penance? Is not this hubris challenging the gods?'

'Ay, it is!' then cried Toxeus, stabbing his finger forth. 'What would you expect from this rash-brained bully? Ay, and all these louts on horseback! He has roused them with some high words, and he leads them all forth to commit mass sacrilege. It is not for nothing people mutter that his father was Ares! He is mad enough to be the son of any war-god! But we want no wars! This Boar was cast on us by the goddess Artemis, because our king neglected her sacrifice. We must suffer it till she lifts it. To go against it would bring us ruin. Pull them off their horses. Pull them down, enemies of the state!'

Now when Meleager heard these words red rage flashed in his brain, and he reared his horse staggering back on her haunches, and his spear he twirled, and flinging it forth split the beam above Toxeus' head, so that the thud and quiver brought a fearful silence. Wherefore Meleager cried in anger, 'An evil tongue and a bitter brain: always, Toxeus, you open your mouth for poison! Insult me if you will, but spare my

6

parentage, or by the gods, your paunch I'll rip, and throttle you with your own entrails!'

But the other uncle held out his hands, and said, 'Nephew, you have strong arms, but as for policy you had better leave that to your betters. Well is it known your pride and abruptness leave you few friends, and those you lead are rather cowed than faithful.'

Then Meleager cried, 'These hunters are faithful. You need not trouble about their feelings. They are my men and they will do what I say!' And thus he swung about his horse, and sought to spur on his men, but all of them had turned to look up to the gallery.

For the steeps of blue hung silent above the frosty forest, as there echoed the clatter of the city-gate being opened. The crows that pecked about the fields were scattered in alarm, and the doves flew off with fear over the farms. Through the smoke of brands and braziers then, with fluttering robes of black, bearing a flaming torch of her own, there stood upon the gallery the queen, Althaea, mother of Meleager, staring about with black eyes blazing.

'There is in my power,' she cried to the crowd, 'as most of you know, always the means to override Meleager. Always within his mother's hands lies his fate and life, and woe would be the day that he forgot it. I hear my son is again in madness! He goes against my express demands! Well, as ever I have that which stops him. He rouses the fury of all of us here with rashness and pride. In Meleager's skull indeed is not brains but flames! But see his defeat!' And Althaea stopped, and reaching in her robes, lifted up a bundle for the people to see.

A violet gift, a wrapping was it of mysterious weave, mauve silk bound round a box she held up high. Then did she cry, 'You all do know what I bear in this casket. See, in the frosty sunrise a purple talisman! By this long ago I saved Meleager — you most do know the story, and for those who do not, let it stay a secret — but in here lies his means of life. Destroy but this fragile object and you destroy him, send him to the bitter shores of Hades. So

7

hear me, Meleager, and harken my warning: I shall cast this to the flames, if you ride forth this morning to hunt the Boar!'

Now Meleager, as all looked upon him, spat in anger to the ground, and sat panting on his steam-breathed steed. And he debated in himself whether to cry forward to death, or whether to heed the words and threats of so many. But now there came a voice within him, bidding him to quiet, and the orders of reason ran forth before him. So he turned his horse, and rode past the columns of the market-place, and went through the echoing portico to the stables. And Althaea cried in triumph, as her son gave way, and the huntsmen stirred, cowed with their hounds, in the agora.

And when the goddess Artemis saw this, rejoicing with hoots like an owl, she launched herself from the painted temple-top, and looped white-winged away from the town of tiles and trellises, happy with all, then shot over the sea. For far off in Crete, on the Mount of Dicte, where the white cloud-cattle graze, Zeus, the sky-father, bided her answer to his summons, for some time since he had sent for her on business concerning strife-torn Hellas, and there impatiently he stayed her coming.

Yet Meleager, having left the square, raged with exasperation, and quitting his horse, ran again up the stairs, and into his room he went, banging the door, to sit stunned on the bed, tormented to hear his troops thudding back towards the stables. And plunged in dismay, he sat with his hands knotted together before him, his russet cloak thrown back in fury from his bare chest, and he sighed and sighed, and groaned in his soul, shaking his gold-locked head, staring down at his bare feet on the stones.

And Meleager said, 'Alas, why in my rashness do I not halt for but a moment, take calm thought, and plan my deeds under the light of reason? For had I but thought, I would have told my huntsmen to assemble at the edge of the pine-forest, and to find me there in secret with their hounds. But no, fire-hearted, I had to meet and shout to them in the very agora, giving time to my mad mother, and

8

those timid priests! Oh, wretch that I am, to be so bound in, so vulnerable to a woman's will! Why, so it is all my schemes are tempered. I must abroad, in another country prosper, for here there is not any but knows of the power she holds over my days!' And Meleager rose, and went from his room, and looked out over the city, and the huntsmen were gone, and the marketmen raising their stalls.

Chapter Two

Now when Artemis arrived in the warmth of the winter morning upon the sea-churned shores of Crete, she found Zeus waiting gloomily for her in his red-pillared palace overlooking the mysterious cave of Dicte. Here was it long ago, Rhea, the mighty mother, flying from the blood-lust of Kronos, hid the little son which the prophecies had foretold would be the downfall of his father. By the nymphs of Ida was he fed on honey, and lest the murderous Kronos overheard him, the dancing Curetes, the children of the rain, would leap and noisily clash their swords on their brazen shields. But Zeus sat brooding now, his hyacinthine locks, black as night, tumbling on his blue robe.

Wherefore Artemis approached him, and smiling said, 'All-father Zeus, hail, O defeater of the cruel Titans! Obedient to your summons I have flown here across the wintry sea from the mainland of busy Hellas. I hear that you are talking with each one of your children, and are much troubled by men's warfare. Apollo did I see hereby, and messengers come and go, bringing news of the latest conflicts. Indeed, father, the rough Achaians and savage Dorians are ever bent on battle. Lust and greed run riot. What would you then with me? Men are pestiferous creatures. Surely I would sink them all in the ocean!'

Now as Artemis sat by Zeus, cajoling him with her hand, for she was sweet and maidenly enough with her father, there came through the door bright Phoebus Apollo, her brother, and his blond locks shed light all about him. Wherefore he opened a leopard-legged chair, and throwing on it a purple cushion, he sat with naked body bronzed and gleaming, and cupping his one knee in his hands, he leaned back and smiled, nodding his head at his sister.

But Zeus sighed and said, 'Daughter, you have surely seen war, the war which is rife in Elis. The troops of men have clashed by the city itself, and Heracles, my dear son, has led the warriors. He, alas, has had to retire, his forces were turned back, his own brother has been killed in the fray. And my heart grieves for him, as he lies sick with disease, which so far none has been able to shift from him. My daughter, you have the skill in your fiery darts of sickness: go to the hero and take from him his fever. For the sake of your father now, fly with your skills to the land far off, heal Heracles and strike down the Eleians!'

Yet Artemis sighed, and said, 'Surely will I not. And why do you ask me especially, father? For with a shake of your locks you could hurl Augeias into the ocean, defeat Heracles' foe and his fever. Why then do you hesitate? Merely because you fear to upset the other gods, and you would rather your dirty work was done by you. children. Well, monarch of the sky, I hear your words, but I heed them not, for truly I have no patience with any of these fighters. Too far, too fast, too greatly, too stupidly do men waste their might in warfare. We goddesses are firm in this opinion. Put a stop to these battles. It is a waste of human virtue!' Thus Artemis concluded, and Phoebus Apollo smiling nodded at her speech, and stared with ironic eyes at his father.

But there came now a nymph to the terrace, bedraggled and distraught, a dryad of the type of auloniad. With dripping chiton, and speckled with wood-moss, she tiptoed fearfully into the presence of the immortals. Then did she speak, 'Excuse, great father, a humble lass flown from the land, but a long journey here have I made across oceans, and I have come with an urgent message for my forest-mistress, and here at last I have found the goddess Artemis! Oh mistress, mistress, come quick now. In Arcady there is danger. Your devotee, Atalanta, is in peril.

'It is well known that in Tegea the virgin princess of the city has become of all your devotees a favourite. This beautiful and long-legged huntress, swifter than all other mortals, has kept herself a virgin in your honour. Long ago

11

when she was born, her father from spite of her sex cast her out cruelly to die in the forest, but luck was with her, and your deity saw that a bear lumbered by, and by that she-bear was she suckled and cared for. Being found by shepherds at last she was saved and returned to the repentant palace, and the king and queen took again their daughter to them. But with such upbringing it is hardly surprising that the girl mistrusts men, loves the woods, and shows a wild and a savage nature.

'Yet who knows not also that with her sisters, she is pledged to virginity, and also has a prophecy guarding her: for it was spoken among strange secrets whispered about her cradle, that whoever should take her maidenhead should soon see death. These prohibitions have been kept secret from the populace, but we of the woods know them well. Proud is her spirit, and never to men's embraces would she slip. Such stains of base servitude are hated by us of the woods!

'What then is the news I bring you here? Dire it is and horrible! Goddess, goddess, come quickly and protect her. For this very wretch, her father, King Iasos, he that first turned her out, has decided that he will give her in marriage! Imagine it, great forest-goddess! Atalanta married to a man! Is the whole thought not a disgrace?'

'It is indeed!' Artemis cried. 'Nor can I delay here further. For from hateful men I must fly to save my girl! Zeus, my father, farewell now. Good brother, good bye. Another time perhaps we may talk of these matters.' And the goddess sped forward then, and taking the dryad by the hand, launched herself like an eagle into the air.

Now when these women had gone from the heaven, Zeus turned to his son and said, 'Lord Apollo, what firebrands these women are! Are women not meant to be amenable, ductile and considerate? They accuse us of brawling, but they are just as bad! They complain of men's wars, and truly I also grieve over needless slaughter, but is not the female more vengeful than the male? And where will it lead, this

12

female vigour? Are not things upturned? Will it not be a deluge follows this ferment?'

And Phoebus thought at this, and for a while his grey eyes stared at nothing, but then he turned to his father and said, 'Of the future who can tell, but the sibyls, my Oracle at Delphi, and yet to ask them is also to ask of a woman? The times are troubled: great power is there, and strength overburdening to men, and some way we must find to contain these impulses. Yet for all that, I think not, Zeus, that these things presage an end. Rather do they lead to great feats forward. If we can but hold the reins in check with a little wisdom, then could we see a Golden Age for Hellas.'

'Where buy we wisdom?' then said Zeus. 'Of that our women could provide, were they not dashing about after their champions!'

But now there hurried towards the two gods another nymph from the mainland, a dryad of the pines, bedecked with green needles and pine-cones. And this nymph cried, 'Great gods, give me hearing. I come seeking the lady Artemis. For I have dire news for her of Kalydon. Only this dawn she visited it, and scattered there a rebellion of illegal hunters among the hot youth of the city. But now I have fierce things to tell her that will cause her much rage, and surely do I dread what the goddess will do.'

And Apollo looked at her, and said, 'Well, nymph, this minute has your mistress gone, and there is no hope now of heeding her wishes. Yet if you will tell to me your news, I will return with you, and perhaps in Kalydon I may act for my sister. What is it occurs there?'

'The prince,' replied the nymph, 'rash-headed Meleager, he was quelled in his quest this morning, but now in secret, impervious to his put-down, he is acting against her wishes by once again planning to go hunting! Alone this time he seeks to ride, armed with spears and arrows, to hunt the Giant Boar in the wild hills. And if the goddess does not come, her beast will be affronted. There is no end to the madness of these men!'

The nymph finished pantingly, and Phoebus Apollo

13

smiled upon her worried face and quietly said, 'This will be best dealt with by me. For in this matter I can quell Meleager as well as any sister, and prevent the hero from upsetting the gods by overweening acts. Lead me to Aetolia. Let us see how the prince proceeds. All will be well, nymph. Do not you fret.'

And the kindly god then took the nymph, and smiling back at his father, flew from the terrace and hastened westward towards Hellas.

Artemis and her dryad, however, hurtling across the morning seas, in the misty air that bred with the chill of winter, came to the mountainous mainland of Hellas, where the grey ranges step down to the azure gulf beyond the Argolid. Climbing in the steepy blue, they rose up above the hills, and crested the silver peaks that bound in Arcady. Glistering in the clear winter air, the swoops and gulleys of virgin ice dazzled white in the motionless world, till the shriek of the unleashing eagle should upon the shuddering pines plunge down, the avalanche engulfing.

Now in the city of Tegea, where the road winds on the plain beside the temple of Athene of the grind-stones, the maiden devotees of Artemis were hurrying in the palace, with their woollen cloaks pulled tight about them. From the wide hall they streamed in panic, and crossing the courtyard, hastened up the stairs and along the gallery. When they came to the princess's room, fearfully they burst into it, to where Atalanta, the oval-faced, sat with her peacock arrows, sharpening them on a little whetstone.

And the virgins of the forest-goddess came to her and said, 'Atalanta, it is true: your father has decreed the horror! Even now the messengers leave to make the winter journey, threading on foot and sail through the crags of Hellas! You know the decree? He has sent the messengers to every kingdom in Greece, summoning this very spring princes to the court. They are to come and bid for you, to offer him deals and alliances for your hand, to come and eye you, like some cow at the market! What greater insult: a horde of young men ogling you with their eyes, sizing your parts, and slapping their gold on the table! And this spring too! I died with horror. Yet Iasos, the King, is implacable! Nor has your mother spoken against it. On the altar of marriage you are to be offered, despite all your vows to Artemis, your sylvan soul, and your upbringing among the woods.'

Now when the virgins had cried their news, Atalanta looked up, and her face was dark with anger. But she did not reply to them, only rose from her chair, and fetched a bright-bordered cloak from beside a smoking brazier. This did she scarf about her, and went into the air, and strode long-legged across the courtyard, to burst open the doors of the hall, which swung on their bronze hinges, and let her pass in among the counsellors and warriors. She found King Iasos seated on a lion-legged throne, harkening to the accounts of the season.

And Atalanta said, 'Father, if such you can be called, who have so thoroughly misused a daughter, have I not made it plain enough? I am not of your city-dwellers, nor do I accede to the ways of men. My upbringing was secret and savage: among the animals I was raised, and ran free in the echoing wildwood. How might such a one tamely submit to the indignities of marriage, and be borne off by a pranked-up gallant to a slavish home? No, rather would I choose to fight. Or else in the dead of night, rouse up to stab my would-be husband. Therefore King Iasos, I bid you beware. Do not risk destruction by seeking to have me cast upon a husband.'

Now King Iasos was wrath to hear this, and looked up from his throne and said, 'Do you dare to come and interrupt our councils? Is it not plain that you are a girl, to be kept in the women's quarters, not to go braving about like some man-killing warrior? You know nothing of the state, girl, nor anything of our perils. There are Tegeans even now fighting with Heracles! The wrath of those opposed is likely to fall upon our heads, if we cannot by policy find some assistance. On these things we have deliberated, and we have come to a plan, and you, my daughter, are to be

15

a help to your country, for we have made in order to forge
an alliance with our neighbours, a decree that you, ingrateful
one, are to be married. To the princes of our neighbours
you are to be offered, and they called to bid, and what is
offered given consideration. And you, though nurtured by
a bear, for this time will be sage. Go back to your room.
Now you have a use, you will be put to it.'

Now when the king had spoken this, all in the hall were
hushed, and Atalanta stood coldly, fierily staring at her
father. But as she stood broodingly thinking of his words
and how to answer them, there entered in flowing robes
Queen Clymene. The queen came to her husband's side, still
carrying in her hand the wool deep-dyed which she had been
winding, and when she stood by the throne, sighingly she
stopped and stared at Atalanta.

Then did the queen speak. 'You need not tell me, my lord,
what words have been spoken. Your face and that of my
daughter says it all. I anticipated as much, for Atalanta has
a morbid fear of marriage, and loves merely to hunt and
dance the choruses with her sisters. Perhaps all girls are so,
for I think in my youth I was much against matrimony, yet
the affairs of state saw me wedded to an Arcadian. And I
have not regretted it, remote though the country is, and un-
tutored its peoples. Wherefore Atalanta, I bid you accept
this sweet ruling. When you see the princes which the fame
of your beauty will bring us, surely you will relent and long
for some handsome youth, with whom you can taste the
delights of Aphrodite.'

'You have a choice, daughter,' then abruptly spoke King
Iasos, 'you can either be married or immured, for I swear
by my counsellors here that if you take not a prince, I will
wall you up in a cave to perish. Either a living bridegroom
take, or the King of Death. Be off, and ponder on the fate
before you. All Hellas is menaced by war. Our city is like
to be taken. An alliance of blood would give our people safety. To think that a stubborn girl should put her fears before
this! Be off, be off, you ingratefulness unparalleled!'

When the king had finished his speech thus, Atalanta

16

stood, once more in harsh thoughtfulness staring at him. And for a while the counsellors looked on her, amazed at her proud bearing, tall, with eyes that blazed like beacons on a headland. On her robe were also sewn eyes like the prow of a ship, yet blazing from her sleeves in radiance. But while they stared at her nervously, Atalanta turned, and with a spring from her lithe thighs, she ran then from the steps of the hall, across the courtyard she fled, through the town, by the blue-painted temple of Athene. And leaving all her sisters behind, did she run along the newly drained marsh-land, and over the wintry stubble towards the hills, where coming to the fir-forest, with solitary berries frosted, she walked till in loneliness she reached her goal.

A deserted temple in the mountains: that was the place she sought, gloomy, and the haunt of forest creatures. A rain-worn curtain flapped across the entrance of that fane, and in the sanctum a bear looked up in wonder. Atalanta drew inside. Beasts did not fear her step, for she was of their kind, and the forest wildness. Rime-covered was the upright image of the wooden goddess, crowned with a crescent moon, and faintly smiling. Atalanta stopped before it, and with her breath steaming fierce, gazed up into Artemis' wooden eyes.

And the princess said, 'Great goddess of the wild, that long has been worshipped in the woods, but especially are the protectress of us in Arcady, hear my prayer now. Let not your servant be cast into the slime. Let not my fire-pure heart be quenched in man's seed. The thought disgusts me! Rather death shall take me, ay, and him who seeks with his lust to defile my body. Yours alone I am, alone, solitary like the wildwood! Artemis, great queen, hear my prayer.' And lifting her hands up in supplication Atalanta sighed, her patterned cloak falling from her heaving breast.

Now quiet was it in the woods, and the sun-clear air brought the bark of the fox from a distant dale. The dipping spruce-branches hung their needles, with spiders' webs rimed over, and the stiff pine-twigs tenderly tinkled with the frost. Hanging then in beams of sunlight, the robes

17

of a divine girl burnt blue and amber out of the air, and a vision of the goddess came, embraced by a wood-nymph, about whose thighs there clung the rimy ivy. In fear did Atalanta freeze, her limbs knitted up in holy dread, and the voice stuck in her throat as the goddess addressed her.

'Hear me, virgin Atalanta,' such were the deity's words, 'mark well the injunctions of Artemis. The plight that you, princess, have come to, this is all known, all found, nor need you pray what needs not to be spoken. The word for your marriage is given. The messengers have gone forth, the princes are summoned to Tegea. But be not afeard at this. Submit to your father's will. Accept his rule, and let the suitors come to you. But when they are all drawn to your palace, they will not prevail, nor they, nor any man shall marry you. When the time of the choice arrives, pray to me again, Atalanta, and then will I reveal my strategy. For no man shall take your maidenhead, without soon finding his death. And there is a way to shame these suitors.'

There came a thunderclap from the blue. The forests shuddered and rolled. Across Tegea the bolt sent the crows scattering. The goddess was gone. And Atalanta surged forth from the fane, and inspired returned through the wintry woods to the city.

Chapter Three

Apollo, meanwhile, had gone in haste across the Corinthian Gulf and spurned the dusty headlands that butted the purple sea. Towards Kalydon he rattled his arrows, and coming to the town, dived down like a cormorant towards the city. As the savage sea-bird, armed with sharp bill, plummets and cuts into the waves, to thrash into the murk after the silver bass, so did the sun-god, falling on Aetolia, as the clouds were massing above, and the high-piled dark frowned on the town. But searching the streets, the god could not find Meleager in the walls, nor his chamber, nor the palace seemed to hold him.

But when bright Phoebus had studied the fields, and seen from the banks of grey, the cart-borne travellers hastening to the safety of the city, gazing back fearfully over their shoulders, for it seemed soon snow would blow in the west wind and drive its drifts upon them, then he saw the hero running along the flat, leading his horse by the bridle, beneath shivering poplars seeking to get clear of the town. And Apollo saw the hurrying prince come to an old orchard wall, and seeing it screened him, stop and look back at the city.

Now when Meleager ducked out of sight, Apollo floated near, and stared as the hero knelt down and undid a canvas bundle, and the god watched intrigued, as he took forth weapons, and laid them ready before him: a club, two well-oiled lances with shining points, a sword set fast in its leather scabbard: all these did he check and handle, his eyes burning bright with hopefulness. A wide-brimmed petasos he set on his head, and looked up at his horse, like a Thessalian traveller over the plains. Next did he take the lances up, and the club, and about his naked waist bind the blade in its scarlet leather, then vaulted onto Thunderbolt, and urging her forward, so did he set forth hunting, while Phoebus Apollo hunted him in turn.

And when Meleager had travelled some way along the level road, where the fields lay fallow under the frost, he came to a sheltered farm which lay before a tree-girt valley whose whitening top led up to a mysterious ridge. By the fence did he alight, and coming to the hut, called in to rouse its farmer. Yet there was no mortal answer. But Phoebus Apollo saw to it that he had some reply, and muffling his locks in a cloak, and with a shambling gait to disguise his great beauty, he in a disguised voice also addressed him.

'Young Prince Meleager,' he said, 'I know you well enough, and the Boar you seek is rootling up trees over that hill-top. Wherefore you can catch him if you ride now by the wood. But indeed better were it to remain at home. For surely you seek a monster far beyond your strength, whose hide cannot be first pierced by the lances of men. The tempest approaches, moreover, and high in the hills snow mantles the ways, and shivering death hangs in the passes. Go home, go home, impetuous youth, bide the words of your mother, or the great Boar will you devour!' And the figure of the god moved into the hut once more. But Meleager rejoiced, and leapt again onto Thunderbolt.

By snow-dusted woods Meleager then cantered, as all lay hushed beneath the cloud. Along the white shores of the vast lake he glided, reflected with the snow-peaks moving upside-down. Up into the hills he climbed, where the streams steamed from underground, and the black bears prowled, scraping the bark from the oak-trees. And Meleager gazed down the wooded valley, as the snow began to fall, and all was quiet and fearful in the mountains.

And Meleager said, 'Why, though I ride excited, how still do I feel, and how secret is this blessed forest! All is untroubled by raving women, and uncles with religious fear! It is almost as if they speak to me, these summits, and these resin-scented temples of the wolf-pack. Oh, to live in these woods like a forester, with a wife to wrap close and snug in the pelts of snow-fox. See, that nestling wood in the whitening valley! How sweet to live there, and bend its trees into a leafy cabin!' And Meleager looked down smilingly at the wildwood by a stream, where the water breathed vapour strangely.

But then the wood moved. It shifted its back and looked up from its drinking. It lifted a steaming snout and sniffed around the summits. And Meleager saw then that fatefully he was beholding the Boar-Giant, and Artemis' sacred beast was before him. How vastly did its bristles rise, much like a ridge of firs, how wide its flanks filled the dale! Meleager's eyes sparkled in his head, his brooding mouth fell open, and musingly still he watched the Boar move away.

But when the hero had woken from his daze, fire was in his heart, and his blood raced and thudded to be at the monster. Urging his mare forward, he snatched up his spears, and held them ready. But the horse was stubborn to ride. Fearfully did the mare start, smelling the beast in the valley. Whinnying round, she refused to make forward. But Meleager angrily jabbed her sides with the blade of his lance, and furious forced the steed down into the glade.

Unnoticing, the browsing Boar made its shaggy way over the ridge, and the bristles of its back were lost in the firs. Meleager thundered by the brook to pursue it. He galloped towards the crest, and over the summit gazed on the widespread ranges. He saw before him nothing but vast, white plains of snow, a landscape bleak of forest and filled with silence. Clattering after, Thunderbolt-borne, galloping by a cliff of icicles, the hero sought the monster in the white world. The mare neighed terrified. Then did he see doggedly trudging through a drift the black back of the Boar sliding forward.

At the neigh of the horse, the Boar raised its snout smoking from the snow, with tusks that menaced the iron sky. The Giant smelt Meleager. With burning eyes it turned, and gave forth a hornlike roar that softly echoed long over the summits. The snow was falling about the crags, teeming with gentle flakes. In spuming white the Boar rushed forward. One spear was cast. The monster plunged on. It reared and plunged in the drifts. The other lance winged and bounced from its back unnoticed. Meleager drew his sword. But the snow now was blazing and swirling now in a blizzard, and neither hunter nor hunted could see the other.

In the cloud of ice, shining like the sun, Meleager then beheld Phoebus Apollo, blond-haired, bronze-limbed, bare in beauty. The god raised his arms, flashing-muscled, and struck forth with his fist towards the Boar bellowing through the mist. The tusks of the beast did Phoebus seize, and twist the Boar from its course, and with his bronze foot he spurned it forth among the snow-drifts. Then did he lash it, driving away the monster from the peaks, and rout it, sealing its path once more with snow.

Phoebus then turned, and frowning at Meleager, in these words did he speak. 'Presumptuous youth, how are you full of hubris! Do you, but one boy, seek to bring down the ferocious bulk of a giant? With your flimsy spears do you credit to bring it harm? Know that its back will never be pierced by the lance of any man, nor will it fall except to a fleet of heroes. Wherefore I tell you: fortunate are you that my sister is hence, for surely had she seen this, you would have perished. Yet hear me, Meleager, if you would seek the means to bring down the Boar, then further than Kalydon must be your journey.

'Know that in Arcady, where peak-ringed Tegea raises its pillared porches, there is a fair-faced, proud princess, Atalanta. Long-legged is she, and loves in the forest to hunt with her sisters. Yet now has her father decreed time for her marriage. To his city therefore he has boastingly summoned from the bounds of Hellas to come compete for his daughter's hand the best princes. And if you would find a band of men to bring down the Kalydon Monster, then there in Arcadia this very spring will you find them. Be off therefore, if you have courage, cross the Corinthian Gulf, seek for hunters, and bring them again to these hills. Should they be men of this age and Hellas, they will rouse to the task. And by these means you may have a hunter's fortune.'

And Phoebus Apollo smiled and faded, and Meleager marked his words, and thoughtful in spirit turned his mare and made homeward.

Chapter Four

Now while these things were progressing on earth, and the winter plying its course, and the pageant-car of the seasons lumbering forward, far off in Ida, the mountain of Crete, where Zeus, the sky-father, had his palace, the company of the gods was gathered together, and they sat on terraces in the sun, enjoying the warmer winds that brought on the speckled springtime. And Zeus looked about the gods with pleasure, surveying the brawny men, and nodding at the beauty of the goddesses.

For there did Hera, the ox-eyed queen, recline on a striped golden couch, wife of Zeus, and goddess of marriage. Beside her there pecked her strange pet, the shimmering-myriad-eyed, the green-shot-feathered and sumptuous-skirted peacock. Much pride and wrath had Hera for her wifehood, and angry was she over Zeus if he should go wandering, but though she frowned about at first with a majestic brow, she smiled when she saw all was satisfactory.

There also was quietly sewing Demeter, the mother of crops, that urges the wheat and barley greenly stirring. She wore black robes of a beautiful sadness, but was crowned with ears of corn, and a torch did she have to light the darkness. In sacred Eleusis was she worshipped devoutly, where cluster the holy pilgrims, ready to taste the mysteries of the goddess. None of those who has ever been there has ever told of the mysteries, and none who has never been has ever heard.

Last of the trio of goddesses on his right was sweet-faced Aphrodite, the goddess of love, inspiring of lust and play. Gaily chatting to Ares was she, the stubborn god of war, and shaking her milky bosom with ivory laughter. Flashing were her intimate eyes, brilliant her crimson lips, silky and glowing was the skin about her. A temple white in Paphos she had, and glittering-citadelled Corinth, attended softly by her sacred prostitutes, and from the copper-veined isle of Cyprus she urged her chariot forth, drawn by doves in the silky sky a-fluttering. Such were the beauties Zeus stared upon, and such that cheered his heart, though deep inside it was wracked by perplexity.

But when he had looked about the goddesses, then did Zeus frown again, and thoughts of trouble once more descended upon him, for opposite him sat smoky Hephaestus, smith-god, and maker of weapons, and over against him Hermes, the messenger of battle, while still there laughed by the love-goddess the boastful and muscled Ares, noisy in wine, and rowdy did he make the meeting.

Wherefore Zeus said, 'Well, gods, we sit here, while over the waves the spring comes, and the earth begins to smell again of flowers. But yet for all the beauty about, and the goddesses' happy laughter, afar off in mainland Hellas are men still wracked by war. To the west of the mainland, where the Ionian Sea lies coolly folding its breakers, and the rain makes the coast green and fertile, there is trouble still in Elis, and men are ever driving their ghosts to Hades. What can we do to stop their wars? Surely they have fought enough! Is there no way men can be strong and live in peace?' And so Zeus spoke, and the gods all thought, and there was a long pause, for surely none of them had a sudden plan.

But then spoke Demeter, and she said, 'Great Zeus, there is much in what you say. The men in Hellas brawl and battle. But we sit here in peacefulness in the rich realm of Crete, and they with their battles seem far away. It is easy for us to forget them. Maybe we should wander in Hellas more, return to the mainland, where once was our power. Here we could sample the fruits of the wisdom of men, to see what they may prophesy, for truly some men are wiser than others. This would I maintain, for now spring comes, it will be well to journey, and I with my torch can light the way.'

Then spoke Aphrodite, 'Yet father Zeus, can we not use wit too? Are the battles of men far beyond our solving? Set us then a task to devise a way of settling men in peace. If we all put our thoughts to it, there may come an answer. For my sake, dear lord, I might say let men fight their battles in bed: in my arts let them strive to prove themselves heroes, for truly the ways of love show men's vigour just as much as war, though your wife, I fear, looking at me askance, disagrees.' And the love-goddess laughed then, for imperial Hera quelled her with a frown, and ignoring her words, turned at once to her husband.

And she said archly, 'Yet, my dear lord, you have only yourself to blame, for I and the goddesses have said all this before, but never did you pay us any heed. Rather have you spurred men on, made them keen for fight, for with battle indeed you breed a host of heroes. And truly your own son, beefy Heracles, he is most offending in this wise, for he has no whit ceased his depredation, but now he has recovered from his wound, battle with bloody hand he wages, as glowering from the back of black-maned Arion, he rouses up the men from Argos and Arcadia and forms an army to attack those who he claims slew his brother.' And with that did the goddess cease, and pluck a grape from a bunch, and pop it in her mouth with satisfaction.

But as the gods sat talking thus, there came strange thunder from the green-shored deep, and the budding land shook with a fever of earthquake. The north seas beyond the coastal range poured vast waves on the beaches, and Knossos the many-tiered was blanched with fright at it. Then from the raging sand-filled breakers there hurried, calming the seas behind him, with dripping trident, Poseidon, sea-divinity, and angrily to the heights of the citadel and through the huge walls he swept, then confronted Zeus and the others with fury.

'The news from Achaia,' he cried. 'have you heard? That bull-rampant stable-cleaner, that bunch-muscled oaf and swaggering lion-tamer: Heracles has set an ambush upon my sacred procession, and the Eleians has he killed that honoured my festival! The sons of Actor, the Molionids, them he has slaughtered both, my protégés, my godsons — how might this outrage be avenged? I come to you, brother, demanding reparation, demanding hardest punishment for this blasphemy! Heracles must be destroyed!'

But up leapt Hephaestus at this speech, and cried, 'No, you old man of the sea, why should such a mighty hero be punished? Punishment enough has Heracles been given with his twelve labours, laid on him by the Delphic Oracle. What he has done, if your news is true, is fair by the rules of war, and is merely deserved by the cowardly Augeias, for he denied to give Heracles his due reward for his task of cleaning the Augeian stables. You might jibe at him: stable-cleaner! but you live in the sea, and you have no need — strange though it seems — of washing!'

And here spoke Ares, 'Ay, let him attack! The hero is mighty in war, and never has earth seen a hardier fighter! He was wounded unfairly, and now recovered, it is his due to battle, and great deeds will he do to make all Hellas ring! Ah, let me see him! He strikes with his shoulder. Thus does he stab and fling! Ah, what a fighter! Oh, let me go and see him!' And Ares now danced about the terrace, fighting, full of fury, until the other gods fell laughing.

But then spoke Demeter. The motherly corn-goddess looked up again from where she sat, sewing calmly a strange mantle with fringe and scales of leather, and the goddess said, 'Why, Zeus, my lofty brother, thus you see how things go, for how can we urge peace when we are so warlike? It is not a question of ceasing merely the battles between cities on earth, but striving to tackle the fount of belligerence itself. Strife is rife. It has ever been so. And when we are guilty ourselves, how can we blame men for battles, attacks, counter-attacks, ambushes? We must set ourselves to gather some wisdom which will hush all conflicts. If we do not, what will become of Hellas? None will have heard in a thousand years of Greece or Athens or Sparta. Our race will be but butchers without a name.' And the goddess ceased then, and all the company were silent at

her words, and brows were wrinkled with the frowns of
thought.

But Zeus then looked up and mildly he gazed, and then
with care and sympathy he addressed the sea-god Poseidon,
and he said, 'My brother, you know well with me that
Heracles is both a son and a favourite, and much have I
cherished and nurtured him through his troublesome days.
Nor can I think that you would have me destroy my own
boy, or that any god should be asked to be so bloody. Yet
as you say, he does rouse battle, and when the fury is upon
him, great sins he incurs in the madness of his strength. I
will think therefore of some further penance, which might
at last bring him quiet, some rigorous task which might still
his eager soul. For surely we gods must not fall out as often
as do men, or else what good has been our mighty victory?'

'Be sure you do it!' said Poseidon at this, and stalked at
once from the hall, before any there might offer him
hospitality.

Now while these blissful deities were debating thus in Crete,
in Achaia was Meleager at his recruiting, for taking the god
Apollo's words, he set forth from his homeland, and left
his city secretly for adventure. His servants he told, but silent
kept from his mother and father, with instructions to give
them news but a week from his departure. And so he rode
southwards and made his way through winding paths to the
sea, and crossed by fishermen's ferry the grey Corinthian
Gulf.

But when he had come to the rocky shores of ancient
Achaia, he stayed not long there gazing back to the northern mountains, but struck inland, and climbed the slopes
along the traveller's pathways, and urged his horse forward
into unknown woods. A week from his home, he found
himself in deep forests and leafy valleys, where the farmers
spoke in accents foreign to his own. And warmer it grew
as the spring came on, and leaves rustled on the trees, and
the swallows were now curving in the air.

By the forested tracks, converging one day, two heroes

he met on horseback, that seemed like him to be of some warrior breed. Wherefore he greeted them, asking their names, and giving them his own without guile, and news of his destination. Wherefore he heard they were Dryas of Thrace, and Acastus of Iolcos, bound both towards the land of Arcadia. And they like him had heard of the contest for the princess's hand, and were making their pilgrimage to Tegea.

Now when Meleager had note of this, he laughed to himself and said, 'So, bold riders, you bid fair for the princess? Yet tell me true: is it wives you want or is it rather adventure? For many men come questing for the sport not the catch.'

Then answered Acastus, 'Adventure me, for tired I grew at home, and news of these battles in Elis attracted me. Wherefore I am game for any contest, as is Dryas also, whether it wins a princess or settles a quarrel.'

'Then follow me after,' said Meleager, 'for I have a challenge of such might that usual heroes would blanch at the sight of it. A monster Boar we have striking the land of unfortunate Kalydon, and I am looking for men to hunt it with me.' So spoke Meleager, and the two heroes liked what they heard, and happily along the track they accompanied him.

Now the swaggering travellers had not gone far, when in the trembling woods, a scream they heard, as if of a pursued woman, and across their path there hurried suddenly a girl in distressed state, and behind her there came hotfoot an eager-eyed hero. When the girl saw the others, she ran another way, but the youth in pursuit of her stopped and smiled at the riding warriors.

And Meleager called, 'What is this urgency? The girl was not to be won. Who are you, brutish youth, seeking rape in the forest?'

And the other replied, 'What business of yours? The girls hereabout run first, but once you have caught them, they do not seek to flee. They may show their heels or turn their backs, but that is not the same.

29

You need to be skilled in these matters to know this.'

'If you are such a woman-killer,' then spoke Dryas with a smile, 'come with us along to Arcady. For there is a princess, long-legged Atalanta: her father has made a decree, calling all noble youths to Tegea to bid for her hand. If you command respect, come seek, if not, go leave us!'

'I'll come with you surely,' said the youth with a laugh. 'My name is Lelex of Sparta, the second to the throne. My brother is pious, but I am wandering by the way. For any adventure count me in. But give me a lift till I have a horse. I lost mine now, but have the coins for another.'

And so Meleager hoisted him up, and let him ride behind him, and pleasantly they fell to chatting on the journey.

And when they had come to the Ladon river, where Erymanthus loomed above, and the budding trees clustered about the overhanging banks, then Dryas said, 'It is not yet high spring, and the time for the wooing is far off. Wherefore we have some weeks till the princess is abiding, yet down to the south there is a glade where Alpheus meets with Kladeos, and beautiful is the spirit of that place. It is called Olympia, and nymphs abide there, and harmony is in its breezes, and idle sport could we have by the rivermeads. Let us haste there now, and seek if other heroes can be won to our cause, and from there go on when the spring is more advanced.' So did the warriors agree to this, and they turned towards the west, and sought the groves of sweet-hilled Olympia.

PART TWO

Atalanta's Race

Chapter Five

Now when the gods had ceased their discussions with no solution to their trouble, but still war roamed the land with none to oppose him, then did the goddesses, Artemis and Hera, leave Ida to wander in the world, and with Demeter seek once more the mainland of Hellas. And when they had come there they parted again, and went on separate ways, and Demeter struck north to visit her sanctum of Eleusis.

When Demeter had been there a day, pondering in her precincts, there came to her grey-eyed Athene, and the beautiful goddess greeted her as she sat in her sanctum, and said how she had walked but now on the sacred road, for Athene had that day to her own city of Athens paid a fleeting visit, and sat awhile on the barren crag of the acropolis. But now did Demeter entertain her, and welcome her for the night, and the two goddesses slept in the temple together.

But when the dawn came Athene desired to wander on again, and Demeter told her of Hera and Artemis, and said that a shelter would wait for her westward in the vale of Olympia, for they both had gone to visit Hera's ancient temple. Wherefore did Athene move on again, along the Corinthian Gulf and across the mountains, hieing towards the Alpheus, and there in good time she came to the forested height beside the stream, and arrived with the day young about her.

Lush was the country, with rain from the west, and already in the spring the poplars were leafy by the pebbled streams. She found the goddesses strolling easily in a water-meadow, culling the kingcups, decking with primroses their hair. With gladness they welcomed her, took her back to the courts of the fane, and there once more they talked of the riddle of war, and they agreed it was man that made it, the bragging spirit of man, that ever has to be pushing and winning and crowing.

Wherefore said Artemis men should be tamed by hurling upon them monsters, as she had done upon the land of Kalydon. For if you set upon swaggering mortals a force greater than their might, then did they repent and cease from being uppish. But Hera opined that nothing but a mighty war of all Hellas would teach the hearts of men that battle was futile: a war so dark as nearly to destroy the cities of men entirely, then would they become tame and cease from vainglory.

But then Hera said, 'Yet daily indeed do men grow more full of pride, for my dear, do you know what happened in this my very temple? During my high rites, the men had a quarrel, and fought within the precinct, not only that but broke the wing of my sacred peacock! The poor creature was calling and calling! I went and healed it myself. I disguised myself as an old hag, and was not disturbed. But tell her your story, sweet goddess Artemis: she has an even darker tale of the unbounded arrogance and daring of these menfolk.'

'Indeed,' said Artemis, 'for it happened this morning, as I strolled in the woods, and was peacefully breathing the lonely airs of the copses. A daring young fellow from a tree-branch suddenly leapt into my path, and watched my approach with a disgusting leer. Rather than bowing before my godhead, impressed by my dazzling divinity, he propositioned me! Think of it! Lewd to a goddess! A man named Lelex, a young steer rank from the warriors of Sparta! I nearly flattened his face for him with my fist. He even dangled a hunting-net down and did his best to catch me! These men are indeed a race of braggarts, boasters, lechers and swaggerers! Ah, if we could but find a way to tame them, that were a cause indeed, but truly sometimes I feel it were better to send but a deluge!' So did the goddesses angrily chatter in the shade of the fane, but then as dusk gathered, Athene strolled forth on her own.

At evening beside the crag of Kronion, as the shadows

of the rustling pines lengthened over the pebbles of the river-bed, she strolled then solitary along the banks of the fields of flowers, her bare feet treading amidst the damp buds. Sweet was the air. With misty eve the silence was dank and dreamy, speaking of soft forests on distant hills. Athene sighed, as she walked amidst the rustling reeds by the river, and pushed knee-deep through the juicy stems.

Now there was a precinct, where there stood a ruined temple of Gaia, the earth-goddess and grandmother of Zeus. To this went Athene thoughtfully, remembering the spot, and stood awhile in the leafy place. Then as she knew, she went to a tree, and under the roots of the trunk, burrowed and dug and thrust about in the earth. And there at length in the soil concealed, she found a cavern small, with open womb, choked with grass and pebbles. Herein she reached with slender arm, and feeling in the ground, she pulled forth then a grimy thing in her hand. She frowned at it, rubbed the dust, cleared the earth away. Thus did she smile upon a cup.

Gold was the cup, the cup of Gaia, long-pent treasure of the earth, and with her robe she polished it to shine. Not tarnished by the soil was it, or harmed by the buried years, but glimmered soon with a frosty sunlight. She looked upon it, brooded thoughtful. Within its sleek bowl, there were four eyes graven like lynxes staring. Then she set it close in her cloak, and sighing to hold it so, she continued walking in the dale.

Through the golden dusk, she then heard shouts, and splashes of water shooting, and turning by russet boulders a corner of the stream, she saw a leafy-pleasant scene, burnt into the twilight, with springtime smells and reeds and mauve-flowered iris. Youths were bathing in river-pools, gleaming-limbed and bronzed, and from the trees there darted a blue-winged kingfisher. It was a bewitching vision of loveliness, all hung round by hills, and man in his abiding beauty.

As she approached, she saw that the youths were running naked through the grass, competing in races along the flats of the river-bed. While some strove there to outpace the others, thumping on the trodden rushes, others were striving with leaps to fly further across the sands. Beneath a great chestnut tree, one crouched with a discus, coiling himself tight-muscled, then springing to cast the floating plate over the frothy meadow. Others there were that laughed to leap from the turfy banks into the water, and their heads went bobbing seawards through the evening.

Enrobing herself in a great cloak that covered her head with mystery, she approached one of the youths assuming the guise of a sage. 'What make you here, young warriors?' she asked, making her voice like a man's. 'By the sacred precincts of Hera you sport and play? Have you no gripping wars to go to, or sudden raids to make on the towns or ports of your rivals or your enemies? Whence is this holiday striving, while Hellas sternly battles? Who are you, sir, and who are your companions?'

Then did he answer, 'My name is Dryas. From far-flung Thrace am I come, drawn to the call for suitors for the princess of Tegea. Yet hurrying here like those about me, I met with a hero of Kalydon: rash-brained Meleager, brash and daring in his enterprise. Me and my fellows he persuaded to swerve from our former paths, and rather than meekly lining up for a wife, to pledge our lives to a vaunting deed: the hunt of a giant Boar. And when summer has come, we are to sail to Aetolia.'

When this youth had spoken, another came forth who scowled at Athene suspiciously, and he said, 'My name is Acastus, and I tell the truth. This Meleager he mentioned is overrash, and unfit to lead a band, for he is a tyrant and brooks no equals. If he gets not what he wants, he fumes. Well, he was not to fume at me! I refused to obey his latest whim. And while we spend merrily our time, he has given way to fury, and has run off to sulk among the hills.'

'He will be back,' then said Dryas, 'for who would hurry from this spot? And what better pastime than to compete here in games? Fiercer than war is our contest, yet it spills no blood, and yet as fine as war is its effortful strife. With might and skill a man is tested. Against nature too does he

36

strive. The beauty and power of his limbs is here saluted. And laughter follows, for in ultimate contest with gritted teeth we pitch in, and yet from its battles do all return in friendship. Assuredly here would men benefit to make their battles in Games, and all our Hellas could meet here thus in peace.' And Athene smiled at the words of the youth, and left him with a smile, and hence did she wander tenderly in the dale.

' "All Hellas could meet here!" ' she mused as she strolled. 'In Games instead of battles! "With laughter to follow!" Ay, as eternity plays. And if men should come here, in sport not war, certain summers or so, striving together in games not in shedding blood? And if all were to come here, all cities of Hellas, and thus busily compete, and in peaceful sports put forth their fierce fire and fury? Would olives not flower instead of ash? Would power not instead of blood? Would peace not instead of deluge wash over man?'

She stared at the fields. The dusk had come now, and steamy mists befogged the cypresses and the glimmering-reeded river. The heroes far off now crossed the rushes to join in talk together, their naked beauty embowered by great elms. The top of the hill burnt yet with sunset, the acropolis of Kronos, as if on tiptoe catching a new Golden Age.

Athene sighed, 'O beauteous Hellas, how fair and passionate is man! How blest indeed by this Olympic spirit! I will go to my father. This night I'll go. Of these lads' deeds I'll speak. A tale I'll tell of promise and battle's end. For in this dear district, this sweet-faced vale, indeed could all Hellas come, indeed compete in sports of contest and war. And no bloodshed. In Olympia rather could settled peace be pursued, disputes be resolved, all cities talking together. The sword-seeking issues here could they debate, and sway those of mad mind, the major view finding its proper sway. And here all hotheads might find their cooling, all preachers of spite be matched, all chances of sense be nurtured in common pursuit. And if but a truce could be made throughout Hellas while such Games were pursued, each four years, say, while men in Olympia strove, would not this bring the end of war, and set all Hellas to glory? And would not Heracles be the man to arrange it?' And Athene ceased, and flew to Crete, and told her father all, and Zeus with a nod agreed the shining plan.

But on earth, meanwhile, in the region of Argos, Heracles rode forth busily, for on black-maned Arion he surged, drumming up men for a new army. For now upon coward Augeias he loomed with his thronging forces, and the fierce Oenomaus he pledged to set on the throne. The mighty murderer of the Molionids, the ambusher of the Eleians, ranged widely, recruiting the ranks to march, and many the young men that joined his band, many the spears were lifted, and much the brew of battle that lowered upon Elis. In such pursuits did Heracles wander to the rich lands of the isthmus, where the warriors seethed about him. And here he rested by the shores of the gulf, hiding with his troops awhile, as evening sunk over the smokey mountains.

To him came Hermes, the messenger, bearing his snake-coiled wand, fluttering with silver-winged sandals, and finding the muscular warrior seated by the thin-waved sea, as the grey surge beat with lulling whispers, the god of the cross-roads approached him softly, glimmering in the dusk, his purple robe thrown back from his shoulders. And Hermes said, 'Hail to you by Corinth, great son of mighty Zeus, you seem well enough recovered from your recent sickness. You sit by the shore in towering health, and with your vexed brow and taut arms, it seems you are brooding still on thoughts of battle. This after your ambush of Augeias' men, and the slaughter of the brothers, planning to set Oenomaus on Elis' throne! Surely you do not still affront heaven with belligerence? Do you vaunt still to drill armies about the war-torn land? The gods are displeased that you spend your might in sewing discord among men, when there is greater penance for you to accomplish.'

But Heracles turned to the god with a frown, sighing to see him there, and he said, 'What, are you come, immortal messenger? Do I not suffer enough on earth that I am the son of Zeus, without the gods adding further to my miseries? A troublesome skirmish I have planned westward, because, ignoring the gods, Augeias reneged on his payment for my labours. Could you not rather scold him now, and get him to pay me my fee? Why do you let these mortals spurn your laws? I do but seek to chasten men into obeying divine reason, so read me no lectures, deity, about my virtue. And I'll have no more tasks. Psychompompus and trickster of the heavens, I tell you: I am weary of divine labours. At this moment I drive an army to push Augeias from his throne. Nor anything you immortals can say will deflect me!'

'Stubborn indeed I find you, Heracles,' replied Hermes with a frown. 'Truly you are a grumpy fellow! This war you promulgate: I tell you, proud one, it is but a waste of your powers! Why do you pit yourself against such a coward? Rather I have a mission for you, which is a glorious task. Zeus himself has urged me upon it to earth. He has a great enterprise. If you do it, he will guard you from Poseidon's wrath. Think on that: be sensible, and obey! You are bound for Olympia. By the Alpheus there lie great water-meadows. Them are you to clear and prepare for contest. For henceforth in Elis on each fourth year, when summer has come to the fields, a Great Games is to be held to call together all Hellas. Instead of battles henceforth will Greeks compete peacefully at trials of strength and speed, and a new age of harmony and attainment be instituted. Shirk not this task, I warn you, Heracles. Should I come to you again, stern compulsion and rebuke will be in my greeting.' And Hermes left him, while grizzled-bearded Heracles looked with distaste at the god, and scowled as he poked with sword-sheath in amongst the pebbles.

Chapter Six

Now when the season of spring had come, so that there peppered the dales the campion and the purple iris, and the bucking calf kicked them up as he ran to his mother, and the pollen-drugged bees boomed to the shady hive, there came to Arcadia in lush springtime a host of pampered princes, for all were intent on winning the lovely runner. Wherefore Tegea roared with the laughter and proud cries of young warriors, as the youth of Hellas strode forth on holiday.

Yet watching these arrivals sadly, Atalanta, the swift-footed, sighed to see so many men in such a ferment. From the gallery with her maidens, they enraptured, she appalled, she stared forth on the primped and perfumed strolling the streets. Princes drawn from the Argolid, from Thebes, from Boeotia, they strutted, the sun dazzling their tin hats with bravura. But Atalanta groaned, and biting her lip said, grim-faced at the carnival of Arcadia:

'Why, what a parade of cocksure boys we see here in Tegea's alleys! Are all the swaggerers called from the ends of Hellas? See how that one preens himself, combing his sleek blond hair! Look how that one throws his cloak back to show his muscles! Like stiff-legged dogs they prowl about, sniffing each other as rivals, jealous of each brooch or shield that shines more brightly, and with flushed faces they gaze up here, ogling me and my girls, thinking soon that we will be dishes for their devouring! Well, think again, Hellenes! I will not be won! I will die rather than submit to your inflated, keen-eyed graspings!' And she rushed inside then, to brood alone in the darkness, and the day drew on that was the last of her freedom.

But when night had come, Atalanta took sadly off her

head-scarf, and the fillets and diadem that held fast her hair. And sadly then her silvery sandals she flipped across the room, and her zone undid, letting fall from her waist its gatherings. And mournfully her chiton, many-folded, she drew away from her shoulders, and lay down the brooch and the robe on her desolate chair. And so did she garb herself with fear in one great white sheet round, and barefoot she padded across the room to her altar. For there in the corner, burned a lamp — and had done for many days — before a bronze idol of Huntress Artemis.

And softly Atalanta said, 'Well, O goddess, the time of my trial is come. And the time when with right I am to appeal to you. The suitors are here, the marriage imminent, the betrothal comes with the morn, and to me it seems I am this next day to be sacrificed. You bade patience, endure these matters, and all would be well. You promised me that marriage would not seize me. Yet can it be you have forgotten to bring me the safe way forward? No word from you, no inspiration have I heard! Can it be that the heavens themselves are forgetful? Send me some sign, chaste one! Save your servant! Come, before all is lost!' And Atalanta ceased, and from her altar went straight then to her bed, and she lay rigid there, and stared long at the ceiling.

But the honeyed spring night, with sounds of riot, with cheery songs of wine, in carnival mood under the moon and the silvered mountains, brought easeful slumber at last on all maidens and men in Tegea's walls, and the deep of night was peaceful at last among the alleys. Wherefore Atalanta passed in fitful turnings through sleep to the land of dreams, and there did she behold strange thronging visions.

For she saw as if heaven-borne, turning at her feet the length and width of the world, the islands of Hellas foamed and ringed by moonlight, and the mainland of Argos, stony Achaia, fertile and forested Elis, lay beneath as if but a sleeping city. And in this world she saw shadows marching, rows of folk with waggons, armies or townsmen

41

threading their way through the valleys, and they all came one way, intent on seizing, converging towards one place, and the princess shook with dripping fear at this vision.

Yet as she looked, she began to see that the folk that converged upon the hills were neither bound for Arcady nor in lust of her person. Rather towards Alpheus, by whose riverside they swept, they came in friendship, met and joined in no turbulent battle. For Atalanta witnessed the hosts competing at sorts of Games, for they heaved and they leapt, as boys do to beat each other, and the spears went winging, and discuses glimmered, floating under the stars, showering the darkened leaves of the hill-clustered forest.

There stood a line of men to compete, and she saw each of their faces, gathered princes from the width of Hellas. She found them chilling, unknown figures. But then she saw a youth, bold and handsome, staring straight into her eyes. She started at this, and drew herself in from his prying look, and yet melted too, for his eyes were softly familiar. And strange she felt there grow in her breast a melting and a flowing, as though an old river in her was reawakened.

Then the sight of him passed. The contests began. They flocked now to the race-track. Atalanta found that she was the prize to be awarded. With panic she struggled, yet then she saw herself in the line with the men, and the race began and she also at the running. As the men fled fast, she dashed at their sides. Soon she found with her powers she was in the lead from the struggling runners. Then did she flee over forest and isthmus, ocean and crag uncaught, and liberty was hers in the echoing woodland.

And so she awoke. And she thanked Artemis immediately for this dream, for at once she saw the way that would lead her forward.

Now when dawn had come above the sky, and driven forth her grey horses over the long strands beyond the mountains, about the buzzing city the birdsong pierced the dusky air, and woke a hundred suitors from their slumbers. Up then leapt the fresh-faced youths, flung on their glossy cloaks, combed their hair gazing in the brass mirrors, and off towards the king's hall with vigorous step they strode, hopeful to be the face that was distinguished. Meanwhile, King Iasos himself had risen, sent his chamberlain hurriedly to check that all was well with his flighty daughter, and he to his throne-room came bowing to those assembled, ready to rid his mind of a vexing problem.

But when he came to the steps of the hall, he found already Atalanta, with a bevy of virgins clustering about her, and frowningly he looked at her, and said, 'What is this, daughter? No more of your tricks or delayings, I command you! You may come to my hall with a thousand virgins, but the princes are here, and you are to leave your maidens' number for ever.'

'Father,' replied Atalanta coolly, 'you are unduly suspicious. Have I not acquiesced to your plans to have me married? Have I not agreed to them many days now, all along the way, even though you habitually treat my remarks with suspicion? Do you think I will back down? Do you think I will run away? I have given my word, and the word of a virgin huntress is a sacred one. No father, I come to you with these my friends, since I wish myself to take part, and share with my sister in my betrothal's arrangements. Hear me then, for I have a plan to make this day a happy one, and I am sure you all will applaud its sense and sportingness.

'Now father, you see that in your hall only the great may come in: the people, the citizens are by its hallowed walls excluded. I come to ask that my betrothal and the selection of my future husband may be made in the open where all our town may witness it. That way, truly, you will ensure that I cannot escape. That way surely is the way of princes. And allow me, father, this extra boon, that I myself may select by a test the prince who shall have me in marriage, for I know well you have not been able by any deliberations to settle on the alliance I should bring you. Give me and my girls but an hour to prepare the meadow by the river, and I myself will provide a suitable choice and ceremony.' And Atalanta ceased her speech, lowering her eyes demurely, so that her father looked stunned and stared to hear her.

Then replied King Iasos, 'I grant your request. You may choose your spouse. I will make it known that this is how it is to be decided, and by these means I shall avoid the dangers of insulting the allies which already I have had diplomatically besieging me. Yet daughter, I warn you: no trick now! You have been obedient for some months. This plan of yours seems far too kind and amenable. Beware then that you do not in secret plan some usual outrage, or my ire will be unspeakable!' And the king turned away, and went with his ministers up the steps of the hall, and his laurelled head was lost in the darkness.

Meanwhile, about the lithe-limbed virgin the suitors were forming up, staring with ox-huge eyes and hungrily swaying. The girls in groups with blushing cheeks giggled and fussed about, primping the princess, but gazing at the boys. Atalanta with a shout, surprising all, though, led off her maidens running, and suddenly all the girls were gone from the pavement. And the startled princes hurried to catch them up, thundering through the streets of the city, until they came to the wide stretch of fields beside the river.

Sweet and speckled with daisy and cowslip lay the turfy plain, as the morning sun dried the dew from the grasses. The mist hung about it, fogging yet the blossoming chestnut-trees, while the eager charger romped in the delicious meadow. There followed strange sights, for the girls now ran and cleared away branches from the field, uprooted bushes, and flattened the grass with planks. And others there came from the feasting-hall bearing huge benches between them, and these they set up in lines by the cleared passage. Then with flat flagstones, dragged along by ropes through the hissing grass, the girls set up two lines at the field's either end. And all the while the princes

44

gawped, unable to imagine what plan might explain this strange behaviour.

Now while Atalanta oversaw the work of her sweating virgins, standing by the trees, pointing which way to drag the flagstones, there came up beside her an eager youth, who stared at her fierily, his eyes like gimlets boring into her breast. And the youth said, 'Fair maid, I see by these sterling efforts you are a commanding girl, and not one to be easily cowed by convention. My name is Lelex, and from Sparta I come, not the official choice, but second in rank to my brother, who also is a suitor. But this let me tell you: my languid brother, and all the princes here: they are too tame and pious to be your husband. What, you, maiden, were reared by a bear: you live by nature in the woods. You need someone who can live up to your savagery. Try me then, lady. Ask the girls about Sparta. Lelex is your man. Lelex has fire in his veins, where these have milk. Come into the trees here a bit, and let me show you my mettle.' But here Atalanta stopped the hot youth with a smart slap in the face.

Now while Lelex stood dashed, the princess rushed off with her blood stirring in fury. And hurriedly then while the king was approaching and the dignitaries of Tegea, she went where the grey-bearded ministers had placed the competing heroes in a line. In desperate mood she looked at them, scanning their faces, while in her heart there raged insulted anger. But no man resembling the face in her dreams she saw, but every face was foreign and disturbing. And so she turned aside sombrely, and looked over the field, and addressed the populace around her.

'People of Tegea,' she cried, 'as you know by gathering here today I am to be given in marriage. Moreover, I can tell you that the selection of my husband has been arranged by me for your entertainment. You see before you a race-track, my friends, laid out by my girls, with good laps of grass to run each way upon. Two coverings of that silky patch: that is to be the test, and all these princes are to compete on it. Whoever wins the running-race, he wins my hand. This then is the manner I choose my future husband.' And Atalanta ceased at this, and the crowd applauded her speech, and King Iasos looked with smiles upon her.

'My daughter,' he said, 'you are talking sense. This betrothal has cured your wits. I see you will make a fine queen for some lucky country. Let's see then which land shall win you. Princes, strip yourselves bare. Fling off your fancy clothes and race on the greensward.' And the king and his ministers laughed, as they applauded Atalanta, and nodded at the wisdom of her decision.

But when the princes had heard this speech, and the king called them to strip, with the girls looking on, some of them were reluctant. But the ministers insisted, and about the field now, the princes took off their cloaks, and edged forward with their gleaming bodies. The crowd pressed in, eager to judge for themselves who looked the best, and which youth sported the best figure. And some they saw stockily made, some slender and some measured, some swarthy and some fair as sunshine. But as they buzzed Atalanta herself strode up to the starting-line, and she stood there, as though she would not be moved.

'Tegeans,' she cried, 'and princes all, one other thing I should tell you: it is well to reflect that I am a ruthless huntress. My name is renowned for a virago, that runs in the perilous forest, and hunts alone wolves and boars and bears. Know that my spirit is passing proud. For me to submit to a man: this is a paramount humiliation. And truly I will wed no youth who is not wholly my master, whether in wits, strength, endurance or speed. Wherefore I say I will also race, a suitor for my own hand, for I cannot marry a husband who cannot defeat me. And if I win the race then surely, no prince has won me in marriage, and I am free to stay a virgin!' And with these words did the long-legged huntress suddenly throw down her bow, and pull off the fillet that bound her hair with delicacy.

Then before the princes, whose fast-fixed eyes stared with growing wonder, ogling the vision which was unravelling before them, Atalanta, the princess, tore off her cloak, threw down her golden clasp, undid her belt, tucked off from her shoulders her chiton, kicked off her sandals, slid down from her body the folds of her fragrant dress, and unrobed before the princes of Hellas her body. Smooth-skinned and round and buxom it was, with nothing but a loin-cloth binding her hips, and a tight scarf tugging with fragile grip her breasts. And the air was filled with a mighty gasp, echoing over the river, as the town and the suitors stared at the beautiful nude.

Yet before they could speak, or any protest, or the king call all to a halt, Atalanta raced off with thudding heels over the green. Some princes there were looking startled after, too astonished to run. Some drew in their breath, and hurriedly raced to catch her. Many others there were who with cupped hands cringing had to limp from the scene, bearing away their shame to a secret spot. Meanwhile, Atalanta at the far end of the meadow, raced to the stone marker, whereby she would turn and come back again.

Lelex was running in spite of all, shameless with eagerness. He let no sense of propriety slacken his competing. Before him and after the other princes heavily panted along. They strove to catch up, but before them were distractions. For the sight of Atalanta's back seemed to drain their energy, as it flew sweetly with its bewitching writhing. And then the sight of her front cannonading, as perilously held in, as she turned and returned, made them weaken further.

Lelex stood amazed. His hands clasped before him, it was hard to run, but now he swooned and loosened to see such a vision. His legs would not work. His hips went limp. He sunk into the flowers, and there in blossoming keck he disappeared. Others slid also. Over the field distracted heroes wilted, like falling shoots of reeds going down to the scythe. And Atalanta stormed past the post, triumphant in victory, and at her back the field littered with loons.

47

In riotous joy now ran the maidens and about their princess danced with laughter and cheered her in the victory. Up on their smooth shoulders they lifted her, paraded her about the ground, and braving raucously marched before the king and ministers.

'So father,' then cried the happy huntress, 'by a straight contest I have before the people won my freedom! Let no man seek to wrest what is mine. I have won myself! I am my own woman!' And off in heady glee they ran, bearing Atalanta through the city, and in front of Artemis' temple they capered and sang.

Chapter Seven

But as the spring advanced on Crete, and the blossoming fruit trees threw their red and white petals on the breezes, on the terraces of the gods, the immortals were in surly mood, as they sat drinking and bickering idly. Among the old red-tapered columns of the Minoan heaven did they recline on golden couches, and fretfully they fed on bread and olives and honeycakes, and peevishly hurled their wine-drains at a basin. And all of them had some dispute with the events in Hellas, and yet was Hellas a long way away.

For Hera was there frowning most, nursing a grand resentment at the deeds of the speedy Pelops, for Pelops the young, aspiring hero, had left his eastern realm, and gone in search of glory and adventure westward. Hera thought the boy a cursed one, due to the deeds of his father, and could not overlook the sins of Tantalus. But Aphrodite quarrelled with her over this hate of hers, and she took delight in opposing the queen.

A little further off on a couch lay Poseidon also brooding, for everything in Hellas had gone against him. Towards Heracles he bore his grudge, as he had done before, for in spite of Zeus' word Heracles had not quietened. Rather had he compounded his wrongs, incensing the sea-king's anger, and all Elis had changed because of the hero. For King Augeias had Heracles cast unceremoniously from his throne, and in his place had set up Oenomaus, and now a new king ruled over Elis renowned for his cruel ways, a persecutor and murderer of young princes. This did great Poseidon brood over surlily, lying in sullen wrath, and about him all the gods were sighing also.

Each immortal burnt with futility, unable to take action, for far off Hellas was lost in the western sea. And Zeus their leader, without whose nod no action could be put forward, he was away, and none knew of his going. Moreover, with Zeus, their chief, absent, they had none to whom to complain, but all were merely frustrated in their fury. Yet to Hermes at least, the messenger-god, often privy to Zeus' thoughts, they could set forth at large their many resentments. So did they bend the ear of the wind-god, the youth of the golden wand, and demanded where and when would his master return.

But Hermes said, 'Great lords of the ether, deities of peace, where Zeus is, how can I command? Till Zeus has returned, what can I do? True, you may complain to me. But of what you bicker, what can truly be done? Agreed: men on earth abuse your power. They fight, they rage, they swagger and boast, they are overweening proud. But we cannot strike them down willy-nilly. Pelops we cannot slaughter. Heracles we cannot take from the earth. He has made war, deposed a king, set Oenomaus on the throne, but think what trouble would come if we were to try and reverse this! Be patient awhile. Zeus will return soon. He is but gone to ponder. And when he comes back, I also have things to tell him!' And Hermes turned away then, leaving the gods in a pack on the palace, while he himself flew up to the sky to brood.

Yet while Hermes hid, there returned at that moment from his long northern sojourn, Zeus, the sky-ruler, strolling with buoyant hope. To the throne-room he went, and summoning servants, he called forth a tripod to wash, and towels to mop him, and a meal he had brought to him on the coals, and there he sat munching, while one by one, the other suspicious immortals started to shuffle into the chamber. And there they stood frowning, gazing on him with blackness in their brows, while he ate on regardless.

'Now gods,' cried Zeus, 'you have been wondering no doubt on what great plans I have been brooding, while you were lazing about the blossoming hills of Ida. Not idle have I been, not sitting around listening to old songs, or watching the Muses dance before Phoebus, the dancing-master. No, I have been working, and I come to you stoutly, with fiery plans. And you are all to be inspired by my projects. For Hermes will tell you soon how you are to fly over all Hellas, summoning Greeks to a great enterprise. And there is to be peace in Greece and all manner of building, and you to this are to summon the tribes. But you must know that once this is done, northwards are we to go. No longer in Ida are we to languish idle. North to the mainland we must go and the commanding ranges, and there are we to set up another heaven!' And Zeus nodded happily, and seized up from a coal a stick of skewered lamb and tore it off with his teeth and devoured it wholesale.

Now the gods when they heard this speech, stared astonished, for there sat the deity they had hunted, contentedly issuing them their orders, while all of them had for him vast complaints, dissatisfactions to take up the whole day. But Hera cried, 'One moment, my lord, you misjudge our temper. No slackers are we, nor have we sat about in idleness or feasting. The earth is in turmoil! Each one of us has representations to make. Heracles has unseated the King of Elis! And there's this monster, this now-regal insult to the marriage-bed, Oenomaus, that cruelly kills all princes that seek his daughter. And this prince Pelops – '

'Ho, leave these petty things!' then cried Zeus dismissing her. 'What matter's all this? Let Pelops be what Pelops will! Instead, harken my orders. Each palace and temple you keep: it is all to be packed up, all treasure and temples, borne away from Crete. The whole of our tribe are to migrate from this island to a greater kingdom. We are to colonise the slopes of Olympus!

'My comrades, long ago in the twilight, we were but petty things, a downtrodden race, while Titans ruled the world which we inhabit. My father, Kronos, fixed forth all things, and summoned a Golden Age, and we were but pygmies to his mighty ordering. Yet he, as you know, had dispowered his father, cut off his fertility, strewn the sea with the urge of his creation. Weak me and my brothers were to be eaten by this devouring Titan, yet a trick of Gaia saved me for a Cretan childhood.

'My brothers, you know well how after with Rhea's potion you and our sisters were puked up from the dark maw of the aging Kronos. His time was passed, and the other Titans chose for their king not him but Atlas, while Kronos went to an old age in peacefulness. Against those Titans we gave battle. Ten years of wars emerged from that throat of Kronos, and with the great aid of the dwellers in Tartarus, we prevailed. From Orthys they struck us, and we were forced to mount from Olympus our attacks, for only that height gave us vantage over the giants. From these wars and others at length the victors, we looked about a world that was ours, and unthinkingly settled with me in the Crete of my childhood.

'Yet what are we masters of? Where are our peoples? To what kingdom did we ascend when we had beaten back the rage of the giants? For what did the Cyclops, the monster Campe, the Hecatoncheires, hurl forth their thunderbolts with us onto the old ones? Through vast, flaming forests we beat them back, we drove the old gods from our realms, even to the very confines of Chaos, and for what inheritance? Why, Hellas we gained, golden Hellas which lies all to the north, and which in the distance we peer at, with low, myopic sight! This isle and this mount have no commanding quarter from which to reign and know. Our wars then have drawn us to the wrong capital. To the site of our victories we must go therefore, set up our heavens in the north. The immortals must rule Hellas from Olympus!'

Now when Zeus had ended, Hermes came and entered the glossy throne-room, and the gods were all silent and stunned about Zeus. And when Zeus looked, he saw Hermes, and said, 'Welcome, O messenger-god, I have just told the immortals my great plans for Olympus.'

52

Yet as he spoke, there came Aphrodite, and she held her head on one side, and said, 'Yet, sweet father, before we fly off to the cold north, will you not hear me out, for this Oenomaus that Heracles had made king, he is an illegitimate spawn of faithless Ares, and − '

'Tarry one minute,' said Hera firmly, 'that is of little moment. Have you forgotten the crimes of Pelops' father? I repeat my demand. This unprincipled youth cannot be let go west. It is all − '

'No!' cried Poseidon. 'My demands are fiercest! You promised me you would shackle this Heracles! But he has made more warfare, and defeated those he struck with sacrilege!'

With wrath did Zeus gaze on them. He leapt up now, and from an alcove in the wall, he plucked forth a cup and showed them the gold goblet. To Pallas Athene especially he looked, nodding that this was her cup, and to them all he revolved it, gleaming with gilded spheres. Then did he speak, 'You see this cup, gods? It is the cup of *logos*, which Pallas here brought to me from Olympia. Drinking ever from it, I have learnt much, for balanced are its bowl and stem, whole and golden, holding the universe. This cup I call now the cup of *logos*, for reason is drunk therefrom, and all things are looked on in it with reality. From this cup's fumes I have drunk deep, and these new visions I have had, and thus is it I see great future for the Hellenes. Wherefore henceforth Olympus will be the heaven of *logos*, the cup. And its shining light our world and worth shall sustain.

'So much for Olympus. But as for Heracles: he has received a mighty penance. Hermes, tell the sea-king what you have bid him set forward. For this cup of *logos* already inspired us to begin a new age, and Heracles has a greater enterprise than has ever been. Harken, O brothers, this will content you! For he is to set up a Sacred Games, wherein every tribe shall compete, every kingdom and state in Hellas. It will be a deed that will unite for good all these squabbling heroes, and one stroke of reason will satisfy all your gripings. Indeed, indeed the light of *logos* is sacrosanct upon earth, and all is builded from its transcendent purity.' And Zeus was done then, and strode off lightly to his resting-chambers, and there was light shining all about him.

But as stunned as the gods had been to be told the substance of Zeus' first plan, so doubly stunned were they now to hear this news. And as worried as Hermes had been to see Zeus first laying down laws, so doubly worried was he now to hear this last pronouncement. And the gods in silence stood a moment, staring after their chief, but then they all turned to look at the messenger-deity.

And Hermes said, 'It is indeed so. The Games are already set forward, and you are to summon all cities to the contest. Wherefore by the summertime to Olympia all heroes are to come, and compete with their fellows in the Olympic fields. A truce is to be over all the lands, and this the message you must take, once I have returned myself from the mainland. Farewell then, gods. To Elis I go, to consult with great Heracles. When I return, call all to the Olympic Games!' And Hermes smiling vaulted from the terrace and flew out over the sea, and busily did he seek the rocks of the Ionian. Yet the gods stood staring, stunned with wonder at everything they had heard. And it was long their open mouths could not speak.

But the son of Zeus, the mighty Heracles was grossly slumped in Elis, lying beneath a table in the feasting-hall. Though midday it was and all bustling, still he slumbered there, for he sunk there to oblivion after a night of quaffing. About the hall lay littered flagons, wine-cups and pitchers on their sides, dishes of ox-ribs upturned by the muzzles of browsing hounds, and here and there servants began to clear the deluge of the banquet, as also in odd corners the feasters began to rouse.

But when came Hermes into the halls, he was soured to find the hero sunk in debauchery. And coming upon him among the debris of the eating place, he looked down a while at the snoring dribbler, and sighed with frustration, but with a kick did he awake him.

And Hermes said, 'What is this slothfulness, Heracles,

54

you liquor-brained sot? Is this how you set about the king of the gods' own bidding? Did I not come to you a season ago with an enterprise for you to enact that would win glory for yourself and peace for your nation? Is this how you treat the gods' commands? You turn your back on their vision, and indulge yourself in petty battle, vengeance, and carousing. But up at once, and lest you have forgotten, speed to Alpheus straightway, and there in Olympia haste to set out a race-track. For you are to summon all the men of Hellas to meet in that place this summer, and to arrange a festival, a universal truce and a Panhellenic Games!' And Hermes stared down at him most reproachful, while Heracles blinked open his eyes, and with dry mouth chewed the air in bafflement.

But then Heracles said, 'What, is it you again, O busy divinity? Do you not wear out your wings with all this flying? My head is panting more than my chest. Oh, we have been feasting here! It may be I shall have need of that dish beside you. Yet what is your message? Set forward a Games? Why, you told me of this in the winter! I am about it. I am indeed. Long ago I sent forth the messengers. All kingdoms about, ay, and even the islands I have bidden send their heroes to the Games. The competitors are alerted. They will be coming. But first I had to secure Elis. I had to settle the site. You cannot hold a games in the kingdom of an enemy. So when the spring comes – well, it is here, I agree – well, when it advances a little, sure enough, Hermes, I will see about your enterprise. Is it March already? March, I think. We shall be ready by high summer. Tell the gods –' And here Heracles paused to stare past into space, and then he whoofed like a hound into the bowl.

The messenger-god looked down upon him, smiling in spite of himself, and then he said, 'Well, Zeus-born, I leave you to your heavings. But be sure at once that you fly to Olympia and level the ground there smartly, and set up huts and sleeping-places for the competitors. This is no little village sports-day to which you must put your strength. No, here are you to lay universal contests. And by these clashes, you are to bring — O heartiest of men — good comradeship and harmony among the tribes. For the men love best who fight each other. Quarrels and matches are life! Set your shoulder to it, and so, great puker, adieu!' And Hermes then floated up from the debris of that banqueting-hall, and shot once more to the high airs over the Aegean.

Then went the inspired gods to their work, for once Hermes had returned, with Zeus he despatched the immortals to the call of Hellas. Not time was there now for restless bickerings, not space for minor conflicts, the whole of Hellas was to be forged in one. So flew the many shining-ones east and west, to the northern Thracian slopes, to the scatterings of the independent isles, and they called on the leaders of Greek-speaking tribes — those scarce speaking to each other — to join for the summer in one sumptuous spree.

To Ionian islands did they fly, where the grapes grow thick, or Paros and Naxos shine with ivory marble. To the Aegean bays, where the oleanders blush, and the tulip and the crocus by the springside. To Delos the long-haired Apollo shot, where markets throng the amber hills, and the white lions guard the path to the temple, and Aphrodite the Paphian, to Cyprus, bowered with erotic woods, to kindle with fire the coppery veins of her soil. The Sporadic islands, rose-bearing, ship-building, oil-pressing, the others pressed to send their heroes to compete at Olympia.

When these were roused, to the towns of the mainlands, Asian- or Thracian-based, the deities flew next whipping the Greeks to sport. Chill were the fir-clad slopes of Thrace and Macedonian mounts, though gold lay buried in the Pangaian peaks. Vexed the Propontic and Hellespont lay, where the impulsive currents with peril swirled their waves in the Bosphoran straits. Yet bright on Aeolian shores of Asia, or where Ionia smiles, the cities of delicate elegance glittered their hills: Tyrrha, Miletus, Ephesus, where the Persian silks were worn, and purple dyed the wealth of the merchants of slaves.

Last to the west the immortals flocked, to Dodona Zeus himself, to drum by the oak-tree that spreads its millennian arms, to Epirus Poseidon, where stallions gallop, thundering over the plain with the rapid attack of the cataracts of their hoofs. To Attica then and Boeotian hills, to the eagle-hung Delphi they flew, where the wildcat slinks his path among Grecian firs, and the gorge-deep forests of haunted Thessaly, the spine of rugged Pindus, that hovers like a sea-beast above the clouds. Such were the rich realms the immortals visited, the land- and sea-isles of Greece, to summon competitors for the first Olympics.

Chapter Eight

Now when Atalanta and her maidens had sung their song
of triumph, gleefully they danced by the temple of
Artemis. With branches and ribbons they capered like
imps, joining hands in lines, running and weaving amidst
each other. The dust flew up happily from their feet
pounding the market-place, as they tapped and flung their
pearly-gleaming ankles. But about them there came
clustering curiously the crowd of citizens from the race-
track, for here was something even more intriguing.

But Atalanta called to maidens, and said, 'Girls of the
free forest, we have vaunted the virgin well on account of
her victory. But look: the people peer about. Some women
clap us, some scowl, many men stare angrily upon us,
while at the palace trouble brews. Why then do we dally?
What is for us among these pressing men? Should we not
rather run wild and take to the woods and mountains?
Should we not maintain our virgin purity? Come, string
your bows. Pick up your spears. Don your hunting-capes,
for I am for hunting all day in the greenwood!' And the
princess whooped then, and swinging about, gathered up
from her maid her robes, and laughing she ran from the
city.

Now as she hared off, dumbly the crowd watched,
amazed at her racing heels as they once more flew into the
distance. Meanwhile, there came the angry King Iasos,
glowering after his daughter, and ministers who frowned
with set faces at the girls. But in shrieks and laughter, with
bare feet romping, dancing along the goat-tracks, the
virgins followed quickly in a rout. And soon beyond the
farms and meadows, they skipped beneath the trees, and
soon they set echoing the mysterious boughs of the forest.

Like roe-deer that leap, dapple-backed, among the sun-blotched oaks, streaming in a herd to sniff for trickling waterfalls, so did the rout of flush-cheeked maidens crash and flash through the ivy, breaking the branches and waving fern and hazel. And then they gathered beneath the looming beeches with smooth limbs, and stared with eager eyes about for quarry.

Straight they found game, for snorting with fury and cantering from a black dell, there leapt up a great boar from the rotted leaves. With bristling back and snarling snout, tusks huge, old and yellow, he roared and ran through the rout of girls towards the canyon. The maidens yelled cheerily. Those in its path ran with a screech to the trees. Lifting their spears, others steadied to cast at it. But the shrewd little eyes of the bristly boar saw his swiftest escape, and burrowed through the tangled brambles by the cliff. Atalanta leapt up and treading a boulder, watched the track of the beast, and then with whooping halloos did she issue orders.

Thus did she cry, 'You girls on my left: Beroe, Chloe, Metaneira, you take the left flank of the hazelled dale. Those on my right: Nephele, Evadne, and you, milk-white Galatea, run by the right slope and seek to cut off his escape. Close in behind, lasses. I'll to the summit, chase him round about. Oh, this is more fun than running away from men! Boys can..ot catch us, but boars we can catch! We are the hunters now!' And Atalanta ran off to head off the quarry.

In the sun-drugged noon, where the fresh green leaves were held by the mounting heat in the drowsiness and dust of the warm springtime, while the bushes lay still, and slanting sunbeams smokily pierced the foliage to fall on the moss and the violet fuming sweet, the boar seemed vanished, and far away the knocks and calls of the girls, sleepily lost amidst the forest's echoes. Atalanta paused a while to breathe, and with satisfaction she sighed, and thus did she think among the trees.

'How sweet it is to hunt again, free in the virgin

woodland! This is my own dear heart's existence. I was bred a forest-beast, suckled by a bear, and surely the taste of the leaves is in my limbs. In the deeps of the greenwood there is freedom: no pressing or petty duties, no trivial tasks with the well-behaved. Oh, better this freedom than the bondage of marriage to an irksome prince! Now I am clear of that fear for ever!

'Yet what joy it was to see so many princes at the race-track, and oh, their beautiful discomfiting! The faces of those startled men, their expressions of shame and lust, their wonderful shock, failure and confusion! The goddess Artemis put in my mind the lively stratagem with which I defeated a horde of heroes. The goddess set her virgin princess above all the brood of men. Oh, glorious to be the victor over mankind!' And thinking these thoughts, Atalanta closed her eyes, about to laugh, but then a noise startled her of shaking leaves.

Following the noise through the thick creamy blossoms of elder, and past the shrubs, she found herself now in a sun-dappled valley. Cool-green and hazy in sheltered pools, the sliding stream flowed here with sun-dried boulders smooth amidst the emerald. Narcissus hung above the surface, and dipping sycamores, shedding the sticky bracts of winter. Atalanta searched, while the ferny forest hung over her head, and the green beetle scuttled over its reflections.

But now a sudden dismay seized her, and as she gazed about, she thought, 'Alas, yet I seem to be searching strangeness! For now I have the feeling again I had at the race this morning: searching and finding but disappointment! Seeing the princes ranged there in their line as my suitors, I was dashed in my hope of seeing something there. The man of my dream! Where was he? Would he have raced against me? If he had, might he have beaten me? If he had beaten me, what then? I should not be here in the forest, but at his side, or in bed with him from the wedding! What then would I feel?' she gazed about, then gave a scream of horror. Staring from the bushes was the man from her dream!

Straight did the hero run at her, lifting up his lance, with a shout of triumph laughing from his teeth. Yet the hunting-virgin leapt to one side, scattering the waves, and splashed through the pool to find the way back to her sisters. The man sped about. He closed her path with his warning arm, poising the lance to cut off her steps. Atalanta turning hurled her spear, which hummed through the hushed air, and catching his cloak thudded into the turf. The man raged keenly, tore off his robe, and naked looked about. Then chased the girl from the pool and through the gorge.

With terror did Atalanta run. The race before was laughter: now did this race with bitterness seize her breast. He came on fiercely, for fire inspired him, gleefully watching her moves, as the girl he hunted like a forest-beast. In busy flight the racing pair set splashing the sunlit waters. Beneath warm rocks they hurried in their hunt. Below the bending willow-boughs frantically they leapt and ducked, over the boulders jumping to thrash through the brakes.

Now had the virgin few clothes upon her but those she wore in the race. Yet through the brakes even these were torn from her. With fear of Fate, she felt herself naked, exposed all to the air, and vulnerable like a nightmare to the man. He chased her hard, cutting through the boughs with a swashing arm, chuckling among the bluebells with sweating chest. They burst through a gorge and into a channel, leading to deep pools, where swans went flapping with black legs from the noise. Struggling to climb, she found a great rock, dislodged it from its bed, and groaning cast it down upon her pursuer. The hero crouched, clung to the side. Atalanta slid down on the shingle. The rocks splashed the stream, and the man again came after.

With lonely sense of capture now, Atalanta found herself closed, hushed in a canyon, where hazels dappled the sky. In tearful pleading she gazed about, hoping for signs of her maidens, praying for rescue even from Artemis. Cool and grey-green the lagoons of the river lay now all about them. There was no way for her to escape their banks. Into the water she plunged, waist-deep, and he behind her panting. They chased and splashed, bare-chested amidst the lilies. With gleaming skins, among mud and lotuses they waded onto the bank. Yet here he seized her, the bare man from behind. His arms slid round her. He pulled her down. His hands tugged on her breasts. She bent her neck to look back on the face of her dream. Then down she fell, panting and held, his legs twined fast about hers, and flatly now she knew that she was caught.

'You will be cursed, if you take my maidenhead!' yet she said in his arms. 'For the man that takes it shortly will see death. Such was the prophecy spoken about me, with other gifts, at my birth, and you will be dead, if you heed not its words! You have overpowered me. With fear and surprise, these thick brakes and weed-strewn ponds: with these you gained a victory not your own. You willed my defeat! But have a care, for the kingdom of Tegea, and the goddess Artemis will take revenge inevitably upon you! Death will be yours if you seek to take my protected virginity! I would give it you too, if I had place enough to fight.'

'As to that,' smiled then the man 'whether death you mean or your maidenhead, you may truly give what you may. But if I would take you, wishes or prophecies were no compulsions! There are always paths about prohibitions! How moreover may I know that you spin me no useful lies? Why, anyone can invent injunctions to guard them. Your prophecy does not make me pause. But yet: are you a virgin? What, and running naked about in the woods? Strange is this habit for a virgin, even of Arcady! You are strange quarry to find in such parts. Your voice also and looks give heed that you are no country lass. What is your name and your parentage?'

'I am the child of the she-bear!' then hissed Atalanta at him. 'And you smooth-talker, I will reward with savagery! Why do you ask me these formal things, when you have me pinned to the ground, wrapped in your body, defiled by your hands? Have done with your honeyed words, highwayman! Spare me your good feelings! If you would rape, rape then and be done! With a spell you trapped me and outraced me. This is no fair strife. You would not beat me on the flat.'

'With respect treat kindness, ingrate!' then replied with anger the man. 'He that would deflower you, let him have his will. But come you here, sweet. There is some pleasure that can still be had, and your foul spite can be taught a little.'

And the man held to her then, and twisted round and crouched over her thighs, and pinning her arms down above her head, he kissed her sturdily, fleshing his lips on her angry mouth, and covering her face in taunting kisses. Then sliding down he toyed with her lustily, relishing her fine curves, and riding with sweet lust about her legs, till casting them up to catch his shoulders, he tugged her into a knot, and slid on her merrily swimming against her thighs. But then as she gasped and squirmed beneath, he flattened her with a spasm, and cast up his seed over her breasts and chin. The girl cried out, then lay still staring, and he with a smile sank down, and sighing with lust stroked her and kissed her cheek.

'Why now,' he sighed, 'you are some girl to meet in a forest! Never such a hunt could I imagine with another. You run so fast, and look such ice, and spite is in your very teeth. And yet also is wisdom in your eyes. If you were a man, I could wish you my fellow, for I have good work, calling for fire and speed such as are yours. Well then, rejoice, girl, for you have still your virgin seal intact. You can keep that for a future chase.' And the man sat up then, and looked around for his spear again, and was about to rise and vanish in the forest.

But Atalanta said, 'You have defiled me! Where can I go now? And where go you alone in this great greenwood? The deed itself you have not done, yet what of that? My heart you have scalded with eternal hate! So you abandon me, having brought upon me my defilement and ruin, thinking, just like a man, you are magnanimous! Upon

63

what basis is this pride with which you regard yourself? Is it perhaps some god has deigned to half love me?'

The man replied, 'No god am I. Meleager of Kalydon: this is my name, a prince of the distant, peaked Aetolia. I am in Arcady seeking men, to raise up a mighty band, longing to hunt great quarry in my kingdom. I came to Arcadia, hearing word that princes were flocking hither, hoping to win the hand of a fair virago. I scorn the lady, but yet the men I would have in my company, since our prize will need the best strength of the best.'

Atalanta looked at him, and with a smile, lying beside him naked, said, 'So you have scorned to race for the princess of Arcadia? You must know, sir, that Fate determines things, and try as you might, you cannot avoid what is destined. Yet tell me more of the quest you mention. How does it progress? And what is this quarry you are hunting?'

And he replied, 'A Boar-Giant, girl, a monster of vast size. I have seen it in the snows of the mountains. It roots up the farmlands, sets down the vineyards, throws great houses on its back, and slaughters the poor people of my country. For this I seek heroes of boundless spirit, men of might and fire. Here is a quarry for any hunter.'

And Atalanta grew dreamy and said, 'Ay, that it is, my hero, Meleager of Kalydon, I could do you much good! None better are there at tracking quarry, or sensitive to the forest. An instinct I have, that might bring down your boar. Where are your fellows, and what are they? Are there many already, or is there room for another hunter?'

Meleager smiled. 'Another hunter? I like your inquiry! I left them a certain distance from these woods. We were encamped and they by shepherds were being entertained, while I grew impatient and came forth hunting. Some five already have we in our group, but surely is there room and much need for further hunters.'

But then she said, 'First tell me a little more of this boar you hunt. They are the toughest and wildest of forest-foes. He is a giant? How did he come? Has he been known of long, or was his coming sudden into your woods?'

'Sudden was his advent. Deadly and cursed!' the hero then replied. 'For he was sent upon us by goddess Artemis. The vengeful deity of the forest: she set it on our land to punish my father for neglect of her sacrifice. The priests of her temple, my own uncles, they cry in defence of the monster. They sought before to stop my attempts to fell it. Hence come I recruiting, for none are there in Kalydon that dare to cross them, and go against the good will of the deity. But here we are heroes. We dare all. And you will dare all too. Be you welcome, for truly you have fine spirit!'

'Alas,' said the maiden, 'my mind changes fast: thus it is with women. For what you have told me now dashes all my zeal. Devotee of the goddess Artemis am I, nor could turn against my protectress. Did I not tell you she would punish my assailer? If then your boar is sent by that goddess, I could not hunt. To spurn my deity would be to incur death. Alas then, stranger, our talk is pointless. We cannot hunt together. Fly I must, before you tempt me further. This morning if you had gone to Tegea, who knows what might have been? But now farewell! You were my huntsman in vain.' And while Meleager stared sadly at her, she at once rose up, crossed the water, and sought her sisters on the other side.

Now pain stabbed the heart of rash Meleager when he saw her go, and thus did he exclaim, 'Why, now is sadness! O beautiful maiden, smooth and fiery, what loveliness is in your flesh, and what a sister I find in your mind! Why, with you could I hunt through the woods of time, running in joy together, with you could I greet each day with a new quest! And are you gone? O vanishing form, soft-skinned among the blossom! Never has been my heart so wracked before!' And with dismay now, the hero sat, and sighed by the bank of the river, and all his fire and spirit was overwhelmed.

Meanwhile, Atalanta also sorrowed, as she walked on her way, and thought, 'Alas, what strange turnings of Fate! How have I been this day whirled about from doubt to ecstasy, and now here pitched into a fearful new world! Meleager of Kalydon: his was the face was brought to me in my dream! How strange to meet a vision! What may it mean? Yet what

65

grief feel I! To meet this man so suddenly in the forest — one moment to hate him, then in friendship to talk — but now to leave him! O fearful goddess, should I be so abrupt? Should I turn back? Yet how can I think so? The man pursued me, beat me by false means, laughed at me, part-raped me! Is this how I treat the most braving of males? Oh, let me put his face behind me, and seek my maidens again. Surely have I been stirred up to some shame!' And so did she go on again, striding now forcefully back through the bushes, and listening in the stillness for sounds of hunting.

Yet as Atalanta climbed the hill once more towards the others, in a shaft of sunlight she saw gazing at her a crone. A strange old woman was standing by the trees, as if she waited her. From a veiling cloak she waved, as the maiden approached.

Then did the crone say, 'A naughty lady walking naked in the forest! Some lover has no doubt put out of your head the thought of clothing. Here take this necklace. It is good beads: it is of myrtle-berries. Settle it so about your lovely neck. Now you will not be so exposed, but dressed in best fashion, walk more confident in this new path.'

And the crone said, 'Back then. Before he vanishes. Seek Meleager again. Do you think Fate has brought you two together for nothing? You cannot go home now. The wrath of the suitors, the ministers and your father is set to have you forcibly married to whomsoever. This man you found here: he ran against you, overtook and caught you too. Remember that, and recall your vow! You vowed to pledge yourself to the man who beat you in the race. Well, you have found the man you vowed to take.'

And the crone smiled softly. 'Yet also, maiden, listen to your heart. Do you not today hear another music sounding? You are new to these woods. Put your trust in Nature. Go again to your man. Let things lead you on the sunlit way.'

And the crone ceased speaking, and like smoke rising from her falling rags, she glided on sunbeams into the fragrant heaven.

'O dreadful goddess!' then gasped Atalanta. 'Aphrodite,

was it ye? Do you seize me now from the guard of sweet Artemis? What fate then awaits me? How can I bear to know to what dread am I led? Yet Meleager, oh indeed, I must hurry to find!' And the virgin ran forth, and dodged by the pool again, and sped along the ravine, and sought once more her impulsive pursuer.

Him soon she found, for the hero sat still sad by the shuttered stream, casting the pure pebbles into its deeps. The dangling catkins hung above him, the showering pollen on his shoulders, the moths and water-flies sported over his head. Atalanta came rushing. At the splash he roused, and looked through the dappled leaves. Then did he joy to see the naked girl.

She stood before him and laughed softly. 'Comrade,' she said with a sigh, 'I am henceforth to be your huntsman.'

'Then welcome, campaigner!' replied Meleager, moving towards her embrace. 'With you at hand, my spear will ever be ready.'

But the virgin aside stepped from his arms, and walking on ahead, led him through the forest towards the fields.

PART THREE

Heracles' Games

Chapter Nine

Now billowed the smoke by the towering trees, oaks and
flowering chestnuts, now sounded the shouts of shepherds
by the sheep-cotes leaping. The bleating of flocks came as
goats ran fearful through the flames, the yapping dogs ran
eagerly about them. The great-horned ram snorted
furiously and amidst his sheep lowered his horns, but he,
even he was driven onward, as through crackling twigs and
hissing flame, they hurried the woolly ones on, sheep and
goats, tumbling in cloven panic, till they streamed
complaining, yet more peaceful, into the open hills, and
sank at last to browse on the damp clover. So did the
shepherds purify their flocks of Arcady on this the day of
their spring festival.

Yet by the cots, where the rows of beans were planted
neat and springing, where the lettuces grew and salads of
tender green, where the cat sprawled dusty, hens flew
about, and on old sticks puppies chewed, there also was
hurry and feasting under the sun, for the garlands and
sprays of the day of blossoms were decked about the eaves,
branches of blooming hawthorn and crab and peach-
blossom: these were nailed on the smoky-black beams of
the wattled cottages, and under the pointed leaves of the
sycamore tree, for the tables were set here on tied tressels,
and daisy-chains laid by the bowls, and benches pulled up
with cushions for a flowery feast. For here did the swains
of Arcadia see their shepherdesses laugh, as they tricked
out the day of celebration.

Yet amongst the shepherds were other folk, warriors
with tall spears, and shields marked in the emblems of their
tribes. Dryas was there, the Thracian prince, and Caeneus,
from Magnesia, with Peleus of Phthia, heroes of far lands.

For here was the band assembled by Meleager, the rash-headed, ready soon for the Boar-Hunt of Kalydon. But with shepherds, guests for the festival, they stood and watched with smiles, as the frisky flocks were driven to the fields.

When this was done, and the rowdy beasts idled in the shade by the stream — for the goats on the arbutus browsed as a favourite food, but they chewed also thistles and briars, and the sheep upon the dewy clover — then did they spill them water in oaken troughs, and while the purling stream diverted laughed in a new channel, far off in the sun there came the noise of summer, for about the poppies droned the bees, and in the rustling poplars whirred the cicadas with their dusty wings. But now the shepherds and their guests returned to the shady table, and all were set to enjoy the feast.

The heroes had presented the shepherds with a great bronze cauldron, in whose turbid tummy the broth seethed with oats and rye. In its swimming depths the shepherdesses now set their swirling ladles and dished out soup in bowls by the roasted meats. The women had pounded the garlic-paste and set on the scrubbed boards loaves white-floured and olives, plump and juicy. A feast of mirth and earth's good will: such was the country fare, and all about was rural happiness.

So that Dryas said, 'Why, here is pleasant, Damon, to live amidst these hills, and order your sheep with the turning seasons! When time dictates, you purge them of insects, drive them to the mountain pastures, bring them home, shear them of their fleeces. In winter's rage, you pen them close away with dry footing of straw, and with your hounds and stones keep wolves from the pinfold, and so begins the year again with washed wool and cheese to market, and salted larders and hives all full of honey. It is a deal more free from cares than our warrior's life, sailing looting seas, or with watchful troops biding the peril of ambush. Enchantment indeed is in Arcady hidden arcane away, embowered from the clash of tongues or arms.'

72

But Damon said, 'Oh? Then come you here when snowdrifts hold the pass, or Boreas blows cold through the cottage clean, or sores on the sheep spread uncheckable, no matter how sulphur is burnt, wax smeared on the skin with black bitumen and hellebore. Come you here, Dryas, when plague holds the flock, and the larder is empty of all, and the hills are high and nothing to trade in the market, and the wolves come closer and nightly snatch the bleating youngling from the fold, and the dog comes home from the master up the mountain alone. There is as small mercy in Nature's dice as there is in man's. You are a fool, if you think happiness is here.'

Now they broke off here this debate, for a sight across the field made them pause, for there they saw approaching more warriors with their spears, clad in bright cloaks, and fillets upon their brows. Wherefore did Dryas rise from the bench and cry, 'Lo, here they return, our heroes!' But then he stopped and stared at them puzzled. And thus did he say, 'And a sorry lot they look too! For now what has become of their bravery? They went forth finely, bound each one in quest of a golden prize, mad with lust to win the lovely princess of Tegea. But oh, bold suitors, how have you failed to become the husband of this girl? Whence do you return with failure sitting on your helms?' And Dryas smiling swept aside some places to sit them at the table, as the new warriors strode through the barking dogs.

But Acastus said, when they were sitting, and the shepherdesses had brought them broth and bread, and set about them salads of dressed herbs, 'Dryas, and you others, admit to our number now for the quest another hero: this, noble Ancaeus of Arcadia. He in disgust at what we saw today and what we all suffered, has quit his homeland, and for a brave future is come to throw in his fortune with ours. He is a fine hunter, and will swell the numbers of our boar-hunt, when we voyage to Kalydon on our mission.'

And Ancaeus, the new man, then bowed to the others

73

and said, 'It is true, O Hellenes, I have left my home-town Tegea for ever. I will join you, if you allow me, and I rejoice in such a band of men, untainted as it is by contaminating presence.'

And Dryas replied, 'Then are you welcome, sir. Surely our band grows apace, and Meleager, our leader, will be glad at another hero. He is at present restless, sir, and has gone chasing in the forest, but surely he wants all strong men that he can find. Do you know of any further heroes, that we could bring to our band, for as yet we could do with a greater number?'

But Ancaeus shook his head, and sighed and began eating what was before him, just as the others sighed and ate forlornly. And Peleus and Dryas stared at them puzzled, wondering what might have occurred at Tegea so to dispirit the heroes.

But now through the trees of the rustling greenwood, hieing across the turfy meadow, there now came wearily another hero, a messenger, bearing a staff in his hand, as if upon some kingly mission. And when he saw the others he cheered and speeded his step, and panted up crying, 'Ho, heroes, which is the way to Tegea?'

But when the warriors saw this king's official limping over the grass, they begged him sit and eat, as courtesy bid. And then as they all clustered about him, when he had fed himself, they asked him what was his embassy, if he could tell.

'Ay, surely I can tell that,' then replied the messenger. 'For my news is general, to all young men such as yourselves. For news I bring of a festival to be held this summer in Olympia, that will bring all Hellas together in one place. And from all cities are all your heroes bidden come compete in running, leaping, throwing, to come pit yourself in sport against your fellows, and drink the mad tension and joy of the race. For a Games is to be held greater than ever have been held in the world, and this will mark the beginning of the worldwide union. Every four years shall these Games be made, and the champions that therein win, they will be renowned over all the earth. Will you compete?'

'Ay, that we will!' cried the heroes now in glee, and all their faces brightened round the table.

'Yet you must excuse me,' continued the messenger, 'that this message is late I bring you, but I fell ill by the way in the mountains of Arcady. Nor have I brought yet my message to Tegea. Wherefore I bid you point me the way, and with that news my embassy will at last be completed. Yet truly you look already, sirs, like a company of athletes, all set as if to try your strength on the track. You will find under Heracles a mighty sport going forward, and many of your great mettle will you also meet.'

'Indeed,' said Dryas, 'we will go to the Games, and we will seek there further heroes, for surely there will be the pick of all Greece. Fate has given us now a chance to make our band against the Boar invincible, for no other way could we discover such strength. Now messenger, stay with us tonight, for the evening hastes upon us, and tomorrow we may point you the way to Tegea.'

'I thank you, sir.'

'And so,' continued Dryas, 'the high days come upon us! Our company grows and soon we will show our prowess. Yet will no man tell me — I burn to discover — what happened with the princess of Tegea? What occurred at her choosing to strew so many gloomy faces? Surely you could not all have wished for the bride, or hoped at least all to get her? One man one wife is the general rule in Hellas. You, sir, Ancaeus, the new man amongst us: your own country it was: can you not reveal this morning's secrets?'

'Alas,' sighed Ancaeus, 'a greater shame was never known to man! Oh, speak not to any of us of that dishonour!'

And here the heroes once more relapsed into deep melancholy, and all sat about the table, toying with their food.

Now while the band of Kalydon thus feasted with the shepherds, Meleager led Atalanta through the forest, and he took her to the look-out spot where he had begun his hunting, and where he had left his pole and travelling-bag. Here then did he take his petasos, and stack it on his head, but also in his bag he found a cloth, and tearing this to make a tunic, he gave it to Atalanta, so that she might clothe herself for wayfaring. And when this was done, he smiled at her, and looked into her eyes, and then he paused and spoke to her in earnest.

'Now Atalanta,' said he sadly, 'this is a turning of the ways, and from this point the way is settled forward. Wherefore I bid you choose yet again, and have no compulsion upon it, for of your own will you must on or not at all. You have told me your father lives hereby, an exiled nobleman, a farmer and a forester, with a brood of many. And as we stand here to the leftward lies the way to your father's cottage, while rightwards the road rolls to my company. Choose then your fate: to join our hunting-band, the journey to Kalydon, the danger of tracking and bringing down the Boar, or choose to return to your father's cottage, and live a dutiful life, a girl indeed, serving a farmer's days. What say you then? I ask again, for never unwillingly would I have you by, stepping forward together.'

Now Atalanta looked back at the prince, and for a while she paused, and then she said, 'I have given my choice already. This is my destiny, to come with you, and hunt in the Kalydon band, and join with men in pursuit of the Titan-Beast. This only constrains me: the beast you hunt is a beast of Artemis, and I am dread of giving her sacrilege. And this constraint further: that you and I have lain naked together, and I am doubtful of your lust towards me. Will you then, Meleager, promise me that still you will keep your kindness, and never seek to take unwillingly my love? In the forest, when there you had me, powerless, at my unwillingness you ceased. Let me then ask you: keep this kindness forward. For as I told you: a

76

savage am I, bred amidst the forest, and there is a protection upon my maidenhead. Whoever takes it will soon see death. These words I know only. Therefore beware of me and of your feelings.'

Now when she said this, Meleager paused, and stared at her a while, but then he said, 'He is a coward that bides old wives' tales, and I reck nothing of them, for who can tell the fate of prophecies? And I could tell you — will tell you soon — of the talisman of my soul, wherein reputedly all my life is kept. But there was a way round such prohibitions in the birth of my days, so may there be round these our present cautions. Yet fear you not. Today I never raped you, nor will I tomorrow. If love is to come, it will be on both sides. But I am calling you forth to our company not as a maid or mistress, but as a hunter, as I have seen you are. So give me your answer.'

'It is given,' smiled the huntress back. 'Where are these heroes? Let us sharpen our spears!' And with a laugh, the pair of them shouldered their lances and packs and poles, and off along the afternoon track they jaunted.

Now when evening approached, and the band of heroes, feasting still at their table, had recovered their cheer, rejoiced at the news of the Games, as the sun now slanted through the amber trees, Damon, the shepherd-swain, addressed them and said, 'Heroes, you are not alone in having contests. With brawny arms and sleek-thighed legs you pit the strength of your bodies, but we with throats and voices compete in singing-contests. For tradition decrees that in verse-competitions the shepherds of Arcady grow their art, and promote the saintly crafts of Apollo. Therefore to lull you after the banquet, hear us at these sports, and after see which you agree has the garland.' And the shepherd then called forth for young Thyrsis, a swain with a faraway look, and urged him to join him in his singing.

Then spoke again Damon, 'Now, sirs, our rules are easy to follow. The lines we sing are by tradition hexameters: the six-beat verses used by our epic poets and by oracles

of the god, here given a rustic holiday. First I will make up
four lines on a chosen subject, and then must Thyrsis
follow, and he must copy or cap what I have sung, and so
we proceed in the quantitative lilt of the rhythm of our
Western blood and the language sung by all our gods.'
And so did the shepherd arrange with his peer to have an
Arcadian match, and soon were they plucking their lyres
thus in the fields.

DAMON

Nymphs of the chill cataracts, grey-eyed and lithe
   hamadryads,
harken and inspire him that brings honeycakes for your
   altar,
curds and cream cool-poured, as Damon prince of the
   goatherds
sings one of his ravishing cool songs, and victory bids for.

THYRSIS

Muses of high Apollo, sunset-winged over the mountains,
lift me upon plumes up to heaven, with coals coruscate
   my
heart, that his own splendours no dust can touch, nor
   come desecration,
for pure is the song of Thyrsis, both humble and haughty.

DAMON

Autumn is merriest season. With barley and oat-stacks
stored roofwards, billygoats butting and fat herds ever-
   plenteous.
Sweet is it at sundown, with smells of mist in the pastures,
to sit around chestnuts in the fire, and speak of the old
   days.

THYRSIS

Wild poppies in scarlet drug me with fumes in the hayfield,
and butterflies, rust-hued, brush my soft hand.
   Meditating
on spring's best blossoming, sadness I see in the flags, and

blue anemones honouring Adonis' grave, bright with his
    anguish.

DAMON

While screech-owls from the old stables, and crows from
    the ash-tree
keep up a long wailing, as if endless night were upon them,
I of the good sunny hill will sing, with flowers checkered
    over.
Life brief as daisies will yield its sweets to the sunlight.

THYRSIS

While trilling in cheap rhymes the sparrow sends songs
    from the barnyard
and rooting hogs grunt, their snouts set fast in the daisies,
I spurn these sunny heights to ponder an hour on the
    canyon:
how deep those creepers that fall like waters of evening!

DAMON

Home, enough of browsing, fat goats, run home from the
    hillside:
on broom and nutty-flavoured gorse, and heath ever-
    purple,
you've fed enough. Mist sinks in the vales. Smoke drifts
    from the homestead,
and vanishing haywains creak over the hill to the sunset.

THYRSIS

Ay, enough of the prickles, enough of these thorns of the
    wayside,
sleep's beckoning, my flocks, and airs of the silvery
    chamber.
With the lavender hanging by the door, with the posy of
    hyacinths,
love throws open a closed window towards slumberous
    oceans.

Now when the shepherds thus ceased their songs, the harkening heroes mused, and nodded in contentment at their charm. But then to seek to decide the winner they pitted their thoughts as well, and argued for Damon and the delicate Thyrsis. Yet they were no critics, and they had not the power to reason like from like, and so they judged according to their humour, the thoughtful and the active inclining by nature to those verses in which their souls — thoughtful or active — were mirrored. But now the dusk was kindling with fire the oak-trees of the west, and the doves already roosting in the elm-trees, when two figures came over slowly through the dewy grass, exciting the puzzlement of the gathering. At first they could not see who they were and squinnied in the dusk, but then there came a clatter of wine-bowls dropped on the table.

For nearing the feast, nodding upon them, holding a hunting-spear, there walked naked and handsome their leader Meleager, but by his side there came wrapt close in a glowing cloak of azure, softly smiling, the princess Atalanta. This sight was enough to set all those who had been to Tegea in startled amazement, reeling from the table.

But Meleager smiled and said, 'Hail, heroes. I bring us a new hunter: a girl who lives with her father in these woods. Make her then welcome, for she has great skills at tracking and catching beasts, and I am gladsome to bring her into our band.' But then he ceased, for all about him he saw the staring faces. 'Why gawp you so?' he said with a strange look.

'Now Dryas,' then said Ancaeus hoarsely, 'you asked us what went at Tegea, and for very dishonour none of us could make ourselves tell. I told you of shame, and shame it was, shame beyond all telling! There is the reason! What does that woman here? Oh, do not you blench to look upon my face, girl, again? Oh, are you ever to make my life a misery? Foul minx, shameful harlot, gross deluding witch! I shall tell the rest what has occurred! This morning that woman took all of these heroes on at a running-race, and beat them by the foul wiles of her sex! She shamed good men before all Arcady by trouncing them in the race, and showing them naked clowns before all the land! Nor that alone, but with her maidens, her girls giggling in frenzy, she danced in triumph at defeating such men, and all these females pranced in abandon, lording it over the strong sex, laughing to bring to demeaning their noble betters! Send her from here! She will not join us! Though I am only just welcomed, I say get her out! She is poison! I know her well!'

'How can you know her?' then said Meleager. 'She is from the woods. How can you — Who are you anyway?'

'His name is Ancaeus. He comes from Tegea. He has joined our band.'

'Then back he shall go if he keeps up this rudeness!'

'No, but Meleager, he spake true! This girl indeed shamed us all! She made us fools this morning before the whole of Arcady!'

'Nonsense!' cried Meleager. 'She is but a forest-girl, skilled in the chase, drawn of a noble but humble household.'

'She is not!' they shouted back. 'She's Princess of Tegea!'

Meleager stood staring at them puzzled.

'She is Princess of Tegea!' they said again.

'She's what?' said Meleager.

'Princess of Tegea!' they shouted. 'We saw her this morning at the Games! Ask her yourself! Ask her if she is not Atalanta?'

Meleager sighed and looked at the girl.

Atalanta smiled at him and nodded.

Chapter Ten

Now when the March winds blew vigorous, curling the black waves of the ocean, Heracles, the lion-killer, strove forward and put his shoulders to his mighty enterprise in Olympia. First did he measure a precinct for his father Zeus on the meadows by the Alpheus, and there he set flat the land and dug pits for the foundations of the chief of the immortals' temple. Next did he fence off a sacred grove, and hallow its rustling canopy, and here among fir-trees and cypresses he made green lawns calm and welcoming. The blustery winds of the young year blew sleet on the hills, and the river flowed swollen and muddy, but the swards of Olympia soon in blithe airs put forth the flowers of promise.

Now by the forested hill overlooking the site Heracles walked and pondered. From the top of it he gazed, sizing out the ground, debating where to fix race-track and hallway. The snaking river swung around. At the pine-bowered foot of the slope, a temple to Hera lay, ancient and vari-columned. The hill the hero named Kronion after the ancient Cretan father, Kronos of the Golden Age. Then to the twelve deities he raised altars six at the copse's edge, and burnt sacrificial thighs on a fire of white poplar. And the April showers brought with abundance the lush, dewy grass springing about each god's table.

But when the sun had climbed the azure sky and shone hot on the sweet-scented blossoms of Maytime, then Heracles was sweating on the plain, flattening out the throwing-grounds and clearing the thistles from the jumping-pits. Plagued by buzzing flies he slaved, treading forth the measures, sizing with his foot the race-track of the stadium, and there he set the turning-point, raising banks on either side, marking the start and the stand for the umpires. And the year grew strong and beauteous, humming with heavy bees, leaping with young lambs and calves and swallows. And so the heady June appeared, blazing in gold, and all was ripe among the flies and resinous.

Yet when the June came blazing forth, to the precincts there now arrived the first contestants for the Games, and the ministers and elders also strutted with thrust-forth chins, and others who fancied themselves officials. From Elis, and the city of Pisa, trooped the many headmen, anxious to oversee their important duties, and they looked about the work of Heracles, found fault with this and that, debated over the adequacy of his provisions. Meanwhile, the menial folk of Elis put their shoulders to stone, and raised the walls, and set the pillars of temples, and along they brought white marble slabs, pure as sacred oxen, to roof the growing walls of the temple of Zeus.

But as the ground began swarming now, Oenomaus appeared, King of Elis, with Hippodamia, his lovely daughter. Decked in pomp had she been brought to join his recent triumphs, and in a chariot did she ride beside him. Nor was the queen there, Sterope, she of the stubborn features, for the daughter was preferred to the mother, and like a dazzling moon she swept by, closed in the wheel's embrace, with the eyes upon her constantly of her jealous father. And these came by and called Heracles to break off all his labours, to entertain them night and day by the tents by the river.

Yet also arrived to the strengthening throng, he of the shoulder-bite, the devoured of the gods: Pelops, one-time Prince of Lydia and Phrygia. He it was in his babyhood, by his father Tantalus sliced, ended up in a cooking-pot for the table. The gods themselves were given the babe, duly boiled and tenderised, and ere they had discovered the perpetration, one of them ate the shoulder-blade of the lost boy: Demeter, the lamenting mother. To Hell pitched they the evil father, suffering never-slaked thirst and hunger, to endure an eternity of tantalising, to life again the son restored, beloved of the immortals, and a shoulder-blade of ivory gave him replacing. And Pelops from far Asia came now, and the Paphlagonian sought in mainland Hellas to make his future.

But soon as Pelops had come to Olympia, eager to compete, his eye fell upon shining Hippodamia. As keen as blades cutting his heart, he felt himself again pierced through and sliced in pieces, but by love. The eyes of the princess were proud and haughty: high among horses she loomed, guarded about by powerful stallions. Her frozen white face showed sleek and implacable, with her ringleted hair wild and bound, glittering with diadems. And Pelops yearned to become her suitor, longing to hold that dream, and to the king he came, and addressed the new monarch of Elis.

'Oenomaus, King of Pisa, I, an exile but a prince, master of many, hail you, sacker of Elis. Yours is a new realm, now distinguished by Panhellenic meeting, and yours is a living crown indisputable. I see beside your breast a vision, more goddess than woman, yet a vision you cannot hope ever to cling on to. If you are so minded, let me put my name before your gaze, as a suitor for the hand of Princess Hippodamia. For me I would win the stuff of yearning, for you strength and protection, riches in my gift, and the championship of my prowess. Accept me then, monarch, as a son, and in these Games let me prove myself, for surely I will never rest, till I have the lady.'

'Impious wretch!' replied Oenomaus. 'You are a stranger here, and had it not been, your presumption would have proved fatal. For you have dared where daring is forbidden, and where darers have visited death short time hereafter. For who knows not Oenomaus guards his daughter before all other men, and that those that ask her hand are cursed to destruction? For I tell you, prince, as many as have asked her: each man has met his death, for I myself overcome their braving. We will forget you have made this approach. To you as a stranger, we must extend the protection of hospitality. But never seek to ask again what you have asked today. Nor let others hence speak of it.' And the angry king whipped his horses suddenly and clattered away in dust, while Pelops watched the monarch curiously.

Now while these things were going forward in the Olympian dale, towards Alpheus there marched another company, for the band of Kalydon, pledged to hunt the Artemisian Boar: these made their way through Arcadian forest. In the vanguard there marched Dryas and Acastus, striving forward stoutly. Behind these came Caeneus and Lelex. By these and some others Meleager strode fierily, at his side Atalanta, rejoicing to stalk as a hunter with quiver of arrows. But glum at the back and with surly features the woman-hater Ancaeus stomped moodily. And when they stopped, he made complaint to the other heroes.

And Ancaeus said, 'Now hear me, brothers, I know I am only just joined your fellowship, but I am pledged like everyone here to hunt the Boar of Kalydon. To this I agreed, when I left with the others the farce of Tegea town, and Acastus and Lelex here will bear me out. But one thing to which I did not agree was to join in a band with women. I cannot think you mean truly to bring that woman with us?' And Ancaeus, as he said this, pointed with contemptuous finger at Atalanta.

But Atalanta said to him, 'Who do you not, dog-face, keep silent? Or either that, or go back to Tegea. Though I have left my girls in that town, still you will be at peace there, for you will not have me to egg them on against you. But I have joined this band of Kalydon, because as I have shown you: I can run faster and aim straight as a man. So why should I not be part of this hunt? If you would kill the Boar, you need me, a fine hunter, to assure it. We go to Olympia. We seek the Games. We are aiming to find other heroes. Good then, let them replace this doubter. But I say this: if we find a hero who can run faster than I, then surely I will go home, and you can on without me.' And the huntress ceased there, and no one further wished to stir up trouble, and so after eating, they again pressed forward.

Meanwhile in Olympia, still there arrived heroes from over Greece: from the Argolid they came now and the islands. Some streamed from the north, winding their way through Achaia's grey-sloped crags, some from the coast travelling the reeds upriver. From Sparta too the warriors approached, with long spears and round shields, conical pointed helmets on their heads, meanwhile their commanders came with helmets crested in wide-fanned plume, scarfed in dark cloaks, menacing and intent. All these arrived in the pleasant plain, and set up their warlike tents, and the fires began to twinkle in the valley.

Now when the dawn came, and touched the hill of Kronos with warm beams, chasing the dewy shadows from the laurel copses, then did the warriors take to the fields to practise their athletic arts, and the meadow was filled with the sunburnt strivers. Here did the heroes oil their limbs from lekythoi of perfumed olive, and gleaming-anointed, stretch their legs in exercise: some to coil round for discus-hurling, some to bend back the spear, some to thud and leap through the silver air. And the coaches came, old grey-beards who had seen their racing-days, and now barked keenly to make others skip before them.

But amongst these athletes, as Heracles with frowning brow busily walked, hurrying to where his next enterprise was a-building, there came to him furious a one-handed man, Trophonius, of gloomy aspect, who said, 'Cease there, O braggart and usurper! I come to this place, Heracles, disabled as you see, and protected by the truce of the Games approaching, knowing that if not by strength at least I may by argument show you to be a coward and ingrate. Augeias you have pushed from the throne of his rightful rule in Elis, and set up instead this braver, incestuous Oenomaus. Yet I challenge you to debate with me the right of your case, and all these Hellenes I call upon to give judgement.'

But Heracles said, 'Be off, Trophonius, I know you of old, and you were always a spreader of doubt and misery. You and Augeias had your day when with armies you vanquished me, but now is the tide turned which you set sail on. Be content with defeat then: death is worse. Not again will I compete with your cause, unless you or some others will partake in the contest, for at athletics I will challenge any you care to put against me. And this is the spirit I expect of all at the Games.' And Heracles went to the wrestling-ground where they built the gymnasium, but gloomy Trophonius walked to a bevy of warriors.

And he said to the men, 'You see how he braves? I said it would be thus. Yet he is wrong to refuse debate in council. Be ready then, comrades, by straight means or crooked, you men I appoint to his challenge: at boxing or wrestling, pounce upon him and wrench him. We leave not here with Heracles' neck safe upon his shoulders. He is to be made to see the other way!' And the comrades went off, glancing sidelong, intent on conspiracy, and they envied all the building and striving about them.

Meanwhile, upon Alpheus the band of Kalydon came from the hills, and daylong marched along its miles to the seaward. Through the gorge from the Megalopic plain they threaded with echoing crags to the forested hush of its northward travel, thence pierced the limestone hills wherein with sullen roar from the dark, the river disappeared from the sight of sky, in fir-hung silence running subterranean with most far-off turmoil, only to burst rejoicing again to sunlight, and foaming at its pebbles' edges to glitter a new path, and laugh again in pursuit of the ocean.

But when they had marched by its banks enough, so that Olympia was close, then once more the surly Ancaeus addressed them. And the warrior said, 'This very day's march takes us to the Games, and soon in a pack we will be swaggering the field. I put to you again: how can we go there? We will be a laughing-stock, because our band has in it a woman! I have spoken of this, but nothing has come of it, since it seems to me, you are all afraid to cross your

87

leader, Meleager. Yet this he must vouch, and she as well: there is no arguing with this: a woman cannot partake in the Games of Olympia!' And when he had said this, Ancaeus was silent, for he saw all about him silently nodding in agreement of his speech.

And Acastus spoke now, and said, 'Ay, indeed this is true. Best if she turns and goes home. For also I think it is an injustice that she should be here, for we all march alone with no company but each other, while Meleager has his doxy following him. And her he prefers — I have noted it — to all of us in his leadership, ever harkening her words and giving her the best quarry. If we are a band, then we must be men, and men alone too, for always there is trouble around women. So I say we insist: let him expel her. Why should we bow to her! Let her go, or let him go without us!'

'Surly, snout-faced wretch!' then cried Meleager. 'Do you challenge my leadership? Press on yourself then, on, and be slaughtered by the Boar. I prefer her, and harken her words, and give her the best quarry! You jealous fool. I do not. Why should I be swayed? Nor do not you seek to be treacherous and move my men against me. They are mine, as also she is, all part of my company. I will fight you for this, pugnacious rebel. And Ancaeus, you join him too. The pair of you arm yourselves. I am not for forgiveness. You lying hounds: she is no doxy, nor do I treat her fair, nor has there been any friction from her coming!' And Meleager with tears of rage drew forth his sword, and set up his round shield, and crouched ready to fight any or all that came.

But Dryas said, 'Let us calm ourselves. How foolish it is to fight now, when a little more march and we have reached the Games. Here is no time to quarrel over such things. We must be on our mettle, seeking more heroes, distinguishing ourselves also. Therefore, rash Meleager, take not offence. These do but speak their minds, and no criminal deed is this to give vent. Yet it is true also that they speak sense, for this very night Olympia will be gained, and surely we cannot go there with Atalanta thus! There may be some women attending tribes, or settled about the camps, but she cannot appear as if she were a competitor.' And Dryas spoke calmly, laying his arm on Meleager's to steady him, while all about him nodded their heads.

But Atalanta spoke easily, 'My comrades,' she said, 'I am a girl. No one seeks to deny it. But as you have seen I am still a hunter. I can run and spear and read the tracks of beasts. In all these forested things I am as good as any man. Why do you think then on matters of policy, I am an abject fool? Why do you consider I have no brains in my head? I can see in the Games of Olympia there will be no contesting for a girl. This struck me as soon as in Arcady we heard of the contests. But since I have a brain of my own, do you leave me to cope with my problem. I am well able to see to these things. No one will notice a girl — this I pledge! — among the band of Kalydon. But now let us on. Olympia I long to behold!' And with that the virgin bounded up and raced by the grey-green stream, and the swans flew up excited at her sudden surge.

Chapter Eleven

But when soft-bosomed dusk was cloaking the Altis, and spreading checkered clouds on the horizon, into the grove of Olympia, raging and loud, with a crash of chariots and thudding of horsemen, there arrived King Iasos in haste from Arcadia, with black face looking thunder. Nor did the king stay and greet those he met, but straight away he rattled with his team of horses, and through all those that threaded among the olives and the cypresses, he set his manic wheels a-whirling.

First amidst the ranks of course officials did the monarch fume, seeking and throwing aside those who displeased him. Next among the athletes went he peering about, studying each face, seeking for any that were in Tegea. Then did he race his chariot along the tent-poles and the fires, and search among the servants and the camp-followers. But finding nothing, he swerved again to the precincts of Zeus, and there he encountered a kingly party.

For here was Oenomaus, walking in state, surrounded by his warriors, coming from the new altar raised to Zeus, and Oenomaus saluted the King of Arcadia, expecting to welcome and be welcomed by his monarchial brother. But angry King Iasos after brief salute turned away, and sought again busily among the gathering. Then raced off once more, leaving the king standing, as off he and his horsemen hurried, the dust lit russet by the sinking sun, to race along the site of the gymnasium.

Now sweating still, laying flat the practice-ground, and founding a bath-house and an oil-store and a changing-room, there slaved great Heracles, even at dusk directing the hodded labourers, or setting to himself with bulging muscles. Now burrowed he out the pits among roots and

boulders for the timbers supporting the roof, now laid he
forth the pavements along the string-lines for the inside of
the colonnade. And a fury of frowning energy seemed to
fizzle about him, so that all around him men were fired to
action.

But King Iasos drew up, and he called from his chariot-
train, and he yelled, 'Heracles, lay off your labours! Here
am I in fury, King Iasos himself, summoned from Arcadia
by reports and messages of dire menace. To you I come,
to challenge you: make reparation swiftly, should you have
any crime against me, for if you have my daughter,
Atalanta, princess of Tegea, this Games will be by warfare
blown asunder!' And the king yelled so, while Heracles
stopped and looked, and with weariness sighed and
stomped towards them.

And Iasos continued, 'You know me, I think, Heracles,
and assuredly both of us respect each other's prowess.
Wherefore I warn you, if these reports coming from the
forests are true, I will hold you and these Games in account
for abduction! For the word has reached me that Princess
Atalanta, my daughter, skilled in the chase, has been
ravished away, and that the Prince of Aetolia, rash-headed
Meleager, has taken her, and harkened to her pleas to
bring her to these Games. All this I can indeed credit. You
respect no king. But if she is here with that man: you, sir,
will pay for it!'

Now Heracles when he had heard all this, looked at
Iasos with a groan, and said, 'King, I have more work here
for myself than stealing daughters. If you have a princess
a runaway, let that be your care. Over family quarrels
make no war with your neighbours. Your girl I have heard
of. From what they tell me she is a lass of spirit, who nicely
trumped recently your schemes to have her married, and
beat at running several princes, who here might hope to
win. All this would endear her to me, if I ever met her. But
I tell you, king, take your rash accusations to another man.
I have no time for these petty squabbles. Go to King
Oenomaus: he will sympathise, for he himself is like to be

soon in your pickle. Meleager is not here, nor Atalanta, and as for your fantasies: go and howl them solitary in the woods!' And Heracles turned his back on the monarch, and went again to his work, and all about him the labourers smirked and spaded.

Now while these matters kept the eastward end of Olympia in a ferment, other arrivals set other parts on fire, for into the west, by the newly set race-track, with wondering eyes there came Meleager and his band, reaching the site just in daylight. Meleager, fiery-eyed, strode in the front, Acastus at his side, with Lelex and Dryas peering about behind them, and the heroes gaped at the race-track ready, and the newly turfed embankment, and the stone-dressed place for the judges' tribunal.

And seeing all this, Meleager said, 'Why, look here at this battle-ground! Sure enough here we can have some contest! For here we could drum our feet on the ground with all Hellas watching, and in sight of all win laurels for our brow. And see those fires smoking beyond the embankment: the tribes are already assembled: greater champions to fight than could be found in any war! Why, here is the ultimate place indeed to win yourself glory! Oh, would that the Games were now, and me to run them!' And the hero prowled about, peering on the starting- and turning-points, till with a shout deserting his fellows, he ran the length of the stadium, and they saw his heels whipping away smartly along the greensward.

Now when the others had come after, and all together the band of Kalydon raced on the Olympic track, first of the runners who reached Meleager was a long-legged boy, and they scrambled then together up the embankment. From that turfy perch laughing, eyeing each other merrily, they looked down, the boy and Meleager, upon the humming vale below of green Olympia, wherein the heart of Hellas was now held. And they saw fresh temples and pillars, mules and teeming labourers, great pits and shafts dug among the sunset-kindled trees.

Beyond a row of canvas spread out like a line of market-stalls, they and the others who now reached them, saw the Altis, the sacred grove, wherein among pines and firs were altars of Zeus, heavy with the woven garlands. Beyond these sacred panoplies, and the wooden images of Gods, they saw the dug mud and stakes of the palaestra. Past these again were bustling the tents of the officials and the athletes, the labourers and mess-tents murmuring also, and a wealth of fires lay by the hills, like fire-flies on the meadow, while the untroubled Alpheus glided westwards.

Now cheered by this stirring vision, the band of Kalydon dashed down, and laughing nodded and joked with those they encountered, and through all the busily working army they swaggered and stared, rejoicing as at a fair to see so many. For down on the ground they met with beggars, already hobbling for alms, and oil-sellers and makers of spears and discus, and from the stalls there clattered and hummed the sound of a carnival, with reed-pipes eerily shrieking and shaking cymbals. And through all this they passed by the porch of the new temple of Zeus, and came to where was a gathering of nobles.

Now at this gathering was Pelops, and he had the ear of the nobles, and held in his hand the speaker's mace. And Pelops said, 'Hear me then, Hellenes, for at the Games of Olympia, all may speak without fear of causing war, for here is universal peace established throughout the lands and islands, and none but the impious would seek to break that truce. Wherefore I again come to the presence of King Oenomaus here, and without fear I speak what I did in the Altis: I sue to maintain the claim I made there for the hand of Hippodamia, his daughter, nor will I be put off by threats upon my life. Let him then tell me what pain he puts upon her would-be husbands, for I am content to endure anything for her sake.' And Pelops finished, gazing afar off to where in the camp of the king, Hippodamia was sitting with her handmaids.

But Oenomaus scowled at this, and before the throng he strode, and picking the mace up turned and surlily addressed them, and thus he spoke. 'The claim of this youth, Pelops here, a refugee from Asia, this, my friends, I have great reason to ignore. All know in this gathering how my daughter is most precious to me, and never lightly do I entertain thought of suitors. Yet when she is challenged, I do my best to dissuade the youth from the task, for by the rules of our tradition, they otherwise meet death. So do I with Pelops: he has suffered, and he is loved of the gods: I would not lightly seek to harm him. Thus I turn my back on him, and bid him with virtuous thoughts: seek well a kinder father-in-law!

'Yet know this, Pelops, were you to take the path of the other suitors, and challenge me inevitably to the decision, you would come to compete with me in a chariot-race, for whoever wants my child must defeat me in that most dangerous of sports. Always in that race in the past not only have I won, but the suitor himself has met a grisly death. Do not tempt me therefore to bring on you a mangling of horses' hoofs, and dismemberment at the flying spokes of a war-cart. Leave well alone, for as you say: here is universal peace. Let us all be Hellenes and friends with one another.' And Oenomaus ceased at this, while Pelops looked keen to hear more. Yet before he might speak, Meleager and his band were abruptly noticed.

For King Iasos, that attended these issues thoughtful and siding with the king, now suddenly saw them, and with a great shriek pointed, and cried, 'Look, where he stands, the very man I spoke of! Rash-headed Meleager! He who like Pelops lays impious hands on a man's daughter! Who has not heard of his impulsive ways, swaggering in his own country, spurning the priests of the cult of Artemis? Come here, you runaway! Answer me this: if you lusted my daughter, why did you not come compete for her as other princes? And where have you hidden her? Tell me outright: in what cave or secret grove have you set my daughter, escaped from us to the forest? I will arraign you in this assembly before all the tribes of Hellas! Here at least there can be no avoiding!'

But Meleager cried, 'I challenge you to fight, coward-caller King Iasos! You will rue accusing me of weakness before these warriors! If I had wanted your daughter, ay, indeed, I would have come for her! And won her too, not like the slackers that competed! I did not come, because I had no liking. I am in search of men, not women, men to take on the Giant Boar of Kalydon! And then I had not heard that the princess was indeed the equal of any man, as equal as she surpasses all men in beauty. But if you think I have hidden your daughter, and have her skulking in a forest, why then, call me coward indeed, I'll own it. If I have the princess, then here she is: you see all my men present. No more nor less than them have I assembled.' And as Meleager ceased at this, stout Heracles approached, his day's task finished, repairing to the nobles to see what was toward.

But as soon as he saw him, King Iasos again raged. 'There is his accomplice!' he shouted. 'You, Heracles, you told me this minute before witnesses, you had no part in Meleager's being here, nor was he here at all, and look: look how you lied in your teeth! This Olympiad of ours: what a blessing it is, for here is assembled all Hellas, and these disputes can be seen truly for what they are. I appeal to my peers then: King Oenomaus here, and others of Sparta and Argos: have I not occasion now to have Heracles fined? Fined, nay imprisoned! Imprisoned, nay rather given some dire penance! I will not submit to these lies and deceits and insults! On him must be some penitential labour!'

'Oh, run and submerge your face!' then said Heracles. 'If any man seeks more penances for me, I shall kill him! Have I not enough with the Labours of Hercules, killing lions, stags, cleaning stables, without any other custard-headed king employing me? Is it not enough, wretches, to have this Olympic Games: all arranged for you, half-builded, set out? Do you want also my blood painting every stone? I did this because Zeus, father of the gods, himself demanded it! But tempt me no tittle with any more talk of penance! Or by the gods one demand further from a bead-eyed cockerel like this king, and I shall run mad and savage you all! This Meleager is new come. Hail, Meleager! I have never seen him before in my life. Now shut your traps, for Heracles is going to sleep!' And Heracles furious stomped his way off towards his camp, and sickened flung himself down on a couch and into dreams.

But Telamon of Salamis now took up the neglected mace and said, 'Hellenes, the day grows late about us, and tomorrow we are to begin the first competitions of the Games. This is no time surely to settle disputes. Yet the Games themselves, as has been claimed, are resolvers of contestation, and what I propose is that all this is therein tested, and by a game decided one way or other. So let Heracles sustain the challengers we have heard of earlier that have come from the disgruntled Trophonius, and let king Oenomaus, when the time comes for the race of chariots, seek to compete in his usual fashion, with this son of Tantalus, and let the king and Myrtilus, his charioteer, do their utmost to decide who shall keep Hippodamia. And as for Meleager, let him partake in what games he will. While the truce is on, King Iasos may not seize him. But whenever and wherever the last contest of all is played in the arena, once it is done, then let him pay the reckoning, for truly it seems Atalanta is somewhere, and why should these not know? King Iasos has told us what the shepherds told him.'

And with this, since the moon was shining now over the turbulent plain, those assembled agreed, and seized that moment to go to bed.

But Meleager went a while wandering by the riverside, and the long-legged boy stepped with him pace for pace. And the boy with him wore a tunic, belted, that came to his knees, and shapely and delicate were his smooth legs. The hair of the lad was soft and golden, but tightly bundled up, so that most of it was crammed beneath a travelling-cap, a petasos, whose wide brim keeps off the tumbling wayside dust, or the heat of the plain in

Thessalian summer. And quietly they laughed at all that had gone before, till Meleager spoke, as he splashed in the stream.

'Now Atalanta, hidden maiden and runner unsurpassed, by Fate we have been thrust into the throng of things! No time was there to worry if your disguise would be accepted, no time to dread if Iasos was hounding you, no time to wonder if he had heard anything from those we left behind that you indeed had made a part of our company. Of all these dangers we were given the lot on the dot! And meeting our troubles in one heap has so solved them!'

'It is a wise father,' said Atalanta, 'knows his own child, and Iasos, my comrade, has not shown great wisdom. He does not do well to make of Heracles a foe. Yet he is of the crew that resent all strength. How I despise this cringing away from all deeds of daring, all new tradition, all that aspires or has zest! And how seeing him here again, with all his court about him, I rebel at the thought of returning home! What, a life of sitting weaving, spinning, gossiping! Then being saved from all this by a loonish husband! I owe him small love. When I was a babe, Iasos set me in the forest to die. But suckled by a bear I held on to life. Thus am I savage, but thus also I owe him little duty, especially when he is by fury blinded!'

Now as they strolled in amity by the sky-reflecting stream of Alpheus, as night closed in, there came to drink a roe-deer. Its dappled back was hidden in dusk, yet still its white underside showed soft and luminous, mirrored in the dark waters. Atalanta drew near, and looking up, the deer held her in its eye, nor did it seek to stop from drinking or gallop, and the hunting-maiden approached quietly, and smiling at Meleager, touched the deer and stroked its short-haired back. Awhile the creature looked up at her, as at some tame mistress, but Meleager approaching, it bounded up and away.

'I see,' said Meleager, 'the animals do not regard me as a friend, whereas you, huntress, have them tame and mild. You give them your hand with easy kindness. Yet to me you will not. I see you belong to the forest rather than man. But do I not run with you? Do I not race and hunt at your side? Is it not time to think on me as a friend, and give me cherishing? Will you die if as to this deer you reach out to touch me? Why cannot I be dear to you as well?'

But Atalanta glowered and said, 'Because I am no doe! A boy of your band am I, to hunt the Boar-Giant! Do you think I have run a desperate race, and left my own homeland merely to fall for the trap that I left at home? I want no suitors, Meleager, believe it! Why do you do me that wrong to treat me not as a comrade, but as a slave? Can you not have me as your friend? I want no kisses, no caresses. But you are just a man like all the others!'

And Meleager said, 'Surely a man! That is why I touch you! Would you I were some lolling Persian eunuch? If you were a man, though, by heaven, I'd strike you for these continual insults! Do you take me for a beggar with leprosy? The fact that you are a woman saves you from a drubbing here, for no comrade would so dare to talk to me. Go run and sport with your animals. You are no match for warriors. I grow sick of your lovely face!' And so Meleager went away in fury from her side, while Atalanta stayed sad in the river. And then she sighed and roamed again further along the wash, so that her form in the strand was solitary.

PART FOUR

The Games at Olympia

Chapter Twelve

Now when the light of the orient had flooded the stables of morning, her gold skies feeding the nostrils of Apollo's horses, when laughing Aurora by the meeting of rivers: Alpheus and Kladios, had thrown off her silks of smoky pinks and russet-greys, and to leafy Olympia's elm-wooded farms and olive-fertile hillsides had Helios shot the beams from his chariot-wheels, then leapt men eagerly from their tents, washed and got ready for contest, for first was this of the days of the first Olympics.

Into the camp from the further forest there now came shuddering a cart. With growls and roars there lurched the wooden cage. Happily did the hunters bring it forth, parading it through the crowds, and Heracles from his labours came to praise: a wild boar, huge and bristly, was in there, suitable for sacrifice, and the swearing thereon of the solemn Olympic oath. With triumph the youths bore the snorting cart into the sacred Altis, and stayed it by the altar and half-finished temple.

To the south of the Altis and from their looped-up canvas nearer the river arose stiffly and coughing the tall elders: judges at the Games, they were named the helladonikai, and in their hands rested both order and triumph. With nodding heads they greeted each other, looked at the signs of the day, and approving the gods, decked themselves out with ceremony. With grave laurel wreaths glossily leaved about their bald heads and grey hairs, they garlanded in pomp and dignity, then scarfed themselves in purple robes, soft wool from the scarlet molluscs dyed, and proceeded in majesty together.

Assembling at the Altis now from all over the plain, there came the athletes of the many peoples. Gathered in tribes and boastful kingdoms, they massed among the trees, each babbling in their different accents. Oldest of these were the long-locked Achaeans, that marched proud into mountainous Greece far in the days gone by of youthful Hellas: victors of Mycenae, defeaters were they of the Cretan empire, and in their talk they murmured in Ionic.

Next to these in wide-brimmed hats of the travelling kind from Thessaly there sauntered forth the other Achaeans: those for whom the Aeolian language lived in more northern parts, where the deeds of sorcery were practised. Third of the tribes of dialects, came from Mount Cyllene the happy Arcadians, land-locked, knowing nothing of seafaring, and such were the ancient peoples that had earliest come southward into the craggy, stubborn-fielded country.

Now from Epirus and Mount Parnassus, by windy Apollo's shrine, there came those who were yet to invade the great citadels, the Dorians with their flower-decked branches, invaders from the west, to fall upon the tribes established. Also there marched from the far-flung islands of Tenedos and swan-voiced Lesbos, the voyaging colonists, all Aeolian-tongued, while those of Cos and Chios further in the purple Aegean unfurled Ionian sails. Southwards of these in times to come the Dorians would shake their shields, and Rhodes and Telos bask in the wealth of Halicarnassos.

Last of this rout there came the tribes that would enfold them all: of Athens, splendid citadel, nurtured by Athene, here spoke they Attic, giving Ionian their own Attic salt, and this was to hold sway over all these much-talking peoples, for Greeks being Greeks would long to talk, dispute, argue over the right, probe, project, cut in clarity like the air. And so was it Attic in future days was to hold its mastery over the teeming islands and bays of Hellas: from wayward-placed Arcadians of Cyprus and Pamphilia, to Aeolians of witch-haunted Thessaly. So did the tribes march in their lines to the Olympic gathering, and all Hellas just understood each other.

Now when these all were gathered, then did the procession make forth, moving with pompous march through the Altis. First there clattered horsemen, with Oenomaus in his chariot, the silver-faced Hippodamia beside him. Behind him there rode the other kings, with Iasos glowering, high on his mount and wearing body armour. A bronze Phrygian helmet he wore from which the plume nodded grim, and on his shield *alpha-rho* for the Arcadian League. With delicate-legged clattering did the many cavalrymen march on their short-maned, proud-necked horses, and bristling like a hedgehog's spines the kamaxes in their hands filled also the air overhead with milling spokes.

Behind the horsemen led by priests with laurels crowning their heads, there came the white sacrificial oxen. For other gods were led forth the rams, nodding their curly horns, tangled now with gold wire and blossoms. Behind these lumbered the creaking cart, wherein still furious the boar dug with his tusks at the stripped bark of the poles. And a priestess came behind the holy men of Demeter Chamyne: she who would watch the contests from the north altar.

In massed ranks now, with purple robes gleaming among the gold, the sage hellanodikai now marched. Behind them walked the athletes jauntily, eager each man to compete, some naked, some with tunics bound. With braying clash and clanging roars the music-men strode next, exciting dancers into frantic antics. For some there were with pipes bound fast and double to their mouths, screeling the reedy wails of their high melody, and some there were that on curling tubas boomed their solemn notes, while cymbals splashed like sounds of a winter sea. Such was the procession that circumambulated the sacred grove, and came to rest before the altar of Zeus.

Then did Heracles speak. 'Hellenes and citizens, welcome now to the Games, first of all that our world has celebrated! Welcome the universal peace now observed upon all seas, and the meeting for contest of so many champions. Soon will we sacrifice the boar, and over its burning limbs swear the Olympic oath of civilisation. Then men, to our work! There are races to be raced, striving to be striven, jumps jumped and much muscle moved before nightfall. Wherefore let us speak of what contests are first, and who must ready themselves, for all of us yearn to be at the striving.

'Know then, there are first running-races, the dromos and the diaulos, the first one length, the second two lengths of the stadium. Also there are wrestling-matches, boxing-matches, all good strife – set to as hard as you can: but no eye-gouging! We have the event: the pentathlon, wherein we have devised that you may compete in a medley of five contests: you may wrestle and jump, run the length of the stadium, hurl your discus a mile and then your javelin as far as the forest: he who does best at all five events, he will win the prize. Yet the grandest race will be the race of chariots. Here in horse-drawn chariots the great may glitter in gold, and down by the river scorch their path to victory.

'Now friends, you must know that none is here to profit in anything but in glory for himself and for his city. The wood we burn our sacrifice upon is white poplar from Threspotia, but there is also another tree planted in this grove. I brought it here from Hyperborea, a type of wild-olive it is: from this is to be made the fruits of victory. A wreath of the wild-olive is to be everyone's prize and the richest of all Olympic glories. The olive of the fair crown: see where it grows by Zeus' temple, by princes cut alone with golden sickles.' And Heracles showed the tree to them, and a beautiful naked youth with golden crescent cut the first of the crowns.

But now the boar with angry thrashing was tugged from his cage, and held down by Heracles of the bulging muscles. His throat was slit to stain the ground with his gushing blood, and when his rampant tusks had ceased their fury, and bristling limbs twitched their last throes, then did the hero slice him up, and hand over his limbs to be burnt in the altar fire. Hot were the offerings handed next piecemeal to the gathered cities, before the sizzling of the white poplar branches. So did all heroes led by the priest take the oath of Olympia, and swear to Zeus to honour the great contesting: no criminal they, nor stained with malice, nor the deceit of their fellows, nor would they cheat or circumvent the spirit. All fights clean! Such were the promises before the half-built temple, and the smoke of the boar went up and pleased the sky.

Now when this was done, sneering quietly there came the one-armed Trophonius, and he looked hard at Heracles and said, 'While I would wish to cast no cloud upon this glamorous ceremony, or detract in any way from these high pomps, I am driven by sense of justice, however, to offer a comment about the way the proceedings have been managed. I wish to complain that all my champions, representing Lebadaia, have been refused admittance to the contests. The officials claimed that the pentathlon has to be completed by one champion, but this is discriminating against the Lebadaians, for in our state we have a legal system where all men share each other's tasks, and we hold it religious to do so here. We ask you, overseer Heracles, to allow us thus to partake in the events under the terms of our law.'

And Heracles said, 'Do as you will. I am no stickler for rules, provided all is done square and fair. Put down this man and his champions to compete with whom they please. None of them looks able to complete a spoon-race!' And with this judgement summarily did he dismiss Trophonius, though the scribes about him looked with anxious eyes.

Yet next there spoke up Pelops once more, who said, 'Great Heracles, pardon for tardiness a Paphlagonian, for truly I have come a long way to compete at this Games, and delay made me fall short of also putting down my name. But the equipment have I, the chariot gleaming, the horses fretful with energy, and I would set down my name to compete in the chariot-race, calling especially King

Oenomaus, guardian of jealous beauty, a coward if he does not compete against me!' And when Pelops spoke these challenging words, a hush fell upon the restless competitors, and all looked with fearful eyes at the Elean monarch.

And King Oenomaus said, 'So be it. Should you complete the heats, then I will race against you by the river. And I have warned you often in public, this will result in your death. So, Pelops, bear in Hell no grudge against me.' And thus Oenomaus turned aside, and where his daughter gasped, there did he go and quietly murmur.

But last rash-headed Meleager of Kalydon strode forward, and said, 'Heracles, I also have a boon to ask: a youth in my band wishes to contest the running. Yet he has similarly delayed. Let his name be put down at this final occasion. See him far off. His name is Rhexenor.'

Heracles nodded to this request, and as the scribes noted it down, 'To the race-track with speed!' cried the lion-tamer.

Now when the thronging Hellenes had surged and spilled about the stadium, the Games were begun at last with the competitions. First to be tested was the running, wherein in heats of four, the dromos was held on the race-track. Briskly did the hellanodikai call out the names of the contestors, and lustily did they line up at the starting-point. An Elean and a Samothracian, a warrior from Epirus, and Lelex and the Spartan stood ready at the line.

But when the four competing warriors were straining for the start, naked and gleaming in the hot sun, there came a sudden hush among all the spectators, for at once they did not run away. The elders were ready, but each man looked at the other, for it seemed there was no one to shout the off. In the still air beneath the hill where Kronos towered with rustling beeches, the field of athletes stood in silent tension. But then came Heracles, and seeing them waiting shouted, 'Ready? Off!' He started the Games, and set the world on fire.

Then were men running. With thudding footsteps the

racers left the marker, and sped along the dusty grass of the stadium. The watchers roared. With waving arms they urged their own men along, each faction of the bank cheering one, jeering others. The runners raised the dust. First was Lelex, and behind him came the Elean, hurrying close to catch the oily hero, as close as when a girdled woman brings a shuttle to her breast, when she draws it swiftly along the humming loom. Behind the Elean the man from Epirus panted into his hair, while the Samothracian struggled a lagging fourth.

Loud were the crowd now. The Spartans hoorayed, seeing their countrymen in front, the Eleans screeched with anguish at what they saw. So near was their warrior, yet Lelex still was striving in the fore, his breast heaving with the hot air. With pounding muscles and gleaming thighs the three front men ran, the wind through their hair fluttering it like flags. Lelex raised his arms, for now was he at the point of his triumph, such eager intent fired his whole being. To his favourite god, 'Now Aphrodite, give me the victory!' he sighed, just as he came towards the final marker.

But here came a catch, for upon some dung dropped by one of the oxen, which had been led this way for the opening ceremony, Lelex slipped, and down he pitched into the middle of a patch, with much disgrace kissing the turdy remnants. Howls went up. laughter rang, whoops from the thronging athletes, as the Elean came in first and rejoiced at his winning. And the crowd went wild, for the winner now was a native of these very parts, and renown for ever was on his name, Koroebus!

Straightway the hellanodikai shouted out for the next contest, the diaulos, for which the heats were to be run. Yet while the purple-himationed elders worked to get this started, the other contestants were arguing with their colleagues. Rowdily did the noise come from the banks where the Spartans sat, but the judges' tribunal insisted on beginning the next heats. And here there ranged four new contestants, a Locrian and an Athenian, with fiery Acastus and the boy, Rhexenor standing ready. Like those before them, they toed the line, eager for the off. But then an elder came to protest.

'Heracles,' he called, 'in the first of the races the boys competed naked, but here are two of them clothed: Acastus of Pelion, and this youth Rhexenor. Why should they suddenly be shy? Tell them to strip their clothes off, and run fair, for this is the tradition. The youth is beautiful and should let us judge his form.'

'Oh, run and have done!' exclaimed Heracles. 'What does it matter how they look? This is a speed not a beauty contest!' And with that the hero who had marched only now into the tribunal platform, sat down ready to watch the runners run.

Now were they off, and busily did the contestors work their legs, and thunderously on the turf did they speed away. The Athenian paced himself cunningly, neither striving for the lead, nor hanging back too much behind the others. With darting elbows and flying knees, the Locrian flew next, speeding ahead from a fine start. But soon was Acastus pounding down, with large legs and furious face, and with manic zest heaved himself into the lead. Hurtling they flew, their shadows leaving the ground beneath their toes, and with bounding bodies they crossed the first stade.

Now as they reached for the first turning, the Locrian lagged behind, and Acastus was set to take the lead. But just as he turned, the delicate Rhexenor came, and playfully nudged him, as he turned about. While Acastus looked aghast, the boy nimbly leapt on again, and swifter than wings of wind or flickering lightning, he flew along the remaining track and way ahead of the others crossed the line and won the race outright. With puzzlement and shouted surprise, the crowd and competitors greeted him, and the judges judged him victor of that heat. They set his name in their tablets then, ready for the next day, and so Rhexenor laughed and waved in triumph.

Now when these running-heats were done, the gamesters

turned to other sports, for the heats of the pentathlon began. With sailing discuses there competed the crouching naked heroes, and with leaping from the line with weights in their hands. Busily did they swing their arms and heave with their sturdy thighs, then leap into air, holding their weights down, and with the weights' swing in centrifugal force they floated through the air, only to land in thumps and sudden tumbles.

Next after these sports, there came the heats of the javelin-throwing, and here Meleager of Kalydon was the champion. From the far-chalked distance, he hurled his lance and sunk it deep in the target, piercing right at the centre of the gold. For these triumphs went his name down, and on to the other heats, as others of his band also won about him. But then dodged he back, and silently trod forth in a running-race, and with second heats of the diaulos came in first. Thus did Meleager go forward champion of the javelin-heats, and unknown to his fellows also of the running.

But now by the rivermeads of Alpheus, with glittering trains and harnesses, there stomped and whinnied the twitching stallions, for chariot-races were the next, wherein the rich competed, and kings and princes set themselves against each other. First eager Pelops lifted his reins, taking the place of another, and in the first heats raced off to victory. Then Oenomaus in the second clattered against a Boeotian prince, and all watched aghast at the usual tragedy, for driving close the king pushed out, and unwatchful the Boeotian crashed, and his body was mangled in his chariot-wheels.

But ripely now the tiring sun had sunk his journey in the sky, and gilded the hills with his axle-car. In zestful spirit and wide-eyed jangling, the crowds discussed the races, and leaving the fields came once more to the Altis. Here loomed there now a sacred chorus, clad in patterned robes, twenty-four heroes standing by the temple, and when were met, the elders settled, the incense fuming forth, then did they give thanks in a choric song. The metre of an

Olympian Ode, the chorus sang in the dale, and with its echoes ended the first day's games.

Monarch of harps, gold-laurelled odes,
let us in hope abundant sing a lyric to the illustrious!
While Zeus, emperor of Olympia, and great Heracles both merit
multitudinous applause,
you, great Kronos, have our pledge here, the aureate labourer,
and our hymn's honey this hour, for the father of the god's father
must have
his taste of our craft's reverent rhythms and delicate,

imaged with odours. The mountain,
wooded in oaks and ash, where Kladeos hails emerald Alpheus,
named by Heracles Kronion, is reverenced in the Olympian
meadows.
So Kronos was in his age.
So those that Acheron has eaten or the black gondolier
ferried home. Never to be denigrated are the past's mournful
husbands.
From his mother's dug Kronos had suckled sweet canniness,

great Gaia, deep-breasted earth. Him she gave
that cup of logos, which is a strength unending.
Kronos in his season hence begot Jollity and Slumbering,
Old Age, and of Fate the threefold Allotters, and of
that Hesperean arbour of gold-charmed apples
the three that had the guarding —

not idle he! While Kronos reigned
was it a Golden Era: springing in unbidden abandon in
unploughed furrows grew delicate ears of oats, barley and heath-
rusty wheat,
grapes upon hedges appeared,
all grew in unaided art. Never for seas fell the pine,
frothing waves in azure foam, never thirsting over flesh came
the iron,
dug from stubborn veins of earth to bring but death along.

The days were lived under hope's star,
and in the pasture both lion and the lamb. Yet alas, all withers,

all changes in time. The unabashed lilies fall in the dusk's
  infamy.
And Kronos that in his hour
had pushed from his appointed hall the planet-eyed Ouranos,
felt himself terror-ravished. The child now fell on the child,
  reached for each one,
each wolfed, swallowed, gulping in hunger his true progeny.

Yet Gaia, fruitful-bosomed, studious of
that cup of logos, with a deceit redeemed all.
Wit ever wins! And from anguish hope gathers again, tempered
  hard.
So hope's immortals set us these Olympic hardships,
in sweet belligerence pitted, that men can all
be victors and avoid death!

Chapter Thirteen

So sang the chorus at the first Olympics. But when these things were done, there went back to their tents the thronging tribes, and happily they spoke together, walking beside the river, discussing with zest the day's games. But next to the woods of Kronos' hill, where the trenches were dug for foundations, there were those who did not share this joy: the heroes of the Kalydon band, for they were pitched in dispute, arguing as they stood by the planned palaestra. For Acastus was there, and surly Ancaeus, with Dryas and Meleager, and grimly did they all speak of the indignities of the sports.

For Acastus said, 'There is no fool worse than the fool of a woman. And Meleager, that woman of yours has made a fool of us! Why, our band here is becoming a laughing stock: look at Lelex falling in the ox-dirt! And think also what ninnies we seemed to be today, when the elder reproached us for keeping on our clothes. This was her work. I'd have stripped off, but that we agreed to shield her. And then how does she repay me for my service? The fake-boy cheats me in the race, pushing me secretly against all the rules, and taking the race because I was enraged. Meanwhile, she makes a fool of you by driving you into dotage, and we must suffer your perpetual mooning over her. It is a thing not to be borne! One more outrage of this sort, and we will leave your thankless band for good!' And as Acastus spoke, there chipped in Ancaeus, rejoicing in this row, who nodded and frowned at everything was spoken.

But Meleager raged and said, 'You coward! You were beaten fair! If Atalanta is swifter, why not admit it? She outwitted all of you! What speed she had! A halcyon over

the river! Such grace and beauty matched with swiftness!
But you are just a jealous wretch, seeking for accusations!
I grant she twitted you a little. Pushed you she did not!
And you will have me pushing you with a fist in your face,
if you seek to repeat this!'

Ancaeus now weighed in and said, 'Acastus, you see? I
told you it would be just so! This Meleager is a milk-sop,
and is so in love, he has lost all sense of reason. He would
cheat you of your victory, just because of his minion. And
he sought to make a laughing stock of you. Do we think
you need to hide your muscles? Would you be ashamed to
show yourself? And then to race and be beaten by a
woman! We will have no peace in this band, I say, nor will
we ever get to Kalydon, if this lovesick fool does not send
the girl back to her father!'

'You long-eared hound!' then shouted Meleager. 'Be off
into the ditch! That is your place for meddling in other's
business!' And he pushed Ancaeus so that he fell
backwards, and into a long trench he went, while Meleager
kicked the dust in after him. Then did the hero turn from
them, and stalk in fury to the forest. But wrathful Ancaeus
got out of the ditch fuming.

Yet Dryas was there now, and bent and helped him, and
thus did he seek to calm him. 'Ancaeus, noble friend,' he
said, 'do not be warring perpetually. Meleager is indeed
enslaved to the girl. Such is often the way of love. But it
surely cannot last for ever. Let us leave it awhile yet, to see
what arises, for after he has made some calmer deliberations, he may regain his better judgement. For see behind
the palaestra there, the youth himself goes off to him, our
swift-legged half-man, Rhexenor, and one thing I will tell
you: she is a girl of sense, wild and competitive as are her
instincts.' And with these mollificatory words, they all
turned about, where disgruntled they watched the youth go
into the forest, and after a while Lelex left them, and he
strolled forth also.

But yet Meleager, the hero raged, and thus he spoke inside himself, 'Why do they round upon me now, my

113

comrades, the men of my company? They accuse me of many things, yet I am sure I have given her no unfair favours! Why should they hate her so? Is it her fault she is a woman, and a beautiful woman? I will defend her against this injustice, even if it means the breaking up of the band of Kalydon. For truly she is dearer to me than a bunch of warriors, and she and I can hunt the boar together.'

Now at that moment to perplexed Meleager there approached Atalanta through the trees, and when he saw her Meleager was glad and ran towards her eagerly. But she looked at him plain and stern-faced and said, 'Why do you thus neglect your comrades? I saw you quarrelling. Ancaeus I saw you wrestle with! Is this a way to lead a company? That man you must know is a perpetual discontent, and needs to be treated carefully. But you lash out like a fool! Have you no brains in your head? What is the reason of your senseless fury? For daily you grow madder yet. I think you are in love, as Lelex has said. Well, you are a fool, Meleager.'

Now when she said this, Meleager gazed, and for a while he said nothing, for there was in his face dismay and hurt, and anger boiling also. But then he said, 'So I am a fool! So I have everyone against me! And what have I done, but sought to protect your wishes, and see that you could compete freely? They say I have insulted them, and brought them to indignity. It is only for you! Ay, I do love you! But look now how you have rewarded me! No thanks do I get, but ever still your coldness! Oh leave me, or I will spill more blood in my fury!' And Meleager walked away again, bitter in his heart, and went through the beeches solitary.

But as he wandered moodily, there came to him Lelex, who had strolled his way to meet him, and Lelex said, 'Our leader angry! Still in a pet! What a girl he has grown with all this loving! It seems, captain, you have swapped your rôles: Meleager is the maid, and Atalanta has become the warrior! But do not rage against me, friend, I know of

114

these matters. I have come to give you advice upon it. Let Dryas and Acastus tell you of fighting, for love I am the warrior, and love is the battle you are engaged upon. Well then, have at it, fierce Meleager! Dally no more about. Set her on her back and in her place!' And Lelex smiled at the angry commander. And Meleager glowered awhile, but then he sighed and sat on the banked mosses.

And Meleager said, 'Of that I had my chance, but out of some foolishness did not take it. But now I am subdued by her so that fear impels me greater than ever I felt before foe or danger. What a strange land is Aphrodite's! The rocks and cliffs are easy, but the soft bowers and woodbine banks hold terror. You take your armour off for love. Thus are you most vulnerable. What can I do? This is beyond my powers! This foe I cannot beat with force as I have ever done, and I have learnt my fierceness has its limits. Why now should I forgo my command, and creep home defeated! Of this I never dreamed when I left Kalydon.'

'Be off to her again,' said Lelex. 'For I know where she strolls. There is beyond this Kronion hill a valley, where among lush elder-trees a pond lies in the moonlight, catching a net of stars in its bosom. Herein do nymphs dwell, water-girls, I have watched but yet I have not seen them, but their delicate presence tempers the blessed place. Be off to Atalanta again. Next day is the final race. She will be overawed with the coming contest. Speak to her softly and soberly. Tender be your stance. And yet, my friend, hold on to the truth within ye. Be further than hurt. Hold fast to the spirit invulnerable within. Her rage cannot hurt, nor coldness touch its sanctity. And in the wooing time of night press on your charge again. Who knows? Meleager may get lucky!' And with a wicked grin then Lelex darted away again, and Meleager followed his path through the twisting creepers.

Now while these things went on in the hill, where clustering oak-trees loomed, in the dark beside the river and the long meadows, Pelops the eager one darted forth, and ran by the massed tents, till he came to where the horses were set in their pens. King Oenomaus' man-eating brood he found rolling their eyes, and carefully did he creep beyond their snorting, then found by the tilted chariots the mangled spokes of the Boeotian, and the torn shield and sockets of his car. There did he seek where the axle-pin should lie above the hub, and in the moonlight he squinnied at the holes. And so dug forth a matter which he took in his pouch away, and glided back in thought from the chariots.

But as he went, there stood forth Myrtilus, the charioteer of Oenomaus, and he cried out, 'Ho there, Pelops, you have been seen. What trickery are you about in the guarded pens of the steeds, or where the chariots bide for the final tomorrow? Some skulduggery is this in hand? Come you then to the judges. The hellanodikai will settle your virtue for good!' And with that he raised his hurling-lance, and set his shield before him, preparing to take Pelops by force.

But Pelops said, 'Let us haste to them, for I have to show them here a brew of wonderful conspiracy. You may deceive Boeotians, Myrtilus: they are a stupid race, but you must pardon a Paphlagonian. Those horses yesterday were unmanageable of the challenger, and their overpower was matched by the weakness of the chariot. Wherefore my suspicions have led me to a great discovery of Oenomaus' evil manipulations. For he had drugged his opponents' horses, so that they went mad, and for the axle-pin of his chariot, he had put a wax pin therein, so that in the heat it melted, and hence the crash which we saw bring about his death. You managed this for him, Myrtilus. It is your wickedness has made Oenomaus boast over an altar of skulls. So many princes lost in the chase of that silver-faced beauty, and brought down by evil under the moon! Come then you quick to the judges' tribunal. This shall be made plain. The gods and the Games have been transgressed by these deeds.' And Pelops laid hold angrily of Myrtilus by his hair. But the man knelt down and clasped his knees in supplication.

And Myrtilus said, 'Indeed it is so. This act has been long perpetrated, and high indeed is the pile of skulls of the suitors. Yet must you not confront Oenomaus with this evil tomorrow. He will run mad, and slay Hippodamia. Only by this have we survived, for dark are his deeds, and there are things hushed that must not be spoken. Take league with me. Pay Oenomaus with his own just evil, for this alone will rid him and catch you the princess. Come watch me fill Oenomaus' axles with this treacherous wax, and give the drug to his wind-begotten horses. The king will tomorrow drive himself, and you may topple him. But for this, you must share with me Hippodamia. I will claim the bridal night, for always I have lusted her. You thereafter may be king and husband.'

Pelops gazed upon the man, and grimly did he nod, and so they went and fixed the pin of the chariot. And then they gave the horses barley, sleek Psylla and Harpinna, which long ago were gifts of indulgent Ares, and therein mixed the crazing drug for the soft-maned ones' last meal, and left them both, and went in separate darknesses.

And shuddering Pelops came alone then to the river-bed, and he stretched his hand out over the waters, and he cut his arm, so that the black blood stained the swirling stream, and then he spoke as the night received it. 'Take my blood down, cavernous Alpheus, to where in the underworld you sank in pursuit of wanton Arethusa. Address my father, Tantalus, implore him in his pain to give his son here the power of victory. What darkness is stirred up by this, let it be unseen. The face of Hippodamia is my luminary.'

And as he looked, a peering shadow seemed to rear in the stream, and the likeness of a head upon it nodded. And a face much ravaged by pain and anguish, hollowed by famine perpetual, looked with staring eyes towards the hero. And a voice from the stream called, 'Pelops, good son, good child I gave the gods, you will indeed tomorrow have the victory. Take then courage. Rejoice and enjoy on sweet earth the blessed light. And from your winning zest a race will follow. The land you set your feet upon: from you shall it be named. In the Peloponnese, Pelops is remembered!' And the shadow sunk again in the stream, and Pelops heard his father with tears, and he rose to gird about him his destiny.

Meanwhile, Meleager came to the valley, wherein lay the naiad's lake, and sadly and with sweet fear did he approach it. Down by the water's edge he saw the boyish Atalanta, still with her hair wrapped up under her hat. She heard him approach, and turned to him, her face softer now, and the hero went gently and sat beside her.

And then did he sigh beside her and say, 'The night is deep about us. On such a time do men come with aspiring. By a lake such as this a lover could take sweetness with his bedmate, and thrill the very moonlight with high pleasure. To you am I yet bent on nothing but to tell you a tale, and to acquaint you with my determination. For on the morrow I am to make a pledge against your danger, and I will either win you or be lost.

'First then my story, for I am to tell you the tale of my very birth. Nor is the story idle in the night. The tale — as you will reckon well — sets open all my weakness, reveals the slightness of my hold on life. Yet I will tell it. Nor would I hide my secrets from the one that I shall either win or lose tomorrow. Indeed I long to make myself over to your mercy, hard as you are against such lovingness.

'When I was born, a son of Ares, within a week of my birth, to the chamber overlooking the palace walls, the Fates appeared, the white-robed Moerae, spinners of men's destiny, and over my cradle they made their prophecies. My mother Althaea sat startled there, her hand upon my cradle, while nurses and gossips sat on either side, and all their silent eyes stared fearfully at the crones in white, for ominous is the visit unannounced.

'Clotho, the first, that held the distaff, she made the first prophecy, and stared upon my baby brow in my nest, and she for me gave promise of generosity in my nature, and free-giving from an unstinting heart. Lachesis next, the measurer, that pulls the life-thread forth, she looked and said I would have surpassing strength. Then Atropos spoke, the one that cuts: she who cannot be avoided, and her words came to horrify all the chamber, for upon the fire in the dusty corner, beside a purple-hung loom, there burnt a brand in the midst of the flame. This she pointed at, and with her finger crooked from its bony fist, she said my life would last while the brand remained.

'All were aghast. My nurse snatched me up and hugged me in her arms. Others ran round, protecting the little slumberer. The Moerae stood implacable, though my gossips in rising wrath, pleaded my innocence, pledged me the only heir. The Fates stood implacable. Yet my mother bowed not to their decrees. Straight did she leap up, and snatched the brand from the flames. And dousing it and wrapping it round, she hid that log in a box, in cedar-wood protecting my outer soul. And so have I survived to this day, won by a mother's wit, yet subject still to her steward-ship of timber. You see how my fate is all from women, and lies in their loving hands. There is small reason for my braving here.'

'Why do you tell me this?' said then the huntress, and gazed at him with a frown. 'For you speak of your weakness here to a stranger. Who knows not but such a talisman is a hostage to Fate, and in the knowledge of your enemies could confound you? Unwise it is to confess such things. Do you not have fear? Are you not wary? True, you are rash-headed Meleager. And what do you seek to gain this night by confiding this in me? Do you expect me to do likewise?' And Atalanta stared at him with suspicion in her eyes, but Meleager smiled back with an open face.

'Before you I am vulnerable,' he replied. 'So are all men in love. Yet I put my trust freely in the soberness of your nature. Of what I have freely told you, I know you will make no abuse. And so in your presence I know I am truth-safe. But now I must also tell you, maid, that against you I run tomorrow, and if I win, I claim you by your oath.' And when Meleager spoke these words, he stared at her hard, and she was stunned and filled with iciness.

And with a look aghast she said, 'I cannot think this is your plan. To compete against me, and if you win, to claim me? To claim me in marriage?'

'Ay,' said he, 'This was your oath. I have outrun you once. Now before all I will beat you. From this there will be no dispute. Fairly will you be beaten, and then you will belong to me in marriage.'

'Well, I will win the race,' then sighed Atalanta frowning. 'But yet do I dispute this trick! Have we not spoken of this enough? Do you still wish to ravish me? I thought you were my friend, my protector. I know that day in the forest was I lying naked by your side, I know I have kissed you, with fire in the fury. But then you forced me! Now you must know I am a woman of Artemis! All love I do repudiate as weakness! Men can I beat! Men *shall* I beat! Not till I win over all can I think of touching you again. This you must stomach. Now especially, since you have betrayed me, setting against me with this trap of the race!'

'Why is it a betrayal, wretch, to seek to have your love?' then said Meleager with a sudden fury. 'Are you so much a beast of the forest that you can take no man? Do you lust for a bear? Is this your destiny? Yet beasts have mates! What passion of yours then that spurns all love of your own kind? Wild it is not, nor savage, nor natural. No, you are not a natural woman! You want to be a champion man before ever you want to be a woman! Cut off your breasts then! Mutilate yourself to suit your mind! You lust to switch your sex − a fool's dream! True I have defended your hunting. You hunt as well as any. Why should you not pit your might to what you may? But I will not defend this dotage of yours to be a misfit, a nothing, neither man enough or woman! You'll race tomorow, or out of the band of Kalydon you'll go. And if I win you, you'll either be a woman or a slave!' And Meleager turned away at this, and leaving her with his back, silently in disgust he walked away.

But she with fury looked up at him, and swiftly hurled her spear. Humming it winged with hungry teeth towards him. Slicing his leg, it spun on. Roaring with anger he turned, and saw her gazing hatefully in the shadows.

'There,' she called, 'trickster! Now have you my trick on you! See now if you can run tomorrow! I beseech you do not seek to deceive me, Atalanta, ever again, for I am savage and brook no traitors! You have your wound in your leg now, captain. Nurse it well enough. You get no mercy from an Amazon!' And with these words she walked away, leaving Meleager stricken, and when she had gone, he turned to his leg with fury.

And he seized the wound and hurriedly sought to stop its dark flowing, and closed it, pressing white the flesh about it. The spear had glanced forth into the ground, where it stuck still swaying, and the wound was gushing blood from its keen slash. His cloak he took, tore strips from it, then bound them round, seeking to strap the flesh into itself. Quickly he worked, and wound it up, coiling the bloody cloth, and then set a knot and tied it and folded it in. But when he had done, he sighed and sat still, stunned upon the ground, gazing on his throbbing calf with bitterness.

Yet Atalanta ran in the forest, and with anger she ran, her blood racing mad in her breast and head. And furiously she thought to herself, 'Why now, he tries to betray me, tricking my maidenhead. Does not death lie that way? He scorns the prophecies. He calls them old wives' tales. Well, let him remember: it is no old wife has given him that gash on his leg! When will these men learn that Atalanta is not to be dallied with? When will they treat me with respect?'

But as she hurried hotly in the forest, her temper began to cool, and guilt crept in a little at the corners. The bitterness of the anger now was melted by regret, and for Meleager she grieved at wounding him. 'Yet why can he not see?' thus she thought. 'I want no submission to lust! Well, it is done. There is now no contesting. He has learnt

121

the hard way that Atalanta is not to be tampered with. She is too wild to brook the pleasure of men. But yet I grieve. I have hurt him. But no more than was needed. I have saved him instead from the curse of my defloweringng. So should I return? Might he need help?' She sighed. 'No, I must go on. Yet where will it end, this dispute between us? I do not want to lose my friend, nor do I wish my leader to banish me from the Kalydon band. Men are so stubborn and stupid and crass! Well, those that come near me: all of them so far have been defeated!' So she strode through the forest homeward, and sought the camp again, brooding to herself, vexed and thoughtful.

But as she came to a copse enclosed, with shrubs of myrtle thronged, and moonlight sliding down in ghostly moonbeams, she started and leapt back, wishing now that she had kept her spear, for something she saw gliding along the ground. In a shaft of silver then she beheld the old crone again in the mist, that nodded at her from a shadowed veil.

And the crone came up and greeted her, and stared into her eyes, and said, 'Once more a maiden alone in the forest? I see you have not taken entirely my former words to heart, when first we met in the woods of Arcady. Did I throw about you a necklace of love merely to nurse your spite, and show you kindness merely to kindle your malice? You have turned against him who was your friend. You have harkened his secret truths, and not a whit have you told him of your own. Have you not a talisman of your own as deadly as the one he told, and did you not keep quiet before his confession? Run home in the forest then. Yet remember: the gods are not all for you, and soon will Artemis herself have a grudge to bear. Run home then haunted!' And with a fearful gesture, the crone shot up in the trees, and floated over the huntress, inspiring fear.

Then did the virgin race back hurriedly through the echoing forest, and the twigs about her snapped their teeth like hounds.

122

Meanwhile sitting sadly, nursing his leg, Meleager remained downcast, thinking bitterly on his night's enterprise. And thus he sighed, 'Atalanta, you savage, you have me defeated truly! Of this I did not suspect — the more fool I! Though I could not be assured of winning, yet I planned my attempt, but now I cannot beat you with but one leg! Yet what is this honourable course you hold, that makes a pledge of fairness, but wounds her friend when his back is turned? I have been well served! Oh, let me learn a little from this rashness, for she have I defended stubbornly against my band, and what good have I gained from it, but hatred in her eyes, and dispute in the men I should be leading? O rash Meleager, learn henceforth to be cautious in your heart, serve only the good, and let all spiteful things be. Farewell then, huntress, this wound quits us. Nothing I owe you now. Go your ways, and keep them far from mine!' And Meleager sighed, and sat in the forest, repenting his soft love, and yet for a while regret was wet in his heart.

But when the hero had recovered, he looked again at his wound, and staunched the blood that seeped down to his ankle. He sighed with bitterness, yet decided that he must limp himself home, put vinegar on his wound, and dress it with care. Then hope to sleep, for without sleep there would be no healing, if there was any hope at all henceforward. He stiffly arose, but as he shifted, and lifted himself up, he saw in the forest, in a shaft of moonlight, an old woman: an old crone standing, staring upon him, and he stopped in fear, and the hairs on the back of his neck were stirred.

Then the crone said, 'What's this? A wounded hero languishing by a lake? Some girl no doubt has driven you to this. A gash I see you have on your calf, unhappy for an athlete! And do I also see a gash in your heart? Well then, my friend, will you take an old woman's advice about these matters? I can promise nothing, but I have some skill in the arts. There may be magic unguents that could soothe and heal a wound, and for tomorrow's race

. . . some racing-tips? Will you let me have on, or are you appalled by the face of age and ugliness?'

'Lady,' said Meleager, 'all good help is welcome.'

And the crone without waiting took off his bandage, and rubbed on Meleager's calf an oil that burnt his leg with a fragrant comfort.

Chapter Fourteen

With braying trumpets and clashing drums now came the last day of the Games. Swarming from the tents with babbling voices the athletes and spectators made ready. Now washed men keenly, now combed men their hair, now oiled men and sleeked themselves vigorously, slavering over their bodies with strigils and perfumed olive, so that a high burnish was upon them. Their teeth they scraped with twigs, their hairs they plucked with tweezers, their biceps they flexed and stretched in gleaming power. And strutting forth with gathered locks, proud in the chill morning air, they streamed their way towards the stadium.

Above the Olympian vale, veiled was the air with the smoke of bonfires. From the stew and burly of a thousand tents there seeped up the fog of humanity. Covering all the plain were canvas and carts, massed figures darting and stopping, stockades of horses, and goats for milk, dogs scurrying and yelping. There glittered the gold-leafed temple trophies, and the guarded treasure-huts of the cities, there shone the makeshift monuments of the victors, festooned with wreaths and rose-garlands. The purple-cloaked procession went with the sacrifices to the altars, and soon from the roasted limbs the smoke ascended.

High over in the clouds did the many gods sit on couches enjoying both the feast and the festival. Blue-haired Zeus looked down, scenting the cooked meats, and relishing the breakfast of his altar. Protective Hera on his right in rich violet robes smiled down upon her ancient temple, while on their either side reclining, their children on cloud-cushions, Apollo the witty, Ares, golden Aphrodite, gazed also below, as did eager Hermes, taking bets from the immortals on the winners of the final races.

'Now mighty one,' said Hera smoothly, 'the last day of the races approaches, and much mirth to the immortals have these Games brought, wherefore I trust diligently that you will renew them, and hold them every four years, to be called Olympiad. I seem to remember it was here in Olympia that the idea by us goddesses was first mooted. It has been good. Much killing has been averted, much harmony and commerce prosecuted. Now my love, pass me there at your shoulder those Hesperean fruits gathered by the bowl of ambrosia. They are delicious. My thanks to Hermes for gadding off so early to bring them to our divine tables.' And the regal Lady Hera reached across to receive from her husband's hand and pop in her mouth a delicate gooseberry.

But as they sat thus happily at ease, gazing at the striving before them, Artemis the Huntress bounded her way to them, and threw herself down upon the cloud-couch, and Artemis the virgin said, 'I suspect these day's events of skulduggery! During the night there have been manoeuvres, which darkness has covered too closely, but some of which I have got wind of. I warn you all, if there is any cheating here, wrathful will I be if it harms any of my champions. My own protégée, long-legged Atalanta, is due for victory, and from this day forth womankind be properly reverenced. But she will win fairly. And let it be so. Or war will there be in heaven. Nor shall I take kindly if chaste Hippodamia this day is cast away on a husband.' And here did Artemis in braving manner reach for a goblet and drink, and turned aside from her fellows.

But Aphrodite said, 'Audacity! This is some cheek! Eternal girl, do you prance in here before your father, and start dictating to us how the races shall be run, and who is to be each winner? Your pride in this Atalanta has grown overweening. Her triumphs have made you presumptuous. I myself shall hope there arises this day a dent or two in both her pride and yours. And as for Hippodamia, delude yourself another way, if you think that she is one of your virgins!' And golden Aphrodite laughed, and seized on a great peach, and bit into its soft skin with her pearly teeth.

Now when Zeus saw his daughters thus he cried, 'Cease both your squabbles! These Games are for man's peace, and gods' enjoyment, so do not you dare to mangle it! I will be the wrathful one if there is any trickery here. Who wins shall win. This is the whole conception. There is no mooning and binding and yearning about it! You women can never see a good thing without wrinkling your noses and starting to find in it some dissension! One more harsh word from either, and by Kronos I'll cast you down, and flog you stripped before the men of the stadium!' So did Zeus fume, and Artemis looked black at him, but nursed her feelings in silence while golden Aphrodite snuggled down in the couch beside the war-god, and chewed her peach with a satisfied smile.

But on earth, meanwhile, the fields of sport were busily teemed and thronged by eager spectators lusting for the finals, for now were the folk ready to finish the match of the great pentathlon, and settle which man of all Greece was supreme. Much clustering of spectators was there with nodding and craning of heads, eager to gaze and appraise the competitors. The trumpets then called all to silence, and the hellanodikai marched with pomp until they came to the centre. A hush fell then, and all were agog to hear what the elders said, and who might be the victors of the heats.

Now in the spectators, disguised as a youth, broodingly watching the athletes, there stood Atalanta, with face still chilled and fearful. As the judges conferred, she looked about anxious, studying all the faces, looking for that of Meleager with sadness and guilt. The crowd and the gods were harkening keenly, when the hellanodikai at last looked up to make their announcement, for when all was ready, one of the elders called out to the people, and his voice floated far on the summer breezes.

'Hellenes,' he said, 'we come at last to the strife of the final two events in the great pentathlon. And for these

127

events there have emerged two final competitors, who have outstripped in the heats all others. Representing his city, Phthia, we have the renowned hero, Peleus. Let him step forth now before the people. And then for Kalydon, let him appear, the other victor of the heats, the prince of Aetolia, Boar-Hunter Meleager. Then without more ado, let the long jump be jumped, and following after that the final challenge begin of the wrestling-contest.'

Now when the elder had called this, there went up a shout of triumph from the crowd and the competitors' supporters. And into the ring there then stood forth Peleus, the mighty hero, and all his supporters vaunted a great cheer. Then did the crowd peer about, and turn upon themselves, looking next for the huntsman, Meleager. And white-faced Atalanta stood anxious by, wondering if she should speak, and tell them that Meleager was wounded in the woods. But then stepped forth the hero himself, Meleager, smiling dazzling, and all his limbs and legs in healthy order. A sigh of amazement cried Atalanta, and those about her turned. But the crowd meanwhile were cheering the Kalydon hero.

But now Atalanta hurried from the throng, and walked alone in amazement, wondering how Meleager might have recovered, for on his leg she saw no stripe or scar of the wound she had made, yet all was whole, as though no blow had ever been. Busily did she think perplexed on the night before, wondering if perhaps she had missed with the blow, pondering then if perhaps some god had stepped in for his aid, and at this thought a chill gripped her heart further. She turned to the throng again, chaste and subdued, and a feeling of fate began to breed in doubt about her heart.

Now among the milling folk and the festive noise of the crowd, there came through the air the sound of another disturbance, for Trophonius approached, embroiled in an argument with impatient Heracles. And Heracles called, 'Judges, this man is a menace! Regard not anything he may say, but have onward!'

128

Trophonius smiled and simperingly inclined his head and said, 'But judges, by the rules are even you bound here. And the rules are on my side, for you may remember that at the start of the Games Heracles granted the Lebadaians a favour: that men from this especial country might enter for the pentathlon one man each for each event, and this I now claim for my countrymen. Stop all this battle of Meleager or Peleus, and let us on to my athletic compatriots, for the heats are open, and these two champions must compete with each man!'

Now there was wrath and cat-calling followed Trophonius' speech, and Heracles and the judges called for order. Wily Trophonius was booed ripely, but he would not back down, and the hellanodikai were thrown into constitutional ferment. Some argued this way, some argued that, while Peleus and Heracles went and sought to make Trophonius recant his claim. But then Meleager strode through the ranks crying, 'There's but one way to settle this.' And he grabbed Trophonius and thwacked him round the ear.

But Heracles called then, 'Stay, stay, Hellenes, before we all fall into a brawl, let Meleager let go of this whiner's ear, and hear now my judgement upon this matter. For Trophonius' competitors: let them all step forward: I'll take the lot on! Anything to get the Games again moving! But as for these two champions, let them compete fairly, and let us have a good end to the pentathlon.'

'Nay then,' cried Trophonius, 'for there's a change: this Meleager has assaulted me, wherefore he is disqualified from competing. So Peleus must take on my five, and whoever wins, either him or my five will be the victor. We Lebadaians are a caring people, and we lend to each other the aid of which each of us is able. Wherefore my champions are formidable: they are the terrors of earth, and I would advise Peleus to concede defeat before he starts.'

'I will concede this much,' said Peleus, 'if Meleager is banned, then I shall compete with no one, for my only worthy opponent is him: he and I won all our heats, and he and I must fight for the olive-wreath.'

'Nay then,' said Trophonius. 'This is not so, because according to the rules —' But there did the Lebadaian get no further, for once more was Trophonius knocked flat on his back, this time by Peleus. The crowd roared in approval.

Now when this last assault had happened, and all aghast had the judges become, and Heracles had walked away to keep his temper, there appeared in the centre of the stadium five strange-shaped athletic forms, causing all the crowd to gasp with wonder. For there was a thin, whippy creature, all bones and no flesh, and beside him a twisted, bunchy thing in a vest, and next to him a ginger-haired oaf with a great gap in his teeth, one thin left arm and one right arm huge and brawny. Looming near him a high, tall pole, with buck teeth and foolish grin, nodded down with unsteady giraffe-like gait, and under his legs a massive fat man, great as several whales, now blundered forth with massive thundering of blubber.

'Heracles,' then called Trophonius, 'here you see your challengers. I defy you to beat five Lebadaians!'

But Heracles looked at them and said, 'All hail, O athletes of splendid Hellas, O embodiments of the very concept of our Games: shining paragons of mankind, of strength and youthful vigour, hail, and welcome to the contest! My friends, I will take on all of these, and quickly will I too, for now is it almost time for the chariot-race. And to help things along I'll fight these freaks not singly but all at once and I will show Trophonius who is a champion. But once I have done, concede me somewhat. Let the next Olympiad be run by some other man than me, for I am not of the sort of temper that bides this sort of thing kindly, and thus do I vent my rage on an easy target!' And Heracles ran then, and set upon the five weird ones, and ran them with great business about.

For the whippy one he beat thundering up and down the racing-course, and flung a discus over the best of the

130

twisted one's. Then threw the competitor after it, and the ginger-hair after his javelin, beating him and skewering him into the target-gold, while leaping out from the long-jump marker, he knocked flat the bean-pole, arising downheartedly from his own failure. And vanquishing these so, he launched himself into the pile of blubber, tying his arms in a wrestling-hold under his buttocks, so that the strange flesh-malformation was Heracles' own to use as a weapon to floor all four athletes as they came complaining. The crowd went wild. Over the moon with joy was Heracles, and flattening Trophonius all left for the river.

So came the chariot-race. Down by the flowery meads, where the summer breeze rustled the willows, and where the light shone clean among the watery pastures, there prepared the glittering teams of the great ones. With polished leather and gold, with shiny-burnished bronze, the chariots shone like black-cloud-breasted lightning. Round were the fronts, with open backs and wheels glossily varnished, and goldsmiths and coppersmiths had inlaid all with patterns, so that with the clattering legs of the horses, the plaited manes threaded with silver, the sleek-groomed flanks, each team seemed divine and sky-born. Yet assuredly were those of Pelops, for Poseidon himself had given them, and the winged car in response to his sea-spoken prayer.

Now when the folk of the Games were gathered to see this kingly sport, then did Pelops and Oenomaus come rattling forth. These alone were shining finalists, and now these alone were to race their circuits of the meadow. By the starting-post they came with their grooms, the startled horses whinnying, each bevy of servants seeking to hold them in check. Meanwhile, alone the king and the hero stood in their chariots, not here as in war with their drivers to hold the reins. By the signal they stopped, whereon a bronze eagle was raised up, and then did they turn and glare at each other.

But King Oenomaus, as he glared, raised up from his

131

side a spear, and staring at Pelops said, 'Mark well you go fast, hero. For with such spears I have despatched twelve suitors for Hippodamia, and if I catch you on the turn, you will I also. I have warned you enough of these things, but you took no notice. This is the easiest method for settling a race.' And then did he lower the spear again, so that the judges saw it not, and Pelops by the start had now no time to quarrel.

For the bronze eagle up now, beside it in readiness the bronze dolphin clattered down, and all those watching roared in eagerness. And the race was begun, so that Oenomaus with a shout lashed his shrieking stallions, and rushed his carriage straight in front of Pelops. Whereat the hero furiously to the side pulled his prancing steeds, and struck out on a curve over the meadow, and keeping out of spear-shot of the king, hurtled close to the river, so that the very pebbles flew up in his course.

Now there was on the racing-course a place called Taraxippus, terror of horses, where on the previous day, each team that competed had shied frightened, though there was none there who might decide wherefrom that terror came. Oenomaus drove close, and at the point his horses reared in panic, Pelops seized this hesitation to drive across his path. Then while Oenomaus fought his mounts, Pelops lashed his own, the horses shied, yet had he them fast gripped, and steadying the course, Pelops flung his chariot brazen over the daisies, and snorting with triumph gained the lead in the race. Oenomaus cast his spear. The blade singing forth grazed Pelops' thigh. Yet he drove on still and forged towards the turning-point.

But the king was both cunning and fast. By the limit of the course he had placed Hippodamia in the gaze of the racers, and as Pelops came towards the halfway, there did she smile at him, dazzling with a look of love he had never seen before. He slacked the reins, for love made him weak, Oenomaus whipped fast his team. He clanged into the axle of Pelops' chariot. The hero was hurled up. Oenomaus saw him toppling to the side, himself forging on exulting.

Yet Pelops even now righted himself, and settling back in his car, leapt to retrieve and untangle the reins. And thus he fought, while Oenomaus flew to the turning-point, and hurtled round with grinding of his axle.

Here was his end. The wax plug heating with the speed of the race, the stress of the turn bearing on the melting lynch-pin, on the further side of the swerving quadriga there flew off the bouncing wheel, and down ground the axle into the mud. The pole shot up, lifting the stallions. In thrashing hoofs they were plucked back. There twisted over and over in the meadow the chariot, whence flew up spewing wood and metal and the blackened soil. And blood in the air, and loud neighs of torn horses. The king was despatched. His flesh cut from him, he anguished in the grass, with limbs awry, to sink down red at last. Such was the end of the chariot-race of the first Olympics, and the blood of kings was upon the sport.

But now when Pelops gazing back came to the finish of the race, there did the crowd receive him in dashed applause. The servants of King Oenomaus rushed forth to their fallen lord. Hippodamia wailed her slaughtered father. Now sounded there on the left of the populace the thunder beyond the hills, and all were subdued at its ominous rolling. Myrtilus with a cry of anguish broke forth and lamented his crimes, and in the path of Pelops stood with shame.

And Myrtilus said, 'Alas, he is gone! The king I served so long! Now is he to Hades to haunt me for ever! Here is the culprit! This Pelops is the sinner; he was it drove the king to death! O my cunning master, you are murdered now by a proud wretch, hailing from Lydia! Hear me, ye judges, cast out this hero. Pelops has killed a king. He may not be crowned a victor of the Games. I repent my crimes, I have sinned in bringing death to the princes, but he, he is a regicide!'

So did the charioteer of the king inveigh against the hero, but Pelops would not let his tongue speak more.

With Myrtilus' own glittering sword, snatched from his scabbard as he cried, Pelops ran him through and cast him down. Into his ribs he sunk the blade, and where the heart was throbbing, there did he grind it, letting forth his soul. Then slit his throat, to lose the servant's voice in surging blood, or ever he might confess more.

'The crown is mine!' cried Pelops then. 'And the woman too! Let no man here seek to take from me what is just! This Oenomaus many princes had despatched with deceit, and to them many barrows shall I raise. Wherefore for the king's crimes no pity. Fate has decreed these acts. Now I shall take what trophies are mine!' And Pelops then lashed round his horses and with his chariot racing, he snatched from the judge's hand the olive-crown, and setting it upon his head, drove forth again over the meadow, and off on the way of the race once more.

With stunned gaze then the crowds were watching, as Pelops' chariot-team now seemed to fly across the bowing iris. Towards Hippodamia in his haste he clattered with wheels whirling, as she lamented, fainting at her father's corpse. Leaning from his chariot with brawny arm, Pelops hurtled towards the maiden. She seeing him leapt and ran. Her silver feet threaded through the rushes, seeking the safety of a marsh, but gloating did the cart of Pelops draw near. He gathered her up in its dark embrace. Now did the thunder clang again. Across the bowered trees, as the chariot flashed into the shadows, the thunder boomed about the hills, and rolled over Alpheus, so that all the crowd were hushed in fear.

Then did a seer come tottering forth, an old man, blind and holy, and through the crowd he came with bitter reproach. And he cried out, 'Wail, Hellenes, wail the evil that has come! The smell of the crimes of generations is upon us! Pelops has sinned! Son of Tantalus, murdered by his own father, served up to the gods, how is he paying all out! On generation and generation shall these evils pass: there shall be wives corrupted, monarchs murdered, there shall be disinherited the legitimate children of the house, there shall be again eaten infants god-offending. Of what greater crimes can man be mindful than these of this grim house, curséd house of curséd Tantalus? Forbid the Games! End the trials now! Let there be no more sports, for all our Games is desecrated by these sins!'

But now came Heracles and he cried, 'Pelops is the winner of this race! The king suffered but the fate he had courted for others. The Games go forward! No wailing prophet will shut down my sports, however cursed may be certain houses! Be off, you blind seer, and henceforward seek to see more happy things. The races are done. Of the dromos Castor is the winner. Of the pentathlon, I myself unwillingly won all the events. Pelops is the winner of this chariot-race. And there is but one more race: the double-length diaulos. Let us all repair to the stadium for the Grand Finale!'

So Heracles spoke and waved to the crowd, and the people cheered by his robustness, rushed back through the Altis and happily towards the stadium.

Chapter Fifteen

But up in the gods, where the cloud-couches were placed for the watching immortals, there was shock and revolt at these events. There had come now for the morning's sport other deities to the feast, and Poseidon was there, and Athene, the grey-eyed. They lay upon their lion-legged beds, propped on patterned pillows, dangling their empty wine-cups from their fingers, and naked boys hurried to and fro refilling with ambrosia the golden drinking-vessels of the gods.

Now was Artemis angry, and she said through her teeth, 'I have never agreed that all's fair in love and war. This Pelops is a murderer surely, and all in pursuit of his lust! Why should such a fair-faced virgin be sacrificed to a regicide? Why, surely now bad deeds have been done: look, a king's mangled corpse lies there in the flowers, the charioteer Myrtilus unfairly killed! What have we been watching in Olympia? It was not a Games, it was a blood-bath, Pelops should be pitched into Hades!'

But Zeus said, 'No one will pitch Pelops anywhere, for he will finish his days unmurdered. Yet upon his house, as the seer said, there will dire things come: kings slain by their wives, and children eaten: a long curse will glower upon the line of Tantalus, but when it is lifted, then will Athens be great, for Athene's city will order the justice which shall purge these sins, and then the great age of Hellas shall begin.'

Then Poseidon spoke. 'Yet brother,' he said, 'I am still perplexed, and my quarrel is still with brawling Heracles, for though I approve of his supporting Pelops, and treating the king well paid by his chariot-crash, yet it has seemed to me that Heracles has been too domineering in

136

these Games. He struts about and orders things as though he were king of all Hellas. This is a hubris and pride beyond presumption. Wherefore I think that now it is time for more penance for him, and I have already spoken to Eurystheus, his task-master, and made sure that he has another six labours ahead of him. Keep great men occupied; this is best!' And thus did Poseidon smile as he drank, and flicked his dregs at the target in the game of kottabos.

But Zeus sighed now, 'Alas, for my son, how everyone heaps him with labours! Such is the strong man, for all use his strength for their own purpose. Yet he has done well here; his burly justice has kept these sports in progress, and after such work, who will deny him immortality?'

Then Hera said, 'I would, if I could, for never has a man been so ill-named! This Heracles is no clear man of Hera! But what I would suggest, my lord, is that these Games we have seen here are drastically changed and civilised. For what we have seen in the name of sport has been but backbiting and treachery, feuding, rowdiness and now murder! And all before my sacred temple! I was here before any of you, and I have had to witness this carnage. I would suggest that henceforth, husband, genteel games and quiet are instituted. Knuckle-bones is a fine, skilful sport, throwing the pebble, and checkers on a board, and for the women there could be tapestry-making contests.'

But Zeus smiled and said, 'Alas, my love, your ideas are perhaps too genteel for Hellas. What are a few murders compared with a whole-scale massacre? We are all making progress. But come, let us watch the last of these races, the race of the two-length diaulos. And from this day forth surely now will the Olympic Games be celebrated with merry battle through the centuries. Peace then, and watch, for the day grows old, and soon all sports will be over.'

Now in the Olympic stadium were all good folk congregated for the last of the events of the athletics. The sun was going down beyond the leafy hill of Kronos, and the shadows fell lengthy on the race-track. About the rustling woods there piped the song of evening birds, and a lazy dusk settled upon the roe-deer, that looked forth on the plain with yearning, yet it would not be long till the forest was once more silent.

Across the sward by herself, wrapped in her disguise, there now strode moodily the 'youth' Atalanta. Nervous and fearful had she grown, more than ever before, and thus she thought darkly upon Meleager. 'He has some magic. Of that I am sure. It is just as it was in the woods. Some spell, some evil he will cast some spell upon me. What if the gods are aiding him? Well, fear makes good runners. This day I will run the best of my life!' And thus did she stride with set face towards the racing-track, shivering with anticipation.

Cheering and talking amongst themselves there now came the Kalydon band, buoyed up with the success of their leader. Acastus walked first with Peleus, nodding their heads and laughing, and close behind there came new faces, newly recruited. With an eager chant they then began to buffet the dank evening air, and others looked over and shouted at them. And over the way did the rowdy supporters of Sparta urge their man, as they neared the shadow-filled stadium.

Now from the trees in solemn mood stepped Meleager forth. He wore a tunic belted at the waist. His arms he held close to his chest, hiding within the folds some burden which he kept from the eyes of men. 'Well then,' he sighed, 'the race is come. Now will I test my strength. And at least there is one of the gods with me! For these bewitchments did she leave me, strange enchanted things, by which – though I see not how – I am promised victory. Yet who can see the ways of Fate? Am I to beat that witch? Surely the witch is swift that I must vanquish! But more than my honour and that of my band depends upon the outcome. She for me, herself and us must be beaten! I'll do it fair. But if that fails, I'll do it foul. Let these the goddess gave me bring me victory.' And thus did Meleager finger the

138

objects held close to his chest, and stride determinedly towards the platform.

Now the crowd were buzzing with eager talk, as the hellanodikai brought the wreaths, and marched down the length of the running-track. The judges to their tribunal platform proceeded with sombre faces, their fillets decked about their grey hairs. Heracles now came forward boldly. Joy and relief on his face, he approached the last race with satisfaction. The throng gave a cheer when Heracles now ascended the tribunal, and the burly man beamed from his bristly beard.

Yet now there neared across the greensward a bevy of menacing warriors, for Iasos with his Arcadians came glowering. Though bearing no weapons, for these were forbidden in the athletic precincts, they yet bore malice and war in their looks. With ringleted hair and shaggy bears, they watched from narrow eyes, and approached the tribunal with suspicion. Then did King Iasos stare about, and his gaze fixed on Meleager, and malevolently he surveyed the man.

But then the hero Heracles raised his hand to the murmuring crowd, and called out to the final assembly, 'Hellenes, glorious heroes, come, our last event is toward, and swiftly let us decide this final match. The Games that have from the corners of Greece brought the greatest warriors at last have here a peaceful culmination. Recall this year, O spirited souls, set fast your hearts on this concord. In friendship win! But now for this running matter.

'Have we the finalists ready close by? Let them come forward smartly. The four runners in the final diaulos. I call them forth, let them step up, and bow to the tribunal, and then let them go toe the line together. The indomitable Polydeuces, representing Sparta; for rocky Pylos, swift-footed Neleus; the noble youth Rhexenor, who has caught so many eyes, and from Kalydon, cheated of his pentathlon final: Meleager.'

Now as the hero called these names, each competitor

139

stepped boldly forth and presented himself to the tribunal. Whereat the cheers of his supported thwacked the air of the glade, echoed in the woods and set all Olympia roaring. And then did the runners go swiftly on, jogging to the starting-line, flipping their wrists and bouncing on their calves. And eyeing each other without yet seeming to, they took gulps of air, and so they stood to their places ready for the strife.

'Now give me leave, good people!' roared Heracles, attempting to drown the noise. 'You must allow me to call with clarity the off! Have some restraint here. We want no brawlers. And let us hope no whingeing seers or malcontents like Trophonius prevent this event. Now all are content to bide this contest, and whoever wins, accept them as victor without argument?' And a great cheer went up at this question of 'Ay!' from the full-throated crowd, except that King Iasos frowning stood forward.

And Iasos said, 'We accept this race: we of Arcadia, but let it be known that once the running is finished, the truce of the Games for us is over. Then we shall on with our justice, and this Meleager will we seize upon, for surely it appears now he has not abducted my daughter, but murdered her! Truly he must, for we have not found her, but her he has buried in the forest! Ay, so it seems from our reports, and so does it seem by his furtive bearing. This indeed is the only possibility, for she would not have willingly stayed with such a rash-headed brawler! Meleager is guilty! So I accuse him! Let no one seek to stay my guards from hailing him back to Tegea!'

'You must settle that as you may,' then said Heracles. 'It seems not likely to me, but just for now, we must postpone the trial. Now is all ready to start this contest?'

But now there stepped Trophonius forward and he called, 'No! For this man has no right to do it! It is all very well Heracles scorning me and my countrymen! But I maintain the Olympic oath has been violated. For we in Lebadaia protest at the discrimination shown against us, and furthermore, my men have been abducted, for merely

140

were they ripping the race-track up as a gesture of protest, when a bevy of brawling Boeotians – '

'Mercy, mercy!' Heracles cried out. 'Trophonius, you tireless pain, do you never have pity on your fellow-humans? You would berate them even in Hades, I think, impervious to their screams! On with the race. To your marks, good runners. Prepare for my word.'

'Nay, stay, stay, Heracles!' came a third voice from the crowd, and as the spectators groaned, recognising the voice of the elder. Maeander came doddering through the pack. 'Yet again,' he cried, 'yet again I make my plea: the rules are not obeyed. Look, there are two of them clothed in tunics: Meleager and the youth Rhexenor; he is a handsome boy; why should he not show off his beauty? Moreover, this Meleager yesterday competed in the events naked. Why now does he now shun the daylight?'

'Oh, go and sit in the baths, Maeander!' then cried Heracles. 'Therein gaze your fill. But as for this race, let us get on with it. I say a third time: to your marks. No delay further. Get ready! Off!' And he roared so that all Olympia echoed.

Now when the runners heard the word, they sprang forth from the line and sped away yearning for the marker. With loud halloos and reverberations thundered the mass of Hellenes, so that all the groves, and all the waters rang. Now flew up wood-doves from the elms, startled by the noise, now did the horses by the rivermeads whinny. The declining sun peeped through the poplars, dappling the runners' feet, as the first mists of evening descended. The crowd were seething: a mass of heads fixed all in one point, a mass of fists raised and waving.

Now first did lithe Polydeuces rush far out in front, for he was the immortal of the twins. Behind him came lovely Rhexenor, whose smooth-silvered legs dashed out and baffled the eyes of him from Pylos. Next came Meleager, who had made through anger a bad start, but yet had crept already towards swift Neleus, and so did the runners fling themselves furious along the grass, and the parched lawn thudded to their pace.

Along the stretch now Polydeuces found himself amazed, for the youth Rhexenor was swiftly catching up on him. Meleager now had overtaken the thundering Neleus, and strove mightily to reach Rhexenor. Meleager yet was clasping his tunic, impeding his speed, for his arms he kept close to guard the burden he bore. But even so he thrust with his thighs to gain on his young opponent, and his kick sent him haring in the breeze.

The spirited feet of Atalanta now felt this gain, and with dread she looked back at her colleague. 'Surely I fear some power!' she thought. 'Yet now I am beating him! And he before he had only caught me in the greenwood, when I was wearied with river-water, fighting him in dread, for it had been no fair contest. Yet still I doubt, I am closed around. The gods have taken against me!' And with these doubts her speed of running slackened.

Yet cheers came from the crowd deafening, urging Meleager on, for cheated of the pentathlon they wished him well. But Atalanta heard their shouts, and seeing Meleager cheered, she grew enraged, and with her best strength strove forward. Soon she was hurtling down the track, her smooth legs triumphing. She trounced them then, and overtook Polydeuces. A hush fell on the dumbfounded spectators, for the youth was faster than ever. Meleager looked grim, and said goodbye to fairness.

Meleager from his flapping tunic now took a shining object, and he rolled it along in front of Atalanta. And the girl in the midst of her running saw it, and slackened amazed, and with horror ran across, and stooped to pick it up. Hiding then the glossy thing, she put it in her tunic and ran. But hurrying Meleager by now had outstripped her. And all amazed were the crowd at this, and again their cheering stopped, and murmurs went round the mass of faces.

Yet angry was long-legged Atalanta, and she breathed fire, and with fury her strength increased still further, and she shot towards the turning-point, and where the hero was reversing, him she overtook and sped away again.

Wherefore Meleager felt once more, and drew out from his tunic another object shining like the first, and this he rolled also past the maiden: a golden, gleaming thing, bouncing on the pale grass in the sunlight. And Atalanta gasped again, and fearfully stooped to pick it up, and Meleager ran past her towards the finishing-line.

Yet now with utter rage, the maiden, clasping the things to her, flew down the turf and strove to win. Unlucky Neleus in the way: him she thrust aside, and the baffled Polydeuces stared with wonder, as she gained again on fleeting Meleager, and glowering overtook him, and wrested the lead a third time from the runners.

But Meleager took the third of his shining, golden objects, and along the ground the third time did he roll it. And so did a gleaming, golden apple go giddily over the running-track, tacking across the legs of Atalanta. Wherefore with a scream she fell on it weirdly, and snatched it up with weeping, and clasped it to her, sobbing and enraged, while Meleager in the lead ran on, and gained the finishing-line. And the race was won, and the maiden overthrown.

Yet Castor and some of the baffled crowd now did cry out against Rhexenor, and they ran at the youth and seized him as he fled. And holding him, they called on Heracles, who was still far off, and they set up a great burly about him. Now did Polydeuces approach with wonder, and Iasos enraged come striding also. Meanwhile, Meleager at the winning-post, panting, was smiling broad, as the crowd went raging and the band of Kalydon.

But the mob about Rhexenor, whose hat had tumbled off, revealing to them long locks of fair hair, pulled on the boy, who frowned and fought with their grabbing hands, and they tugged at his tunic which had fallen open. Then did they hold the youth's hands down, and with a rip tore the tunic open. And the crowd gasped to see the breasts of Atalanta. Then did they call and shout to the others, and show the maiden this way and that, and there was turmoil their side of the stadium.

Meanwhile, Meleager the crowd had taken, and poured about him congratulating, while the judges to talk came, and some others to debate, and all about could he see nothing but milling spectators, as his own company reconciled were cheering him. To him in the press came also Heracles, with smiles and burly laughter, to clap him on the back for being a champion, and all was jesting and rowdy triumph, while those about Rhexenor called and pulled forth Heracles from the victors.

And Castor called, 'Come quickly, O Zeus-born! See another catch, another vexatious problem for your judgement. This youth Rhexenor who ran so fast is no youth at all, but a lovely girl, with budding breasts and buxom. She fights like a cat. She tears with her nails. She has shown us now both fierceness and swiftness. What shall we do with her? She has made fools of all of us! She has shamed all men in Hellas! Shall we give her for the sport of the soldiers?'

'Now stay your filthy hands!' said then King Iasos striding forth, and seizing grimly upon his daughter. 'No man insults any kin of mine, or punishes any. Leave punishment to me, I say, for I am a king to dispense it! And vengeance shall be mine indeed, and hard shall it be too for a wanton, deceiving and insulting runaway! Now have you done enough here, girl. Now are you coming home! Now will you do penance for ever!' And King Iasos then called his guards, and to their looming shields handed over his daughter.

But merrily at the other end of the stadium, on the shoulders of the crowd was victorious Meleager now lifted. And bearing him in triumph thus, they strode with cheers and dancing along the race-track towards the Altis. Yet coming near the brawl of kings, Meleager then saw from where he was sitting, how all about Atalanta there stirred a commotion. And with a shout, he thrust himself down, and ran into the midst of this company, and flung the grappling hands away from the girl.

Wherefore the hero said, 'Cease now, and leave this to

144

my rule, for now am I the man to take claim here. You see this is a girl indeed, and that you have been deceived, and fast as lads can some lasses caper. You know also those who have been east, the princess of Tegea: Atalanta, the swift huntress. Here is truly the daughter of this Iasos of Arcady, who with his insulting tongue accused me of murder! You see how well I murdered her! I have guarded her close, for she is dearer to me than any monarch. Release her then from your ring of guards, impudent Iasos, and let me go freely with this my companion!'

'Ruinous wretch!' then cried King Iasos. 'Daughter-stealer, honour-breaker, are we to preside here over these debaucheries? What, is there to be no faith, no respect, no modesty, but we must let braves come in and rape our daughters from under our noses? No, sir, you will not take this girl. She is mine to deal with, and in Tegea she will be locked away. Ay, a tower or cave shall hide her for ever as I live from the sight of man and humankind!'

'Your tongue is stronger than your arm, loud Iasos!' so spoke Meleager. 'Friends and Hellenes, no crime is here committed. There was no edict put forth against women at the Games, nor is there any against them contesting. Nor is there a crime in this Atalanta coming with me in my band, and journeying now to Kalydon to hunt the Boar-Giant. The king's daughter I did not steal. She herself ran her own way from home, nor am I seeking to steal her or dishonour her, but her will I fairly marry, and marry moreover on the terms of King Iasos' own oath! For in Tegea he swore to bestow her on whatever prince might have her beaten at a running-race. And I am that prince who beat her, as you have all seen, and won her hand, and as a wife I take her.' And Meleager seized the hand of the princess and held it up high, and the crowd cheered with him merriment.

But Atalanta with no such cheering landed on Meleager's cheek a slap that resounded over the dusky stadium and she said, 'You traitor! Unfairly you won me, nor shall I ever give in! Some witch, some goddess betrayed me to your lusts!' And weeping she ran, with sudden flight stunning all about her. And Meleager with equal speed followed after.

Then Heracles said, 'In disputes of men I step in and do as I can. But woman — them to the will of the gods I abandon! Do you wonder? You have seen this spitfire! I can weigh in when men's muscles are my foe, but a woman's fury: let him who will try it. King Iasos, I think you could not hope now to win your daughter back. She has found herself a hero can stand and fight her. Leave her then to the taxed strength of a better hero. But let your injuries quietly heal with time. All daughters must leave home at some time, and what, Meleager is a prince! You have a fine son-in-law! And as for the Games: they are over and done! We'll have no more races this four years. Enough athletes I have seen to serve me as long. But in future days let us make it a rule that no girls may compete, and that to ensure it, henceforth all men race naked! It will please Maeander. But now we must go on to please ourselves, for a feast is awaiting, and all is henceforth indulgence. Well have you done, men! A rowdier Games could scarcely have been gathered! It is true enough: we Greeks do nothing tamely. And so: strike drums, sound, pipers! Let the feasting begin!' And Heracles smiled and waved them away from the stadium.

Chapter Sixteen

Now when in the lily-abundant dales and the milky hills of
Olympia the dusk had come, and the mist had cooled the
burnt turf and hot bushes of the daytime, when the evening's silver fingers had soothed the russet bark of the pines,
the goat-bitten gorse and broom upon the wayside, stealing
among the pine-needles to call awake convolvulus and
stocks, sweet-scented, to the twilight, then strode Meleager
smarting even yet among the woods, and the fire of
vengeance raged now over love's anguish.

And Meleager thought, 'Why now, this girl has branded
me a fool not just to myself, nor just to my fellows, but
before all Hellas! At the height of the Games, when victory
at last was mine, here has she done best to humiliate me.
What is this enemy I have found? Or rather have not
found! Why do I follow where ever is flight and spurning?
I know not truly, but one thing is sure, whether she will or
no, this night will I take her maidenhead.' And smiling
grimly he searched among the songful trees of the dale, but
never a leg or shoulder he saw of his quarry.

Yet when the hero came to the height of leafy Kronion,
then was the sun still catching the highest pine-trees. A
nightingale with chirrup and chuck was warbling her lonely
tune, lamenting ever the ravishment of Tereus. The song
went forth and beyond the trunks, echoing from beech and
elm, it filled the bronzed valley with blue sadness. And
Meleager looked down, where the glimmering river
streaked among its pebbles and the silvery cypresses grew
pale in the twilight.

But then he saw the tents of the Hellenes. The fires now
sparked their homes. In the Altis there was dancing of a
circling chorus. The clash of cymbal and squeal of

reed-pipe came tinnily up from the valley, and purple smoke he saw snake from the altar. Further off to the south where the elders camped, huge fires burnt of sizzling meats, skewered on stakes and roasted with wine and salt. There feasted the competitors, lying round with garlands in their hair, and high was the cheer of their boisterous meeting: Achaean and Dorian, delicate Ionian, Arcadian and Athenian, all in peace for the first time in celebration.

And Meleager sighed and said, 'Why now, what are my petty woes? Was there ever a band as glorious as this of Hellas? I should be down there feasting and cheering the coming-together of Greece, not up here mooning over a flighty girl! I should be there with my band in splendour, for they were roused by my victory, and soon indeed we must make our way back to Kalydon. What leader is this then that leaves his men when he has won them glory? Indeed, indeed, I must bed her and then go down.' And Meleager arose from his high-rocked place to walk down the hill, but just as he did so, a stir in the bushes near him made him stay.

For there was a shifting of branches in the dusk, as in the nearby alder some large thing rummaged about and turned around. Then the boughs jerked up, as from beneath a figure began to come forth. Meleager raised his spear, but there emerged merely Lelex. Amongst the shrubs had he been skulking, harbouring himself for prey, but found in the dusk little to satisfy. And thus he came forth and dusted himself, and smiled with half a yawn, and awhile he looked down to the lights below.

But then he said, 'Meleager, hail! You catch me hunting. But just for the moment the scent has gone cold. There are nymphs in these hills, my urgent friend, grey naiads and lovely dryads! Blessed is the man who can get hands on such a lass! But you, you waster, why do you sit here, when Atalanta is so close? Are you not spurring to take the fruits of your winnings? Be off to the pond and bed her quick. She is now all yours. Believe me, of girls you know nothing! You won her, and she by slapping your face signalled her defeat. This is the strange character of women. And your men expect it. For Zeus' sake stuff her, and relieve us all of this anguish. Then I'll get my nymph and we can all hunt the Boar!'

When Meleager heard this speech, he looked at Lelex and said, 'Your words sound strange to a hunter's ear. If by that blow you think the princess meant to show me love, this is an unexpected interpretation. What, she now hates me, for I have beaten her, in front of all. And she hates to lose, and it was by trickery! Nor do I know by what trick I beat her, for surely something strange happened to her when she saw those apples. Well, it is done now, and she is mine, and in the forest this night I shall bed her, as you plainly put it. I expect not much, for truly I think I shall have to do it by force, but yet we'll see when the moment comes. Our Games are done. Soon will autumn hurry us to the north. How swift and keenly everything is over! Farewell, my friend.' Meleager smiled then, and thanking Lelex, went with saddened steps up the hill and over the crest towards the dale.

But Lelex, when his commander had gone, darted again in the bushes, and crawled his way to where there looked down a ravine, and he studied once more the little torrent that ran between the rocks, and he combed in the twilight the copses and slabs for naiads. Then did he see by the canyon's end a grey shape pattering happily, delicately splashing the water up silver in the dusk, and Lelex at once recognised the nymph he had been seeking, and dashed down sleek and fervent through the bushes. And the naiad was gathering slimy kingcups, when he whistled to her tuneful, and she looked back at him with doe-like eyes.

Meanwhile, Meleager came again, as the night descended, and the sky streaked with gold behind the beech-trees, to the place of the lake, where the cool-stemmed lotuses brood on the dark waters, and all is dank and hushed in a crater of fragrance. And the lake was still, among high-branched chestnuts, lying with petalled face, as the swooping boughs spilled over the banks. There pierced the rushes the saffron evening burning in the water, there frothed the mock-orange, blossoming fragrant and pale. And as Meleager walked on the banks, the moon came over the ash-tree top, and silvered the air about the iris-beds.

Here did he find Atalanta sitting, brooding on the rushes, sighing and staring in lapping waters. With thankful heart he stole silently, his naked foot on the turf, and came by her side without her even turning. Yet she had heard him, for as he sat, she did not look at him, but sighed again, and stared at the water-lilies. And the call of a moorhen clucked in the silence, echoing round the banks, as the creeper-hung trees and jasmine hung round their secrets.

Now Meleager was naked, and she half robed with her tunic half torn off, stripped by the rout that seized her after the race. And when he came near, he set himself close to her warm, long-legged side, and awhile he sat in silence, touching at the flank. She did not speak, but languid looked a moment in his eyes, and Meleager therein saw a sad surrender. So his arm he brought to slide beneath hers, and gently slither round till he held it firm, clasping her breathing breast. And he curled her about, and bringing his face to stare deep into her eyes, he tenderly lifted his chin as if to kiss. And she also, with trembling mouth let her breath mingle with his, and he pressed his lips upon hers and softly kissed.

Then did Meleager bear down upon her and thrust himself swimmingly, feeling the flow of her thighs go limp below him. He kissed her shoulders and round her neck, while she embraced his sides, then did he feed upon her breast and suck it. She flung herself back. Brooding she let him, sighing, bite those buds, and sighing she let him tug her loin-cloth from her. And weakly did she roll before him, coiling up her legs, clasping him and opening her lap in gladness. He came against her, and with sharp bliss, wedged in her tight nest, and into that place he broke and her heart too.

Then was there fury and passion enough on that squelching bank, the water splashing about their coiling legs. Then did the irises rain upon their wet, driving backs the purple petals, as the pair of lovers clasped and clung to each other. Like rams that lock in angry combat, or ibexes of the peaks, that resound the high air with knockings of their horns, so did they close, and thrust by thrust, the new Olympic athletes this time took the finishing-line together.

'So my new love,' then sighed Meleager, 'how you keep pace with me! And how in all things you are my hunting-mate! You would think you had run before this way truly a hundred times, if I did not stain the grass with your virgin blood. Now are we sporters! We are at one from this Olympic day! And Atalanta, what races, what running we shall run! What, are you downhearted? Here's no defeat! Nothing is lost in this! By this act, my sweet Arcadian, you are a woman!'

But Atalanta said, 'Farewell, farewell, dappled creatures of the forest. For now no longer can I come amongst you! I am enmeshed in human life. They'll come no more to me, the fawns and does, they'll not greet me an equal. Farewell, chaste hours, farewell, old danger, my purity in the chase! I am half this man, half his roused lust! To a rearing passion of soon-spent manhood have I sold my soul. Farewell indeed my communion with the forest!

'Yet hail, Meleager, hail, my comrade, rashly precious to me! Hail, my warrior, though by tricks ye beat me. Hail the man who dared set against the spellbound maidenhead, and broke the seal undaunted on the future. The woman I call up from the ground, below us bursting the soil, the dark earth comes in my womb and gives me to ye! The mother of crops: she has awoken hence in my furry loins, and so is your rain sucked deep into her bosom. Wherefore, Meleager, take me again! On the hunt let us not rest! Let us be deer and bulls and eagles between us. My proud seat longs to have your rider spurring to win again. Now my bare athlete, wrestle to victory!' And Atalanta groaned and lifted up her limbs upon the grass, and Meleager she kissed with a lusty fury.

So did he rouse again to the chase, and thrusting his tongue in her teeth, he glued her with passion to his hot-cheeked face. Meanwhile, his hand lashed to longing her thrust-up loins in the air, and roused her like a horse to make his saddle. Then did he mount her, and clasping her back pierced her slimy flesh, and shuddered against her with groaning, lustful thrusts. So did they ride in heady delight on the turf crouching down. So did they sink on their sides and lingering love. A hundred ways they spurred together, and seized in each hand the prize, and with passion they set ringing the sleepy lake.

Across the pond there hovered now an ignus fatuous, a fool's fire that fizzled like a luminous mist. With strange hallooings they heard the voices of the water-nymphs, and the naiads danced a saraband of the woods. In robes of grey and russet gauze, a bevy of sylvan sylphs over the lake capered to fragrant music.

Then did there appear from the high-bowered trees the teasing-eyed Lelex smiling, and to them came with a water-nymph at his side. With grey-green hair looped-up, and reed-stems twisted on her wrists, lilies she bore that burnt mauve under the moon. And the nymphs danced beyond, celebrating the love that was born that night. Like a feasting-hall was the enchanted lake.

Then did Lelex look on the lying lovers, and softly laughed and said, 'So the Games go on! We see you still race together. And are not these the better prizes? See, here is mine, Lacona. She is the reward of my prayer to Aphrodite. The night is bewitched. In Hellas now a harmony of fires, and Kronos from beyond the west yet blesses!'

PART FIVE

The Race of Hellas

Chapter Seventeen

Now when the summer had burnt the fields, and the hot high sports were done, over Hellas there raged the sultry dog-days, so that the mainland and the islands grew heat-weary. The marble sea, as calm as glass, from the waves of its white-smooth pebbles, was sucked up by the sky into its silky air, so that sailors could not divide the horizon. In the shimmering dawn, when the sea-birds glided, the ports awakened lazily to their labours. The fishermen in sultry waters pushed out their swaying boats, as the sun flashed languishing on the dizzy surface. And the calls of cockerels from the hidden farms went echoing over seas to distant islands.

Beyond the deep Aegean where the heat-haze hovered, and the dolphins cruised with warm backs in the morning, there hung a line of mountains, blue-grey with iron clouds, eternal and silent in the ocean. There Ossa lay by the leafy vale of Tempe, and Peneus winding through its banks of birdsong. There Pelion loomed with hugely wooded slopes, whose forests echoed with the hoofs of centaurs. With idly lapping sands the shore was languid in the heat, and the misty breakers approached and departed sleepily, and at ease on sea-weed-wreathed boulders, yawning and combing their hair, the lovely sea-nymphs rolled in lethargy.

But further towards the hard north, looming with craggy arms, grand in azure reign over the wheatfields, the highest mount in Hellas lay, nimbus-bearing Olympus, victory peak of the great war with the Titans. Implacable did it glower down, at watch from the summit supreme over the seas, the isles, the headlands of the Aegean, from wide-swept Thrace and Macedon, from Bosphoros and

Ionia, to the shores where slumber the peninsulas of Paeonia; high-cragged Acte, Phlegra's flaming plains, and the white-sanded beaches of Sithonia, though idly in the morning light, browsing above the cloud, that dragon of earth slumbered through the summer.

Yet approaching now with a wakeful step, cresting the ascent, freshened by airs by the dust of the plain untempered, there came the twelve great deities of the Greeks, looking on new worlds, striding in crisp, deep-phoenixed robes of gold. They trod the peaks soon they were to govern, they came to the summit of Greece, wherefrom without bar all Hellas could be viewed, from whose high crown they were to rule over the daedal earth in the splendour and clashing calm of the Olympics. And when there had come to the topmost ridge the children and brothers of Zeus, then did the cloud-shaker thus address them.

'Immortals of Hellas, brothers of the depths, and children of my soul, as I bid ye, here are you on Olympus. At last returned to the spot from which our recent conquest came, wherein we took our victory from the Titans, downing the giants that sought in rage against Kronos' deposition to throw his son from his rightful throne. Here then on Olympus, whereon from Othrys we repelled the Titans' attack, we do now set foot in stout array, and quitting Crete, the ancient island, refuge of harder days, we come to take up a vaster destiny.

'My friends, you have seen our mortal races meet in union, you have seen them worship and battle in the Games. In Olympia's vales all men of Hellas came and worked as one, in contest and strife finding the greater harmony. The deeds are keen, and of our vision have our followers brought themselves a harvest of glory. Of mortals there is never a race more excelling than Hellenes, and fired by our wills, guided by our wisdom, so they shall go on to consummate greatness. Wherefore as guides and drivers of men, supreme upon earth, we gods must exercise eternal vigilance. Necessity then impels us to seek a

156

higher regard than Ida, and where is a nobler look than Olympus? The Golden Age of Kronos was drawn from ignorance: in knowledge advance the Golden Age of Zeus!

'Here then on this supreme summit we are to take our place, to guide the destiny of these great heroes. On this barren mountain, here where there is neither bush nor bower, we henceforward, high ones, are to make our home. A new haven for a new earth is now to be brought forth. Wherefore each immortal has his cities to build. For a thousand years must man look up and adore these shapes of things, for a thousand years must this be the measure of his dreams. Make Olympus then, fashion a heaven from a few slabs of stone. To work, to work! Destiny builds from today!'

Now when bright Zeus had spoken these words, spurring the gods with his talk, then did he lead them forth towards the heights. The looming Olympus reared like a throne, circling in wide theatre a curving range that looked down upon earth. First to the slope struck out the sky-god, and leading eleven peers, set foot on the crag which stood like an entrance to the summit, and thoughtful he turned, and pointing to Hermes said, 'Here, great messenger-god, here shall you build your city to guard the gate. The conduct of spirit to and fro the world and the commerce of men: from this point shall you supervise such glory.' And thus did he leave the psychopomp to stare about the crags, bewildering in his eyes where he might build.

And Zeus came next to within the range, where a scarpment rose before them, shingled and desolate under the sky, and here where copper gleamed in the rocks, and silver veins running like lightning, the sky-god pondered and looked about his host. Then did he say to the smith-god, Hephaestus, 'Here, lame god of cunning, here your city of furnace and iron shall you build, and from these rocks drag out the minerals, twisting them to your will. Here shall you inspire all industry upon earth.' And the smith-god bowed to hear this command, and with craftsman's eyes a-gleam limped to study the rusty quality of the stones.

They came now to an uprearing peak that looked proud from these slopes, and stared out ugly, covering the gateway below, and there were harsh pinnacles, turreted, and battlements of flint, and adamantine was the face of this crag. Wherefore Zeus turned and spoke to the war-god. 'Mighty Ares,' he said, 'here your city. Build it fast and strong. It looks out stout upon all the land wherefrom our attacks might come. Build here and make all Hellenes supreme in war.' And thus he left the turbulent warrior staring about in wrath, and he leapt to the crags and pulled them about with his hands.

Now when father Zeus had taken his children over these northern slopes, then did he turn, and with the nine that remained, went walking down to the gloomy vale which underhung the summits, a rolling land protected by the peaks, and here Zeus led Demeter the mother, and Aphrodite the golden, and riotous god of the grape, wild Dionysus, and when these three stood at the verge, then did he speak to them, pointing here and there to their new realms.

And the father said, 'See then, my son, sister and foamborn, behold the vale which is to hold your cities. Though barren yet and filled with pebbles, these fields you must make live, and yonder, mother Demeter, is your harvest. Let your farms sprout there, your market-towns, your fields of deep-soiled barley, and fill the shale with bean-blossoms and bees. And Aphrodite, goddess of love, neighbour to this sweetness, there must your palaces rear, and grow your groves. Upon those rocks build baths of pleasure, marble and jade palaces, set temples and dovecotes fragrant under the sky, and let the lovely dusks be humming with loin-bewitching flutes, and lingering looks and anklets clashing madly. And Dionysus, set at hand, share with the love-goddess your vines, and grow them there, filling those barren hills, and let your banquets sound in those dells, and look there: your theatre, see the dancing-floor and seats curved round. Rear your tense towers. Set loud your streets, domes, and feasting-halls.

158

Among rich trees let russet cities flower. So go to your destiny, deities of peace, plenteous and fruitful gods, and let men eat, drink and love in splendour.' And when Zeus the father had urged them so, he left them to their thoughts, and climbed once more the hill to the five that awaited.

But when Zeus returned to those that bided, he looked at Poseidon and said, 'Brother, it is well, is it not, that I build this great kingdom of the air? For not any heaven that has existed in Crete or palmy Egypt or Babylonia shall have such order of beauty. It is well that I do it, for this year we have seen how unruly Hellenes with order can climb the heights of all achievement. Such heroes as we have seen on earth, such bursting hearts and intellects, these must we now guide with caution to glory. Your empire, my great brother, lies all about us. You will not wish here to belittle your vastness in cities. But come, though, to that far height, which is to be my home, the paramount city of Zeus and Hera, and you will have there a second home, whenever you leave the sea, and fly over land to visit the immortals of sky.'

And when the sky-god had smiled at his brother, and he and the horse-tamer shaken hands, he turned and to the frowning summit led briskly the others, and the six of them walked to Olympus' top, inspired by the task they began, and so they came to the crown of the mountains of Hellas. With steepy cliffs, whereon the clouds browsed with misty teeth, with high-curving slopes of snow, Olympus lay back its head in sky, where pure was the blue air, holding all in consciousness, seeing each thing in its place. Here did the six gods come and stare, breathing aloft with fresh brains. And Zeus and his peers wondered at all about them.

For Hellas lay now in its myriad islands bright amidst the sea, ringed round with foam, floating in turquoise sand-banks. The eagles hung above the world, gold messengers of Zeus, and sporting porpoises romped in the purple ocean. There lay Ionia, marble-white, there lay the Sporades, there Rhodes with rose-tinged columns and sun-burnt coasts. And witty Attica, grey-peaked Delphi, thundering Epirus lay all about the summery-azured gulf. And leafy Olympia still was glittering with the spears of men, as the carts and mule-trains clattered their long ways home.

'Why,' said the sky-father, 'what greater kingdom lies under the sun? What richer fields for any of heaven's monarchs? Go then, good Athene, grey-eyed goddess, go, Artemis of the silver bow, go, Phoebus Apollo, that lights the world with his team. You see that great spur that rolls out southward, vastest of all ranges? That is your realm. Rule your children thence. Build there your towns of purity and refuge, Artemis, and hunting-halls, leaf all in wildness and fill the brakes with game. Build there, Athene, your brilliant cities, let them be violet-crowned, set your craftsmen chiselling, your statesmen sounding in debate. And there, Apollo, let teem on that crest your balanced academies, your music-filled halls, and crimsoned dancing-girls. Go forth, my children, in sports of the brain let your men conquer the earth, and from this place let Hellas be supreme.'

So spoke the great sky-god, and to their tasks the immortals went inspired, and forth from that day were they Olympians.

Chapter Eighteen

Now while the gods on the summits of Olympus set their minds to city-building, in the dales of Olympia men busied with striking tents and the loading of carts, for the tribes were departing now, riding away, or rattling with their mule-trains, and the canvas came down, and the casks were packed in straw, and rolled up was the mattress. Meanwhile, the flies buzzed in blackened hordes about the refuse of the Games, driving men hastily to quit the encampment, and Heracles set up an altar to the sky-god, to Zeus the Averter of Flies, and he and the Eleans made there their sacrifices. And Zeus looked down on these fretful prayers from his exalted Olympus, and impatiently he scattered away some of the flies.

But in the morning light, while the men busied about these tasks, there strolled in the lawns and copses by the Kladeos, the woman Atalanta, smiling tenderly in the slanting sun, and looking with joy on the leafy groves. Now as she walked, the birds fled from her, the roe-deer in the thicket bucked up and hurried off with white-bobbing tail. Her friends were no more, yet did she not grieve, for further there joyed in her heart a pleasure in moving her soft limbs as a woman. The air felt balmy, the burnt grass tingled under her woman's feet. Part of the great lap of Nature she abided.

'Well now,' she sighed, 'Rhexenor no longer — for none heeds the costume now, and it is but foolery to sustain the disguise — what do you feel then, Atalanta, the princess of Arcady, the maiden-no-more, the woman made of but a night? What is your fervour? Oh now, come to me, ye little creatures that fly: this is the faith I feel new-stirred in my heart. For just as I lose the kinship of woodland, I gain the compassion for it. O creatures, I feel I would mother you now, not hunt you! Oh then, come softly and let me caress ye, doddering-footed deer, hopping rabbits, come, I'll give you food not darts. Is this then what it is to be a woman? Nature is part of me. This indeed it is to become yourself!

'And you, my husband, I'll think of you thus, though we must wait for the day, and stay till in Kalydon we have slain the Boar, and though my father gives no blessings to the match – surly man! Yet he bided our pledge, when Heracles bade him accept – oh you, Meleager, how from your love now does my heart walk on! How does it flow like Kladeos over the boulders! What power is this love, that like a river binds us to the great land, and flows with the surge of weather from cloud to sea! O my Meleager, with you I look forth now, armed thus on your arm, and see, what visions of riches unfold their towers!' And Atalanta sighed from her soul, and stretched up her arms over her head. But then there came a call to summon her to depart.

From the bower of myrtles, she then made forth, and walking along the stream, approached and joined the band of Kalydon. For Meleager, meanwhile, had gathered about him the company all for the journey, and checked and discussed with each man the trek and the battle-plans. Nor was he in doubt now, but thought and consulted, confirming the best suggestions, as each man sat proud on a prancing charger. Wherefore when the princess came beside him, patting his horse's flank, he leaned down, and cupped her up into his arm, then did he kiss her, while all about him the others joked and chuckled, and set her again down on the white grass.

But now did the huntress leap herself onto her mount held hard by, a new mare bought, for horse-trade was rife at the Games, and tugging it round she formed up with the band, and harkened to the plans, and checked her hunting-spears and shield for the journey. Meanwhile servants busied, packing wine and olives, with loaves freshly baked that morning, and thus were all ready to ford the river to the north.

And Meleager said, 'Well, men, the day has arrived, and it is time for hardship. Farewell must we say to the sweet site of Olympia. We have the stern travel. A-race with the autumn, we seek Aetolia, eager and thirsty to start to hunt the Boar. Yet truly from this summer of search and contest, now we have about us the best band that Hellas herself can muster. Assuredly had we not come to the Games, we would never have found such heroes, for from the pick of the nation have we been choosing. So let us welcome them: Peleus of rocky Phthia, Nestor, from the southern shore of Pylos, and Lelex's compatriots, the twins Castor and Polydeuces; these are all newcomers and heartily greeted. We that are older hands will make them feel at home, and surely all are afire now for the hunt. Let us to horse — but wait, for I see a great shape striding towards us through the meadow. Look, where Heracles comes beside the stream!' And Meleager looked with merry eyes back along the road towards the Altis.

And when they turned, the band of twelve, aloft on their stamping horses, they saw along the white boulders of the Kladeos, in the morning sunlight by the cool-dappled trees Heracles approach, riding on the black mare, mighty Arion. Through the leafy valley, where streaks the river among rushes and dry rocks, while rustling poplars and cypresses cluster the banks, the muscle-wide hero came grinning. His tangled beard sprouting proudly, he saluted them, and doffed his wide-brimmed hat.

And Heracles said, 'Kalydonian Band, whither away so fast? Did you not expect an escort for your journey? How might I allow such a pride of heroes to vanish from tree-rich Elis, without tracing with them some part of their way? The Games are done now. Officials are wrangling still over future arrangements, and I am weary of these lists and rules. You men are my sort. On a bold venture you hare off, all great fighters. Well, if you permit me, I will have adventure too, riding along the way a little with you. Wherefore let me take you as far as Patrae, and wave you across the gulf. And let us drink and rejoice upon the way.'

And Heracles laughed, and beckoning behind him, he called forth now his train, and groaning did the oxen make towards them.

For the band of Kalydon saw now where Heracles had brought provisions with him, in a great cart high-wheeled, high-walled and full of banquets. For two oxen pulled it, labouring away, heaving the creaking shafts, and servants bustled about and presided over it, and the cart was filled with carcasses of beef, great baskets of bread and fruit, long-necked geese, gutted goats, hares dangling over the sides. And the company cheered when they saw such things, and welcomed Heracles, and clapping him on the back, got their venture on the road.

Now the band splashed heartily over the ford, drenching their chariot-wheels in the speckled-trout-bearing stream of Kladeos. Up into the hills they cantered, where the morning sun streaked through the hazels, and caught the green nuts ripening in moist leaves. Now was the summer weary about them, the brambles romped brittle with blackberries, the swallows twittered high over yellowing woods. Craggy Erymanthos felt the frosts of night still upon his shoulders, as he stared on the last smoke from Olympia fuming.

But when the morning had warmed about them, and the band of Kalydon had fallen into the easy pace of their travel, then Heracles on his horse drank wine, and passed the cask about, and cheerily he laughed, as he spoke to the travellers. 'Well now,' he said, 'to Kalydon you go, primed to hunt a great monster, and surely the slaughter will not be an easy task, since the monster you hunt is not an earthly one. You go in fine spirit, many good huntsmen, and one or two huntswomen also. Let me then bid you: go carefully with the gods, for truly there is one you will have against you. Seek always to act with moderation. Do not like me be foolhardy. If once you strike in anger rather than with reason, then will catastrophe fall about you. But you will do well, warriors, for at this Games a mighty spirit was begotten in all our future ventures.

'Yet truly I think, though the spirit was high, there was riotous sport also. Many great laughs did I for one have, nor was I alone in the comedy. I think of my friends, the opponents of Trophonius, and Lelex, here, arse-up in a cow-pat. I think of Meleager winning the diaulos, and his speedier opponent unmasked as a woman! I think of King Iasos when he protested that night to the council, being butted by the ox over the tripod. Well, he is tamed, and persuaded from vengeance, Atalanta spared, the king gone home to Tegea. O glorious days! Why, from all Greece came men for sport, and there was sport enough for any nation. But Meleager, King Iasos has let his daughter go, and you now seem to hold her, but I hope this is honourable, and when you get home, you will make an honest woman of her?'

And Meleager said, 'Ay. For surely Heracles, having won such a prize, do you think I would not make her truly my partner? We'll marry indeed, though it may be without King Iasos' blessing. We can call it the old term: marriage by capture. You jokingly may lecture me, Heracles, but what of Lelex here? He is in the same case as I. The roving-eyed one: what of his union with the naiad? Will he make of her an honest woman? Now Lelex, will you come as far as Aetolia with this nymph of yours, and fashion a joint wedding with me in Kalydon?'

But Lelex said, 'The nymph of my heart, alas, at the shore of the gulf has to turn back towards Elis. It is not permitted for her to journey across the water, for such is the limit of a lake-nymph. But back in Olympia truly she will be waiting, and when our hunt has killed the Boar-Giant, then at once will I return and I will wed her. How might I conceive of any other?' And Lelex turned to smile with love at the nymph riding on his saddle, and she looked back at him with lingering eyes also. But there came a shout of disbelieving laughter from the band, so that he frowned and protested at their groans.

But Heracles said, 'Scoff not, Boar-Hunters, for what Lelex has said he means. And here is no cause to doubt his words. I have some gifts of prophecy, ay, and I can vision the world, when the time is right and the wine brews in me. Soon in the future I see the nymph and Lelex — what is her name? Lacona? The lady of the lake? Ay, I see them marrying. And more than that I see them founding by this union a race, a race of warriors, long-haired and hardy will they be. Laconians shall they be called, unmatched for endurance in warfare, and stern shall they live, tempering their infants in chilly streams on the plains of Spartan Lakedaimon. So bully for him, though he is, as we see, a scallywag, and finished his race chewing on ox-turds!' And Heracles laughed and swigged again some more wine, and they joked until night stole the goat tracks from them.

Chapter Nineteen

In heaven meanwhile, where the bright immortals were tasked with building their cities, with Zeus frowning down, studying the ways of his children, one deity was not about her work, laying out the lines for buildings, or determining place for furnace or field or theatre. Fierce-minded Artemis, that with her bow shoots plagues upon mortal men, and wildly guards the hearts of the forest's animals, she, bent on strife, ran down to where the love-goddess, Aphrodite, was dreaming and her with anger did she accost and caution.

'Now, love-wretch,' she said, 'no doubt you are gloating with your latest triumph, and think you have put me down over the Games. You think you have beaten my protégée, and subdued her to that braggart, you think you have trounced me with that trick with the apples. But let me tell you: I do not look kindly on those who insult my danger, and those who betray my love I never forgive. You have made my virgin corrupted flesh with this braggart, Meleager. You have sullied Atalanta with the embrace of a man. I have borne much, but now no more. You may have have won her to love, but you will never win her to marriage!'

And Aphrodite smiled and said, 'I am goddess of love, nor ever have I been goddess of marriage. You rage at the way of the world, my dear. Such is your divinity. But do not blame myself for what Nature does. Nature was it sprang in Atalanta, and Nature takes her course. Your darts, be they never so hard, cannot remake virgins. So do not seek to punish them who are merely human. Stay in heaven, if you are seeking gods. I have helped a little in the common cause of man. Why should we bow because you are fanatical? The river of mortality flows steadily along, and bears down thickets of denial.'

'You will rue the day you meddled in this!' then called the lithe Artemis. 'This feud will not end merely in the lovers' confusion. You will rue the day those golden apples came into the world. In Hesperia should remain the fruit of dreams. From the orchard of sunset you brazenly plucked at the dragon-watched tree, and hurried away with the forbidden fruit. From such things come a world of trouble. The innocent gold is gone. I am now afire with the dragon's rage!' And the fearful goddess then darted up, and like a thunderclap was gone, and hurtling upon the world she swooped in wrath.

But when the silky evening had come, and the band of Kalydon had slacked their hard journey through the woods, by a grove of evergreen oaks they camped and lit their fires, and here they harkened Caeneus play his lyre. First did he sprinkle on the dusky air a prelude of sweet sounds, with busy fingers plucking the flowers of harmony. The owls ceased their song in the heights, and wood-doves harkened cooing. The foxes peered through ferns with pricked-up ears. And when he had becalmed the wood, with lilting feminine voice, then did Caeneus chant the verses in lyric strain:

> Lovely Cyprus' Queen, that in every creature
> sews the seed's fragrance, and the soft seduction
> of promised roses, let a misty evening,
>   purple in empire.
>
> ring to my triumph, for the hour approaches
> of parades and crowns. Delicate delighter,
> on Paphos' sea-coast with a fluttery team of
>   silvery wood-doves,
>
> your pageant goes by. Begotten from anguish
> of the severed god's seed, glittering the turquoise,
> in scallops you rise. On the beach the tritons
>   sport and adore you,

with ringing horn-calls. Azure-veined the breasts of
Aphrodite, gold-filligreed the nape of
Aphrodite, love-gotten and love-mad, the
    queen and the poet.

Now when Caeneus had sung this lyric, and all were
bewitched by the silky sounds, then did the company drift
to their couches and lie about the roots of the great oaks.
With talk and jest they saw the moon begin her travel, with
wine and garlands they became her fellows. And gently
through the forest did their banter float and crest and die,
in the waves of idle thought and reminiscence. But from
the band crept Lelex and Lacona, and into the thickets
they went tiptoeing, and soon beneath the musky woodbine, where fluffy lie the seeds of the traveller's joy, they
lay back on the banks and with delicious sadness, they
loved a long lingering love through the night.

But also there went Atalanta and Meleager, and they too
came to a bower where they might be secret, and there they
kissed and wound each other about in fervent arms, and
soon they lay and sighed on the dewy grasses. Now the
moonlight lay upon the cobwebs that the dew had caused
to sparkle, and it was as if they were borne on clouds
through the forest. Meanwhile, the autumn crocus lay
below with tender petals, in purple sheen moistening their
bed. Meleager smiled at the huntress, caressed her, and
they lay together, and watched the moon lie over the hills.

But then he said, 'The moonlight beguiles, and troubles
seem distant here. But coming to Kalydon, must we begin
to give thought to our speeches. Our band of heroes are
friends again, and I am cured a little of my madness, and
surely we have seen how tact has a sweet way of turning
things. But these are our fellows here. Through my rash
head in Kalydon I have enemies. Harder will be the task to
placate those who are ranged against me. My mother is
fierce. Of her jealous temper I have told you plainly. I have
told you also of her power over me. She holds in her hands
the brand which can bring me death. In Kalydon you must

be a sweet-talker.' And Meleager laughed a little at this, and chucked her under the chin. But the huntress frowned in reply.

Then did Atalanta say to him, 'I am not a savage, Meleager. Nor do not think you can beat me in soft speeches. For I have a mother just as fierce as yours back in Arcadia, and I have enough tact in tacking to her moods. Yet truly does it irk me, for why should we be slaves to them? Why should I run from one tyrant to another? If there was not this Boar to hunt, I would say: let them all stew! Our destiny will be of our own making. Oh, in the woods is freedom! There all is wild and liberal! The creatures there want not fine speeches.'

'They do not,' then said Meleager. 'But you treat them with spears, and your friendship to them is stabbing and flaying. I have two uncles, Plexippus and Toxeus: they are most truly my enemies. They will be most jealous and obstructive. But you must know they are priests of Artemis. When they hear of your deeds, they will consider you have betrayed the goddess. The vengeance will you have of them for ever working against you. Peril is there in their words and in their deeds. Wherefore you must hope to hide from their ears your erstwhile devotion to Artemis, or seek some good reason for hunting her Boar.' And Meleager sighed, when he said this, and thoughtful stared into moonlight.

But Atalanta fervently replied, 'I will be a liar to no men, nor be lectured on Artemis' devotion. That goddess I have served with truth, and with truth so shall I ever. If I hunt her Boar then I am showing her my respect. Hunting is hers: she is its goddess, and great then are her prizes. She would not that men cower at her monster. But why, Meleager, do you attack me on what has yet to be? You seek to bait me at every turn because of my rash temper! You are so smug because you think you have controlled your own. I think you had better sleep alone on your pile of acorns!'

But Meleager said, 'Stay your ground. You cannot for

ever run away. It is too easy to be a great runner. You talk as if you had no faults and were invulnerable. Well, I have somewhat here that can stab you! So on your back, runner, and keep your legs from running along the ground. You are all big talk. Keep quiet then and face this!' And Meleager then grabbed hard on the girl, and pushed himself against her, and she looked back at him with great scowl. But then she rolled her eyes up smiling in a comical look, and so they fell to laughing and kissing. And soon was their love restless again, and sighing in the leafy bower, while the moonlit autumn wood was still about them.

But Artemis now came down to Aetolia, and the town of Kalydon she gained, and once again she found her priests in slumber. And to the holy Toxeus and Plexippus, uncles of Meleager, she whispered in their dreams with secret news. 'Ho, priests of my bow, harken in sleep, and bide my words with care, for there is hasting towards you threat and peril! Meleager returns, and with him a band, swaggering with bragging heroes, enough to challenge the peace of Kalydon. Moreover he brings a wretched ingrate: Atalanta, once my devotee, Atalanta the huntress, that used to keep herself pure. He has defiled her, and she denied me, the beautiful heretic! These plots of cunning and spite bear down upon you. With spears are they coming to hunt my Boar. Be warned, protect my charge. Kill the girl and offer me her blood!' And Artemis turned, and left these brewing thoughts in the uncles' brains, and softly she flowed away again into the night.

Chapter Twenty

Now when the misty dawn had risen to the mountain-tops to fling her golden spears at the horizon, on Olympus' summit did the gods wake from their couches under canvas awnings in a lonely world. They dressed themselves with stern spirits, they cloaked against cold breezes, for here were some that shivered a little. Wherefore did Phoebus Apollo now fling a great pelt of wolf about him, and girding on his golden sandals, go march to the supreme peak of Zeus. And the sky-father rising he found in contention with Hera, goddess of marriage, for the wife of the presider did not take kindly to sleeping in the rough on crags.

And Hera said, 'Alas then, Almighty Zeus, is this the world you would win us: a cold and barren ruin of a fortress where once you prosecuted battle? Victory it might have won you. Against Titans it is a good refuge, but as a place to live it has nothing! Let me gird my cloak about me, and to the warm shores of vine-fringed Crete go hieing. Not one more night will I spend in these rocks, however grand the view is!' And thus did mother Hera bend the ear of Zeus, who sat thoughtful on his frosted couch.

But Phoebus the bright deity said, 'I come upon a quarrel. And truly now the morning has cooled all of us. We look in colder light at dawn upon the plans of yesterday. Yet necessary it will be to revisit Ida the fertile, for our many servants there, our chattels, our belongings; these at least wait to be ferried to Olympus. And truly there is much to plan which must be done first down south and where we can have better command of our people. You need not live on the building-site to put up a glorious

172

temple. Wherefore Zeus, surely, let Hera and others
about: the love-goddess and other soft ones, return to
Crete and settle there the order and plan of our migration.
Yet Zeus I bid you come with me, for other deeds await us.
And I have things of import to discuss.'

And Zeus the father nodded at this, for barren seemed
the crags, and Hera was thus placated.

Now when the gods had met together, and this plan had
cheered them, there went seaward then the major part of
the immortals. Some did there stay, like Ares, fuming to
grapple with the rocks. Hephaestus also probed the mountain's veins. But Zeus with Phoebus Apollo dallied and
perched on the summit of the world, stared a while about
at the waking Hellas. Wherefore Apollo looked out on the
face of the cliffs and hills of the Hellenes, and then did he
turn and address the sky-father.

'Now mighty Zeus,' he said, 'with this heaven, you set
yourself to rule fair, and from this height all in these
regions may be commanded. Also is it well to break from
Crete, and the mind of Minoan cities, for long have they
held us, but now are put aside. Another Greece dawns. In
our tough heroes, we see future cities springing, we see new
arts, fresh thoughts, trade and greater splendour. In their
rough life, we catch the resonance of a future fineness, for
power alone can sustain the growth of the refined. But we
sit here, the twelve Olympians, in our draughty world. Is
it them or us are vulnerable to attack?

'Great Zeus, he is a fool that fears not. Wisdom brings
caution. To build a big fire first must the spark be
sheltered. We have won a great war with Titans lately, and
overthrown the giants, yet this was done with rebels from
those foes. Their days are gone now. And other foes
always creep about in the world. Never is there peace for
the strong. But what strength have we? We have a fortress,
yet are we but twelve divinities. Who but us can man these
bristling walls? In Crete was protection. The sea all about
us nourished the languorous life. Here, though, all is hard
and high and fine. We need defences. We need intelligence.

173

To Delphi come with me then. For I would have you hear of the coming world. In Delphi there lies a glimpse of the future, which we would do well to seek, for having seen, we will have means to prepare.'

And Phoebus Apollo looked at his father, biding the marking of his words, and when he had thought, the sky-father gave his nod.

Straight then they journeyed, the two high gods, plunging through the streaky clouds, hurtling with thunder-claps among the high-banked cumulus. Above Tempe they sped, whose green-channelled vale twittered with waking birds, through the grey dusk they hurtled of the gulfs of Euboea. Soon did the towering heights of Parnassus loom at them through the mist, and Phaedriades peaks flaming in the sunrise. Thus coasting down in the scoop of olives, silver amidst the burnt grass, to Castalian spring they came and drunk of the well. Here clustered the chestnuts, shedding their leaves, with litter of prickly cases, and the amber conkers quivered in the crystal stream.

With secret steps the great god Apollo led his father apace to where in the cave the fumes from the earth arose. Here hung with darkness did rank-scented breath from the underworld expire, and the cave was sweaty, nursed in the bosom of Gaea. As the god approached, there came a shriek, for sitting here in the rock's bowels there lurked the Pythian priestess with mud-locked hair. About her there clustered tablets and leaves, scribbled over with letters, but the priests had gone that had taken down these words. Alone sat the Pythian, her eyes half shut, inhaling the smoke of Hell. But when the gods came, she sensed them and opened her eyes.

'What tread is this unearthly that comes?' she whispered in the gloom. 'Is this the simulacrum of Apollo? Zeus, is this your shadow before me? On the walls of this cave I see the flickering darkness left by the ideal. Question me then. What is wanted of the gods? The fit is still upon me. Quick, seek, ere the bardic mood is passed.' And the

174

sibyl then lurched about distracted, peering this way and that, as the two gods came and sat on either side.

'Tell us then, sibyl, Pythian priestess, what is there to dread?' so spoke Apollo into the prophetess's ear. 'Look in the coming days and see what perils hang in wait for the gods, the immortals of Hellas, now resident on Olympus. What should we shield against? Where should we seek to augment ourselves? What road is best through the forest of the future?' And Phoebus was silent then, he and Zeus hanging on the old woman's words. She fretted a while, but then was still and spoke.

'When the swimming millipede shall approach, have a care, ye immortals,
with spirit and wisdom can these vast coils be averted.
Twice the feathered genii, bull-horned, shall stamp upon Hellas,
but spirit and wit alone can assail the sphinx and the serpent.
Seek men in high heaven, O ye gods, and bay-winning heroes.

'When dawn is fragrant, and shines Ionia eastward,
let lyric-empurpled her islands cast to Achaia
science in honeyed numbers, songs with their musical order,
and the humming wheel shall throw wide his painted appointments:
seek men in high heaven, O ye gods, and flower-shedding artists.

'When day is brilliant, and violets smile on Athene,
let the dazzled city of many idols, blue from the ocean,
forge matter from the spirit, bring wisdom about in the market,
crown life with measure, and prosecute free rule, many-minded:
seek men in high heaven, O ye gods, and mind-winning henchmen.

'Yet when some fishes have dry feet, and the wolves on the Danube
come swimming in refuge, and the centaurs swarm the horizon,
not men nor gods can withstand doom's fires. Then asunder,
fly, deities, fly the stark storm. Seek harbour to westward,
and men in high heaven, O ye gods, may come to awaking.'

So spoke the sibyl, and when she had done, she panted with head fallen forward, and the gods looked on her, aghast at her passion, and the storm which the prophecy

175

brought to her. But when she looked up again, with unseeing eyes she stared past them towards the cavemouth, and not knowing their presence now she busied about the cave, and collected the scraps scattered about her. So did she shuffle from the cavern. And Zeus and Apollo sat in the darkness thoughtful. Then did they arise and go together to think on these things on Olympus.

But rash Artemis, the goddess of the eager bow, she still raged about the city of Kalydon, and having stirred the uncles, she now approached the palace, intent on rousing Althaea against her enemies. And the mother of Meleager she found at her fires, directing the maidservants of the household, bringing in the logs for winter, and stacking them in the hall, and crackling some already upon the fires. Wherefore the goddess disguised herself, and as an old friend, Persephone, she came to her, and greeted her fondly, as Althaea leant over the smoke to scent the fumes of the fire, and to see whether the log was cedar.

And when she saw Persephone, then did Althaea say, 'My old friend, what brings you to the city? Have you run out of good wool to weave or patterns to depict, that you leave your fine husband sweating at the farm? For this is the busy time of the year, with harvest of wheat and nuts and olives all to be gathered in, and yet you trip there daintily, as if your feet did not touch the ground. And so well gowned too! How is it?'

And Artemis cunningly said, 'I neglect our farm for friendship, and truly, Queen Althaea, you should be grateful. For I am to warn you of trouble approaching; your son, Meleager, returns nor has he lost any of his hotheadedness. He means to hunt the Boar as before; he brings a band to hunt it, and more than that: how this will make you jealous! He trolls with him a swaggering woman, that hunts like an Amazon, bare-breasted, and home in Kalydon is he planning to marry her! Think upon these things, Althaea, and have your devices ready. Such pride cannot be supported.' And before Althaea could ask any further, Persephone hurried away, and when out of sight, flew like a bird through the window.

Yet Althaea was seized with confusing fury at what she had heard and she cried, 'Why now, he has done all this to spite me! He hurried away in the spring of the year, bidding no farewell to his mother. And now he seeks only to plot against my wishes! He hastened away to plot against me and rouse up others for his spite, and beefed by his fellows now he comes to assail me! For thus does he return — so we have heard, a victor in the new Games — and in triumph seeks to have victory where he was defeated! To hunt the Boar, expressly forbidden! What greater insult can he dream? A woman: a brazen, bounding, bare-breasted woman! A swaggering Amazon! Well, swagger as she may, she will not last against me! No bride will my son have against my wishes. First will I seek that minx's death, then deal with my renegade! O Meleager, my son, my son, how you tear the heart within me!' And the queen then walked restlessly, tortured in mind by the news she had heard, feverishly plotting what she might of vengeance.

But now had Phoebus and Zeus returned to the slopes of Olympus, and here they sat together again on the summit. Thoughtful their mood, and Phoebus gazed on the broken piece of pot, whereon he had written the words of the sibyl's prophecy. Over and over he turned the shards, wonderingly in his hands, but then Zeus sighed and exclaimed to him.

'Well, we sit pondering, but we could sit for a century here, if we would wait till we have pierced these riddles. This is the language of tomorrow, and we have not got it. So of what we cannot speak, we should remain silent. Assuredly we will beware of swimming millipedes, and centaurs along the Danube. But as to our task: it still remains. The sibyl did not tell us how we may seek to defend our new heaven. So let us on, and fly again to Crete, and see how the others fare with making the great removal to these shores.'

But Apollo said, 'No. Stay yet a moment. For the sibyl's words do advise us. Always there is keen sense, if you ponder long enough. The prophetess spoke to us, iterating at each four hexameters' end, with various additions: "Seek men in high heaven." These are puzzling words, for what men are here? There is no one on these peaks but you and me, and the striving Ares and Hephaestus. Nor may they come here, for what good would it be to shin up a great mountain, and visit a land peopled by beings they could not see? Yet we should seek men here. How, how so? This is the puzzle for us. Let us solve this before we fly to Ida.'

But Zeus said, 'Ay, solve it, Apollo. Then sit you here, solving. But while we wait for your wits, there is much rule going idle. We have great things to build, and decisions to make, and cities to plan. You may sit here, but I must forge onward. Now truly, my son, you have always been a great delver into your own wits, but not always do they speed forth the happy answer. Seek men in heaven. There are none here yet. So let us away. Why will you dally longer on these barren peaks?'

But Apollo was silent, and looked at his father, and a small smile he gave. And then he said, 'We hail the new age of Olympus. To the shining heaven of snowy peaks do the gods ascend, and with them men also brought to their zenith. There is within the essence of things perfection of form, the beauty of the idea of the existent. Not measured too low is that of man, nor can it be exalted, but in proportion lies its eternal beauty. With this age, father, man reaches forth to that perfection of balance, that moment of coming to focus in the real. Upon that moment does his own nature, the very virtue of man, find in its own beauty its immortality. The deeds of this age, the age of heroes, the challenge of beast and fame: these have shaped forth men in abiding virtue. And when they die, where can these beings, in this essence of state, proceed? Where, father, but to your heaven? Here then is what the sibyl urged. When men die heroes on earth, we shall pluck them, and people Olympus!'

PART SIX

The Hunt in Kalydon

Chapter Twenty-one

Now the palace of Oeneus, when morning came, was rowdy with dispute, and the courtyard filled with angry voices, for in fury to Kalydon that day had come many farmers from fields and vineyards, bringing their bill-hooks with them, bristling with hoes and mattocks, and carts they had full of vines and elms, torn up by the roots, and purple grapes squashed and full of flies, and they argued loudly with the officials, who went busily with their great staffs, but could not placate the turbulent peasants.

Wherefore there came into the courtyard Toxeus and Plexippus, having sacrificed that morning at Artemis' temple, and worried expressions did they wear, as they approached the unruly ones, and stood amazed at the rowdiness within. Then spoke Plexippus and called to them, 'What then is this mob? You're farmers, wherefore do you bring these carts of grapes here?'

And a farmer was called Leos said, 'Well may you ask, you shiftless priests of Artemis. This is your work from the sacred monster. We all come here to demand a hunt, for the Boar-Giant rages daily, and look where our poor vintage is shattered!' And the farmer threw some rotting grapes into the face of the uncle, who flinched and fumed, flipping the things away.

But now came Althaea into the yard, and she saw the unruly crowd, and she raged and called in a loud voice over their heads, 'What is this onslaught? Who are these curs? Have we a rebellion in the palace? Shall I call forth the guards and have these peasants driven panicking into Hades? Ho, Toxeus, why do you let them brave here? Have you no courage to face them? Plexippus, why stand you there with a stained face?'

'Lady,' said Leos, 'his face is stained, yet he can wash it. We farmers have our lives ruined; that has no remedy. Here come olive-growers from the hills of the gulf, here from the plain of Achelous wheat-farmers, and here goatherds from about the lake. Most are we vine-growers; not far hence on the south slopes of Arakinthos lie our rows of elms with the vines a-twining. There came the Boar three days ago. Since which he has ravaged a dozen farms. Here are men and families bereft of their livelihood. If you cannot have courage, citizens of the full-fed town, to hunt the Boar, then we farmers will. Here comes the king. He has heard our plaints. He knows of his people. Let him grant us protection!' And the farmers then called out beseechingly, as King Oeneus approached, and the king stood and listened to their shouting.

But then said King Oeneus, 'Often indeed I have heard your complaints. And daily this monster grows outrageous. Truly is it time he was killed. Yet who is there can do it? Does the realm hold now such a challenging hero? The Boar has been quiet in summer. High in the mountain forests he has sought the cool shade and the succulent roots. Now they grow frosty, the faltering days, he comes down to the plains, to the vineyards he comes, where the vines, my craft, are shattered. Artemis indeed is a fierce goddess. Yet so is Dionysus! So now hear the good news that I bring!

'There have come reports from across the gulf that Meleager our runaway prince has distinguished himself before all Hellas. At the recent Games which were held for the first time in Olympia, it seems he has made himself a victor! Not only that but this very day he hastens towards his home, and he brings with him a whole company of heroes. He and they will hunt the Boar! They have pledged to root it from the land, and the best heroes in Hellas are they to do it! It may be this very morrow Meleager after a long exile will be received by our city-gates! My subjects, let us celebrate then. With a victor's triumphant home-coming, we must deck our streets for the hero's arrival!'

And the king in laughter raised up his hands, and the people cheered at this sudden news, and Kalydon was filled now with rejoicing.

But then strode Toxeus and cried, 'Indeed, indeed, this is all true news! And we as priests have set out temples bustling. But there's better news, which we have for you, just delivered from the temple. We have saved it till this moment to tell you. The Boar-Hunt is not needed now! The giant is to be called off. The goddess has spoken to us in confidence. Only this night she appeared to us saying that she would withdraw the monster, if we and the people of Kalydon made a certain action. What that action is we will acquaint you on the morrow with. But now let us deck our town for Meleager. At the gates before he returns we will tell you what you have to do, and then the Boar will vanish from our land for ever!'

So spoke in the silence Toxeus, and the mob for a while were unsure and still, but then they went away again rejoicing.

But the band of Kalydon on chestnut horses through the autumn hills came now to the shores of the Gulf of Patrae. In buoyant heart, with eager limbs, they gazed on the grey water, and the bronzed hills of the distant side. Under fleeced and sunny clouds lay Akarnia silent, the frosts shining on its western summits. But the heroes dismounted and walked down in the village by the water's edge, where the fishermen and boatmen sat by the glassy sea. Them did they press for ferry hire, and crafts to carry the carts, and soon did there come a flotilla to the beach.

And when all was ready, then spoke Heracles and said, 'Well, friends, it is goodbye. Farewell I bid you into Aetolian hills. This journey of autumn has proved redeeming. Much friendship have we found, and warm is my heart among such a company. Wherefore it bleeds. Alas, alas, how our heart's floor is strewn over with leavetakings! Give me your hands then! Hearty heroes, strike home, and vanquish the Boar! Remember Heracles and the friends of the Games!' And the burly-headed one then set about grasping and squeezing each man, so that all was tearful laughter on the departing shore.

Then spoke Meleager, 'Indeed, great Heracles, you are hard to part with! Truly your powers would be well used in our hunt. Yet to other labours are you pledged, that have already wrought so many. Farewell, farewell, great accomplisher! The Games of Olympia we will indeed hold fondly in our souls, for they were your child, and their success of your spirit. None but Heracles could have brought so many to such fine deeds, nor borne and bullied some few to such good outcome. Let me, great man-teacher, take from you the gift of managing friends. Goodbye, my king,' And thus Meleager hugged the mighty man, and tears went trickling down the cheeks of each.

But last there came to bid adieu Lacona, the nymph of the lake, and sadly she went with Lelex to the waterside, and there she spoke, 'Farewell, awhile, my man of Olympia. Have care now when you walk the forests of danger. Do not go rushing in with the first, nor lag till beyond the last. But keep you to the middle of the combat. Thence to these arms hurry back unwounded, and let us walk again in the summery woods of Kladeos by the lake. Remember you well that destiny we have yet to make. O lovely Spartan, how shall I bear you away?'

And Lelex said, 'Leave all thoughts of bearing till I am come again. Keep safe for me that nest of honey, your heart. With Heracles go now. Stay by his side. None then will trouble your return, and safely stay in the lake through the winter's cold. Among frosty reed-beds you I shall think of, by feathery-seeded ice, amidst dark days when deer come shivering to drink. Keep warm then, and safe. Fly the foot of man, and tempt no god with pride. And have you no fear; we shall meet again.' And Lelex then kissed the weeping nymph, and they parted on the beach, and the company stoutly clambered into the boats.

But Heracles, as he watched them sail, sighed and said, 'Meleager, I fear we shall not meet in life again. Nor of those that cross to the shore will each man come back home. Alas, there shall be sacrifices to this Boar! Beware in Kalydon! Wide and savage the anger of Artemis, and some there are unresting till they have vengeance! The wind blows cold. From Macedon I scent the wings of winter. Nymph, we must home and shelter ye in the dales. Though from your soft loins a race shall spring hardier than any upon earth, tenderly we must shield the stirring seed.' And Heracles turned and led away from the gulf the weeping nymph, and together they rode again into the hills.

But in Kalydon now the great Boar-Giant, the monster savage-maned, raged and flung himself upon the farmlands. By the strands of Achelous, where good husbandmen had sweating threshed their grain, he furied and tore down the barns that guarded their corn. By the marshes of the delta, where fisherfolk live and the hunters of duck and geese, there did he rage and pitch to earth their huts. Meanwhile, his tusks uprooted the fruit-trees, felled the thatched stables, pitched bee-hives down and scattered about the air the wings of dove-cotes. All country labour he brought to nothing, setting beasts savage again, roaming the ruined fields in loping hunger.

Yet worst in the vineyards. October nigh, the vintage was gathering in. Men moved by the vines, culling the bloomy bunches. With creaking waggons and nodding oxen, while amidst turning vine-leaves, they heaped the baskets and emptied them in the wooden casks. Here over the hill there appeared the monster. Children ran screaming from his darkness. Men took up pitch-forks all in vain against his rage. The Boar snarled ireful, scattered the harvesters, mauled their yelping dogs, and tossed to the air the carts of next year's wine.

Stained then with hound-blood, purple-toothed, his cloven feet dripping with grapes, the monster then paraded with scarlet triumph. With snorting song he leapt in the harvest, tossing right and left his tusks, capering hog-backed, lusty from destruction. Those that set upon him, he butted to oblivion, gashing with his tusks, the inwards of men tangled between his horns. Those that ran from him he pounced prancing after, goring from behind, and cattle and horses were tossed up onto his spines. Such was the monster of Kalydon, now sensing the band against him. Such was the rage of the enraged Artemis.

But in the city of Kalydon the people were roused in cheerfulness, for all the houses were decked for the coming victors. With vines and fruit were garlanded the galleries and the eaves, and pranked out every corner of their temples. Long did the people stand upon the walls, biding the band's approach, straining their eyes over the fields among the hills. The king passed by, and the queen also, eagerly watching for news, and thus did Oeneus call to those about him.

'Why here is a sight! Not for these two years, since the Boar-Giant came, have I seen my people so hearty and good-humoured. The thought of the monster passing from the land, and the farms and vineyards being free, this has made them vigorous and happy. Yet where is my son? I long to see him! Althaea, come stand by me. You, I see, are nervous as myself. My eyes are no good. Is that them there beyond the sun-lit hill? But see, where your brothers come from the temple!' And the king broke off now, and looked with the crowd to where along the street there came marching together the priests of Artemis.

For Toxeus and Plexippus now, dressed in ceremonial fillets, in stately tread walked before the populace, and climbing the steps that led to the look-out post over the central gate, they advanced and beckoned the crowd to hear their speech. The priests then glanced towards the king, and the king at the queen, and she with a nod put her hand on her husband's arm, and so did the king incline to the priests, bidding them say on. And smugly the brothers looked about the people.

Then did Toxeus cry, 'Kalydonians, I promised you yesterday to unfold to you the plan to drive out the

Boar-Giant. Now is the time the goddess favours to reveal her prophecy to you, and to grant you the means to scourge her monster from the realm. Give ear then, and set this rule in your hearts. Long trouble have we all borne, since first we had the misfortune to insult the goddess. Now let us seize this chance to placate her, and execute exactly her words. So we may be rid of our trouble for ever.

'In the Chersonese by the icy Euxine, among the distant Taurians, to the goddess Artemis is made a vital sacrifice; the first-met stranger of the year that comes on their rocky shores: he is offered in death on a pyre before the temple. By human life is the goddess appeased. Yet tender for the citizens, she decrees this is the life of a fated stranger. So does she with us. The goddess demands that there is burnt before her altar the body of the first foreign woman that comes to our city. Keep then your wits sharp. Note well who enters. The first female stranger we see: she is forthwith to be offered in death to Artemis.' And Toxeus ceased, while the mob below him stirred uneasy at his words, and the king and queen looked on with different faces.

Chapter Twenty-two

But now towards the city of Oeneus came on the band of
Kalydon, the twelve horse-borne heroes from Olympia.
With clattering hoofs raising the dust in the autumn
sunlight, they bounded across the plain towards the city.
Prince Meleager headed the band, with Dryas at his side,
and Peleus the mighty, holding a spear, and with them in
the rout they carried behind a giant stag, slain in the hills,
and brought to the city as a peace-offering.

In the press there rode Atalanta. Hidden she was among
the men, set back where the train of the heroes was
thickest. But yet she thought, 'Why now I must skulk, and
hide myself away! Once again I have the privilege of being
a woman! And now with these extra precautions forced
upon my unwilling self, I have even less to shine than
usual. Yet what is this fate that comes before us? How
shall it be in that city? What will they think, the mother
and father of Meleager, if they have heard he has a
betrothed, and means to marry her, whether he has their
wishes or no? I must tread warily. Indeed I must. Indeed
I must first be a mouse.' She sighed, 'I do not think the
rôle suits me!'

So did they travel, each man revolving on his anxieties,
pondering courses to take at turning events. But when they
had come by the olive-crowned hill which sloped towards
the town they stayed their steps, and rested with their
lances and bows a-clatter. Meleager drew them round by
grove, and sheltering among some cypresses, he settled
them down awhile to listen.

Then did he speak and say, 'Now friends, we are a mile
from the town, and round that bend we will be visible from
the walls. There danger will confront us, and certain

precautions have we already made; wherefore, Atalanta, do you especially be wary. But let me awhile remind you others how best to act therein, and of the dangers that await us. The king, my father: he will be glad to see his son returned. My mother will waver this way and that. But most to be guarded against are the priests of Artemis, two uncles of mine, who will do all they can to prevent the hunting of the Boar. Much have I quarrelled with them in the past, and no love is lost between us, but yet they will be suspicious of us all. Wherefore I bid you take it calmly: no swaggering or braving, but cool discretion must hold all our converse. And so with careful vigilance, we may win the town to our venture, and hunt the Boar with impunity tomorrow!' And with that did Meleager rouse them, and lead them on again, and round the path they saw the glittering city.

Now when to the city the travellers approached, they bore a stag aloft, for this had Meleager hunted and saved for an offering. Across the fields, as they marched in ranks, they saw on the windy walls the heads of the townspeople clustering, watching. The gate of the city was open fully. A group of warriors stood guard. But then from the gate there came in gilded procession, the king with his ministers, bearing branches, olives and laurels of victory, and here did they stand ready to greet the newcomers. And Meleager rejoiced to see his father, and the son then ran along the road, and cheered by the people, returned to his embrace.

And Oeneus said, 'My son, my son, welcome. It is long you have been away, and the seasons indeed have dragged without your spirit. You have come from the Games! We have heard much of them! You were victor in the running-race! We are prepared: we have a welcome for you! No son of mine will come as a champion back to his home city without the glory of a champion's triumph!' And the king called out now, and from the gateway a berry-decked cart was brought, and Meleager was cheered and heartily thrust into it.

Then did the crowds run and make holiday, as the prince Meleager to the town came in the splendour of an Olympic champion. Not yet did they breach the wall for him to make a victor's gate, but still there were garlands and wreaths and fruit out for him. The rest of his band were drawn up in good array close behind the chariot's wheels, and they also were cheered and fêted. Looking this way and that at the balconies, cheerily the heroes strode, and they bore still the stag upon poles on their shoulders.

Wherefore when they came near the temple of Artemis, Meleager stopped and shouted, 'Citizens of Kalydon, first we must make an offering. For you all must know that we have heard dire things about the Boar-Giant's ravages, and that our band fully intends to hunt him. Yet by this hunt do we intend to Artemis no disrespect, rather are we rising to her great challenge. In token of which we would offer here this great stag at her temple. Let the priests be called and accept the fruits of our hunting.' And the heroes of Meleager then took the stag and laid it on the steps of the temple. But none there came out of it to receive it.

Now when they pressed on to the city square, then did the queen arrive and Althaea in gorgeous robes came thickly attended. About her she had lovely handmaids who sidled in flowing robes, and dazzling beauty shone in the face of each. Wherefore the heroes stopped in amazement, and marvelled at the girls, and Lelex was torn with conflicting passions. But Meleager smiled and from the chariot started to dismount, to greet his mother with a show of duty.

But Althaea said, 'Stay, stay, my son. Who am I to call you from splendour? Make on, make on with your triumphal procession. Your followers too. I see them about you. I and my handmaids bid them welcome. Yet truly is this the whole of your victorious company? I had heard tell that Meleager brought with him a captive slave-girl from Olympia, one that had from her owners in Arcady run away?'

But Meleager smiled and said, 'Why, mother, how

report mangles true news! No indeed, I have brought no slave from Tegea. Yet despite your words, I will bid you welcome with the duty of a true son. What is a triumph of the Games before a mother's love?' Meleager leapt down then, and coming to his mother, knelt to crave her blessing. And she embraced him, and caressed him, and tears were in her eyes.

'Truly,' said Althaea, 'your travel has taught you the wisdom of discretion. Welcome, my boy. Ah, how still your eyes shine!' And she wept as Meleager kissed her cheek, and slipping from hers his hand, mounted again in the chariot for the procession.

Then into the square did the triumph come, with the townsmen cheering their prince, and Meleager laughing the while in the chariot. For blackberries and grapes decked about its sides, and yellow vine-leaves a-twirl, and the women had tied thereon tufts of wool, dipped in dye. Wherefore like a king, with the king walking behind, did Meleager come to the palace, and here the cart stopped, where the door had been wreathed in olive-boughs, and a set of tripods were placed thereby as prizes for the prince, and the chamberlain stood by them smiling at the hero.

But when they were gathered, Meleager called, 'Who here has seen the Boar? This triumph is fine, but we have other laurels to win. Let the farmers be brought or countrymen who have seen the monster these last days, for now we would hold conference about his hunting. We must not delay. The vintage is here, and much has been lost, I have heard. Let us rid the monster before the autumn advances further. Thanks then for my triumph. The moment was sweet. But take care you turn not my hot head. There is work now for us to be doing!' And Meleager looked about, for the crowd were cheering, applauding his words about the hunt, and he sought for who in the press might tell him of the Boar.

But then came Toxeus with Plexippus, and they approached the hero and Toxeus said, 'Leave this vain treason, Meleager. You hunt no Boar, for this is sacrilege against the goddess. So was it when you left, so is it now you return. The Boar will leave us, the goddess had assured us, once she has sacrifice. It will be hard, but all of us must make offering. Now where is your band? Amongst your number we hear you have brought a wife? She, alas, is not to be with you long.' And Toxeus went then, and strolled down the steps towards the band of Kalydon, and he passed over them with his eyes, looking for a woman.

But when he looked close, he saw but heroes there: Acastus and Dryas and Lelex, and then Caeneus, Eurytion, Ancaeus, with the twins Castor and Polydeuces. And much as he might stare at them ranged in their marching order, amidst their ranks he found no female. Wherefore Plexippus came, frowning impatiently, and he joined his brother by the steps to look again at the Kalydon band. But girl they saw none, but Rhexenor, the fair-faced youth, Peleus, Nestor, and there was but Meleager to make up the twelve.

Then spoke Plexippus, 'This is your band? Indeed we were told it was twelve. Yet how did we have reports that you carried a woman? The Princess of Tegea we heard you had brought, and so the report held, were intent on marriage on your return. Where have you hidden her? Though she be here, yet not in Kalydon, still is her life forfeit to the goddess. Ay, true it is. For the goddess demands the first woman-stranger in the city: she must be sacrificed for ridding the Boar.'

And the prince replied, 'You see what you see, and as for ridding the Boar, we twelve Olympians begin tomorrow to do it. Wherefore, come yourself, honest Artemisians; if you would offer gifts, give your goddess the greatest beast in the land.' And Meleager dismounted, and joining his father, who had reached the palace-steps, he went with his band into his old home.

But the uncles remained, and Queen Althaea now came aside of them, and Toxeus whispered to her, 'He has brought no princess! Have we been deluded by reports or is this a trick he plays on us? This Meleager is changed now with his travel. It does not seem we can rouse him as in the old days. He looks at us coolly and answers us with reason. What shall we do with this new enemy?'

And Plexippus said, 'What indeed? He has destroyed our plots, and now the people are again in ferment. If he hunts tomorrow, then the mob are all with him, and the king also! We cannot stop him. What does the queen believe? Has he perhaps the princess stowed away somewhere out of our clutches? We must along and hunt with him, in case he plans some foolery. Perhaps he has her hidden in the woods. The goddess must be honoured, and this braving hero cannot be allowed thus to trump us before the people!'

But Althaea sighed and said, 'O Plexippus, your busy plots! How fretful beside the new calm of my Meleager! Why, I think these scared reports of princesses and marriage are all but the dreams of some mad messenger! Let things go by. Our prince is home. And he has grown from travel. I long to see him quietly and talk to him!' And sighing did she stroll into the palace, while the uncles looked about, then hurriedly stalked off towards their temple.

But satisfied so was not the goddess Artemis of the Silver Bow: she hung in the air furious at this subterfuge. And thus she spoke, 'Why, you vain priests! Can you not see what is under your nose? And Althaea, are you now moonstruck over your boy? You think he returns a virgin soul with no taint of the female about him, but look deeper, O indulgent mother, at that attendant boy! That is no Rhexenor – a cunning name, for he has done "manly deeds". No, that is the woman you dread Meleager's embracing. Open your eyes and see your shame, and you, O priests, your outwitting! See, behold whom you must sacrifice tomorrow!' And the virgin-goddess then rose in the air, soaring in a thunderous cloud, and shook dark anger and lightnings over the landscape.

But to her now did fly her brother, Apollo, of the Far-striking Darts, and with bright face and manly beauty he approached her, and Phoebus said, 'What, glower you still above the land of Kalydon? Is there no other city now for you in Hellas? You neglect your Lydians, your Ortygians, and the Amazons of turbid Thermodon, that draw their bows with their breast exposed, you dismiss all these for a perpetual quarrel over a tusky hog! Will you for ever demean yourself with this row? Why do you skulk here, O once-bright sister? Why do you spoil your brow, once so silver, that now is furrowed with ugly rage? You dog Atalanta, to revenge upon her, and Meleager, for her faithlessness. Where then will there be end to your persecutions?'

And the goddess replied, 'Not till she is dead, sacrificed to me, and him also, that stole her from my service! You seek to colour my doings here with ignominious shame, but you must know I defend the honour that has been tainted. I will have them both. Do not seek to stop me. They will fall to my spite. And it shall be accomplished in the world's pattern. They may have outwitted awhile my followers, yet there is time before the hunt. Eyes may be opened before the Boar is pursued. My beast will not be found unfated. No, there'll be hunter's blood shed in this questing of the Boar!'

But Apollo said, 'Then I see, O sister, your rage will not be assuaged. You will hunt down this pair to their very death. But grant me this: let not your vengeance pursue them beyond the grave. Speak but these words before you bloody your hands.'

And Artemis replied, 'I know not, Phoebus, what you signify by these words. But this I grant you: beyond death vengeance dies. The life of mortals is brief and wretched. They flower an unholy hour, then are they gone, restless wraiths in Hades. No need is there to punish further one who has passed over Lethe. I will not seek more. This is enough.'

Apollo heard, and bowed his head, and backed from the angry immortal, and like a lightning flash he sped away.

But when had come the evening, and soft dusk had put the fruit-trees to slumber, muffling the apple-boughs with a sunset mist, when the ghostlike oxen had lumbered their track through the distant hills, and reached the farmstead for water and straw in the caves, when the crowing of those with long, barred tails, russet wings and scarlet eyes had happily come from the roosts in the wild plum-tree, then along the terrace of Kalydon palace, away from the booming banquet, there walked Meleager and Rhexenor, the disguised.

And Rhexenor said, 'Oh, how weary I am of this lanky-youthed self! Why cannot a girl be a girl in braving Hellas! I press myself in, tuck up my hair, and roll like a boy about, and hard is it ever to hold my tongue while others speak. And you, Meleager, so smooth and wise! You are grown a sumptuous magnate. How victory and beating me have made you a prince! Yet what am I? A perpetual clown, padding after your great strides! Who would think I could beat you on the race-course?'

'If you are ready for sacrifice,' said Meleager with anger, 'step forward and offer yourself to Plexippus! You fret against the wisdom of this disguise, and long only to give way to boasts and shouts and reckless quarrelling. You anger me with this whining weakness. Subdue your surly heart, and recognise the danger that abides for us, for once set me against my mother, rouse the spite of my uncles, and from Hades' shore we will sigh on carnage in Kalydon. Now let us part. It is foolish to walk like this together in the open, and you are set fast with the backward look.' And Meleager frowning broke from the princess, and walked towards his chamber, and gladly to his old haunts.

Yet when he turned, he saw Atalanta standing at the doorway, the sunset streaked in russet behind her head, and the princess said, 'I am a fool, I know. But my swift-footed love, you run ahead of me with all this wisdom. Yet I'll catch up. I am not such a fool that I would say this to others. My spirit is fiery, but you teach it sense. Forgive me then. Together let us rest. Here is the chamber of Meleager, and my love, it is joy to have you home. Oh, we together, my dear Meleager, could hunt eternity, and chase the very stars into our nets!'

Meleager laughed, and took her hand, and sat her on the bed, and spoke to her, as she looked up at him with almond eyes. And he said, 'My time has come round, now you are with me here, and home is this great adventure I begun. For from this very bed I arose to hunt in the frosty season, and now in the autumn as a hunter I sit here again. This only is changed: I was alone. Now I have my love. Welcome then, welcome, my soul's sister.' And he took her in his arms and hugged her, twining her about, and smoothed her hair, setting it free from her cap.

But as he kissed her, set free her breasts from their pressing tunic, and pulled her to him, stroking her with his hand, there came Althaea tiptoeing happily to visit Meleager's chamber, and gladly she saw the door of it open. But as she came in, she stopped and froze, seeing the couple on the bed, and noting the woman Meleager held in his hands. Then did her face darken, and with new rage, she exclaimed at the deception, and rounded on the couple that sprang up from the bed.

'So they were right as ever, my brothers!' shouted the angry queen. 'How well they know you, deceitful Meleager! I was bewitched by your new-found command, and fell for the calm in your eyes, but now I see it was but to make a fool of me! Who is this harlot you bring into the palace with shameful secrecy? Who is she, betraying her lanky body as a boy? Set her out of this palace and city forthwith, or I'll not receive again you or any of your huntsmen friends! Indeed my brothers are faithful to me! They said you had brought a woman! Yet not even they considered you would drag in here a trollop! Well, mistress: my son is unusually silent! No rages from him! Baggage then, what have you to say?' And the queen in fury drew up her height and stared at the long-legged girl, and her eyes blazed as they flickered over her smooth face.

But Atalanta replied to her, 'It is not for me to speak. Yet for myself I regret this deception. If it has made you feel a fool, then queen, I beg your forgiveness, for the aim was more to save any injured feelings. I am a princess of Arcady. My father is King Iasos. With your son I have run this far in hope of marriage. With proper respect and honoured presents we were to approach your good will, once the Boar had been driven from the land. The Boar is perilous, and paramount is his depredation. Against such we thought to postpone the lesser trouble.'

Then the queen said, 'Ay, but now you find me a fiercer kind of boar! Know then that you have set yourself for sacrifice! For the words of Artemis to her priests, my brothers, was that the first stranger-woman to come to our city was to be sacrificed to the goddess! So is it settled. I have but to show what I have found at home, and it is farewell, princess of Arcady! Well, surly son. What words have you to chase those of your minion here? Your hunt is done and your wife is offered on the altar!'

And Meleager replied, 'When policy fails, there is still the blade. Do not think, mother, that I have lost my strength. Tact and subtlety may come first, but for those that courtesy spurn: have at them! Humming comes my spear! Your vex-headed brothers, set them not against me, or they'll be moles in the earth, greeting their old friends on the shores of Hades! Nor do not think to take this princess, or carnage will be in this city greater than the carnage of the Boar. Choose then your path, injured queen, I would have approached you fair. With honour and love I would have sought your grace to marry. But if you have chosen the bitter way, set on, I care not! Make your spite, but tomorrow we hunt the Boar.'

But Althaea laughed, 'Why now, I see my rash-head once again! I wondered how long he could keep his hand from his sword! Threaten me then! Well, we shall see. I shall ponder on these things. Denounce the girl this minute will I not. But wit you well: no marriage will you have, be she never a princess. This will I never consent to now. You may hunt tomorrow, my brothers with you. Let the girl be disguised as before. Take care you do not show them she

197

is a woman. But bring her not to the palace again. After the hunt, keep her away. Venture again here, and you know the consequence. My son, my princess, has his strength very vulnerable to his mother. And with one cast I can have his life burned in the very furnace. Seek not one jot then to try and outwit me, or into the fire goes his soul. I will do it surely. A queen is not to be scorned!' And with that Althaea left the chamber, and the darkness now held all, and the couple were silent in the little room.

Then Meleager sighed and said, 'The owls cry over our roofs. The smoke of night has settled on this house. My love, I fear the words of my mother hold in them my doom. Well, we can but go on and hunt the Boar. Should things go ill, with the rest of the band must you fly again to Tegea. Armed are you now with the gift of measured speech. Should she indeed burn me, to Heracles then in haste for your protection go, and with him seek reconciliation with your father. This eve you did well, my hardy princess. Pride is in my heart. Safe and calm were you against my mother. And if there is no journey forward, well, hither was sweet travel. Till my death I shall fight to defend you. But as you are told, my life is quenched by but a throw of the hand. Therefore it is best to make these needful pledges.'

But then spoke Atalanta, 'Your busy spirit you can rest here. Return will I never to anywhere. Do not defame me with such thoughts, nor seek to dispose your chattels. I am not your wife yet for you to dispose. If your brand be burnt, then dally for me on the flats of the grey marsh. You are not alone in your life-token. I carry myself the talisman by which my life is snuffed. You need not think your fate can so escape me. O my Meleager, through many hardships we travel about this world, but we will marry on one side the marsh or other.'

Chapter Twenty-three

Now when golden Aurora had cast on her bonfire of the sun the smoky branches of the autumn morning, and gathering the auburn leaves she had among the valleys walked, stirring the husky doves and thrushes from slumber, when on the frosty-shouldered mount the wild goats she had roused, and brushed the cold tears hence with russet scarf, then from the farms and villages while even the night delayed, with hoes and pitchforks grasped in brawny arms, there marched on high-walled Kalydon the countryfolk in eagerness, ready for the great hunt of the Boar.

Amidst the square of the sleeping city, while dusk still hung in the backstreets, and washerwomen clattered with their tubs, while still the dogs that lay in the doorways scratched at their cold fleas, and looked up sniffing at the passing labourer, there now came clattering with clear sound the huntsmen from the stables, the breath of the horses steaming among the columns, and above their wide-brimmed travelling-caps, the rising chariot of Helios now tinged the palace turrets with the warmth of venture.

From sober conference with his men, all twelve leaping to their mounts, then came Meleager from the palace. With naked thighs he bestraddled his horse, his blue cloak thrown from his shoulders, and at his side in tunic tied fast rode Atalanta. Now came Plexippus and Toxeus, led on their blinkered steeds by servants from their shadowed quarters, and pleasantly they nodded to Meleager, staring close at the youth beside him, and sharing a sidelong glance with each other. The horns were sounded. King Oeneus from the terrace smiled on the hunt, and then called down to them heartily.

'Good luck attend your hunting, Olympians,' so spoke
the king. 'At last we have the will to tackle our persecutor.
The strength and fire you have found at the Games is now
put to your country's safety. Let us no more cower in the
monster's shadow. No disrespect is this to the gods. They
in their fury and grace send us huge hardship to urge us
into glory. Seize then the challenge. For none of this is
combat against ourselves. May the great immortals watch
over your venture.'

Now when the king had called thus to them, Meleager
waved his thanks, and ordered the cavalcade to spur forward. Out through the ringing gate of the palace with
echoing hoofs they then sped, and through the wide-paced
street to the city walls. Great cheering and belling of quick-
eared hounds was there among the houses then, and the
rising sun flashed on keen-oiled spears. With nets and
bows, quivers of arrows, their feathers tipped with scarlet,
the wide-cloaked, bronzed and naked heroes rode. Yet
when they came once again before the temple of Artemis,
there did they stop amazed at what they saw.

For there sped Althaea, the fierce-eyed queen, bustling
her wan handmaids, driving them to pile high great logs
and branches. A bier did they build before the temple,
where the altar to the goddess stood, and hurriedly they
criss-crossed the wood and raised it high. Now went
Althaea with a jar of wine, casting libations about, decking
the steps and the temple with garlands and leaves, and
when she saw the hunters coming, she stopped and smiled
at them, and she too called to them from the steps.

'Hunt well, young men,' so spoke the queen. 'Be sure
the quarry is yours, and in your zeal be sure you have the
right quarry. To offer what you kill today in the forest I
build here a pyre. To Artemis will your fine sacrifice be
burnt. Be sure then you bring back the best of the catch.
The flames will await your return. In triumph will then we
women dance among the smoke. But know this, Meleager,
not one word have I broken of our talk. No blame upon
me for what today unfolds.' And the queen turned away

200

then, and shouted to her maids, driving them with fury to work, and the hunters rode on towards the gate.

Bright now were the fields with ripening morning. Against the ochre-dry grass the silvery olives shone upon the hills. Across grove and meadow the eager hounds ran, chasing the bounding hare, while the poplars to the plashing stream spilled their leaves. From the distant hills came the countryfolk, under the chalk-blue sky, for the rumour apace went of the twelve from Olympia, and already the scouts came riding fierce from the heights and forests with news of the cunning tracks of the monster Boar. Meleager received them, then led his forces along the boulder-strewn torrent, and so the masses crawled towards the mountains.

Now when they were riding, Meleager brought the youth Rhexenor to his side, and drawing apart talked to him in secret. Thus he said, 'Some strike in the night has been made against us, and we have other dangers than the Boar. Now youth, Rhexenor, it seems to me that my uncles have guessed your sex. Wherefore they will be spoiling for their sacrifice. Turn you then aside when we come to the farm at the start of the valley beyond. Hide there this day. Give this ring as a token to the farmer. So shall we frustrate the treachery of Plexippus and Toxeus, and give ourselves further time to plan our actions.'

But Rhexenor said, 'Nay then, my companion, this can I never do. Atalanta turns not back from a chase. When we are married there may come the time for me to obey your each command, but this divorce this day I cannot tolerate. The goddess is angry whatever I do. To have turned against her, and yet to quit from striking: this would be cowardice. Nor can I do it, wise though I grant it. I beseech you, Meleager, of these things ask me no more.' And the girl was silent. Nor did the hero mention the plan again, but rode on overseeing the train.

Now surged the procession in happy pomp along the thundering brook, where the willows bleached their long leaves by the pools. With trumpet and horn they made loud their way, singing hunting songs, and letting loose to chase any beast that stirred their yapping dogs. From sun-shuttered ponds the ducks splashed up, quacking with sudden alarm, the tall heron swooped looping-winged over the woods. Amidst burrows and banks each happy hound thrust his muddy nose, and flapping-eared went cantering through the brambles. Meanwhile, were the rose-hips ripening fast amidst the silver birches, and the rowan-tree burnt crimson against the sky.

But now came a baying. At the edge of a wood, where the trees were tossed and thrown down, the hounds were running, scattering in terror. Some stood there fierce, their backs in hackles roused with stiffening horror, while the huntsmen could by no means whip them away. The twelve studied the track. The Boar had been there, yet the dogs by the scent were afeard and slunk low-tailed behind the horses. Up a hazelled valley the huntsmen rode to spy from a vantage-point if there was any sign of the giant. No call did there come. So they rode on, whipping the frightened hounds to follow the trail, and came to a gloomy forest.

Dark and bitter was the fir-wood that shut out the sun's light, and spidery the branches of the trees. They hesitated, pondering where best to make their entrance, for the hounds seemed certain that the Boar had gone that way. Round and about with whimpering yelps the dogs sniffed the torn-up earth, till they found at last a great hole crashed amidst the trees, and fir-trees were there snapped from their trunks, by the might of some monster thrust aside, and here through this channel in darkness they rode in.

Like night hung the black fir-boughs about them, and with weirdly echoing calls the hounds made the woods seem haunted by many ghosts. By the broken branches they followed swiftly, the horses sniffing with alarm, and the thudding of their hoofs filled the shady forest. As they drove down a dell, a forester's cottage they came across by a brook, and the forester and his wife were staring amazed.

'Good countrymen,' then said Meleager, 'did you see

the Boar pass here by? Is it indeed the monster's tracks we follow?'

And the man said, 'Ay, here be the Boar: he be passed two hours ago. We feared for our cottage at his heaving sides. Do you hunt him down swiftly, noblemen, whoever you are. We live our lives in terror of the beast. Yet watch, for the Boar be vicious and cunning, and the saying is that his hide against all men be stiffened.'

Meleager bowed, and spurred on his horse, leading his men up again. Rhexenor beside him smiled to herself. And so they passed through the gloomy wood, and came to the hills again, and made in their ranks into a sheltered valley.

Vineyards were here, stretched out on the slopes facing the southern sun, and gold their tired leaves shimmered along the elm-boughs. From far off they heard the hearty chorus of the peasants of the vale, who trod their vintage now deep-dyed in the vats. Linking arm in arm thigh-deep in grape-mush with swaying knees a-lifting, they chanted to squash the purple wine from the fumy brew. To them came the hunters. A clatter of horses made the peasants stare. They looked up grinning with bows bound in ivy and vine.

'Good countrymen,' then called Meleager to them, 'the Boar-Giant have ye seen? We come to bring it this day to its final home.'

But the peasants replied, 'We have seen no Boar this year since the wintertime. Then came he this way, yourself after him.'

'True enough,' called back Meleager. 'His track was beyond the ridge. Thanks, wine-treaders. *Io Bacche*, and have good vintage!' And he turned his horse from the farmstead then, and faced again to the summits, but thereon bounded now the bristles of the Boar.

With a hush of horror the vale fell silent, and each hound and each spear-clutching hunter grew cold to view the power and size of the beast, for now did it jerk by, cresting rashly the fir-woods of the range, above which its spiny hog-hairs stood up like pines. Like masts of eye-painted ships they stood, that cluster in the howling harbour, when the gale drives in crashing breakers from the north. With pelting grey showers the storm comes down, bedraggling the tackle and sails, clashing the hulls ruinously in the spume. So did that monster's back appear. But then with a far-baying snarl, its head flung up. Its fierce tusks hooked the sky.

With cries of alarm the peasants then ran, their vats spilling reeking must, the ground stained scarlet with the bubbling grape-juice. In yelps of fright the hounds went streaking, darting away to the shelter of bush and bramble, peering hence with white-rimmed eyes. In flinching regard the huntsmen stood, looking this way and that, seeking what ground might give them vantage or safety. But the Boar stared at them. It sniffed the air, with pig-eyes squinting to the distance. Then sensing trouble it jumped up on the summit.

Bunch-necked and mad did the bristled flanks of the beast root in the woods, like a copse of firs burnt by forest-fires. For a while it trotted along the top, romping with hog-back, its hoofs scuttling huge slabs of the peak away. It was descending to a valley beyond their own, its feet were sliding on the ridge. But then with impatience did it spin about. Snorting in sudden rage, it turned instead and set towards the hunters, and bounded down into the valley of vineyards.

In fury it thrust its tusks about, or ever it came upon them, this way and that lashing down the trees and the vines. Ripping the labour of the year, it tore up the elms and their vine-plants, tangling the bunchy leaves and grapes about its snout. Eyeing the peasants it pounced at them, seeking to pass through to the valley. It bit and savaged the hounds and the beasts of burden. With dog's guts splashed, with horse's blood spattered gleaming along its sides, it upturned the vats and covered itself in wine. Reeking crimson the Boar roared, murder all about, the bowels of an ox tangling its slaughter-red tusks.

So it swept past. Meleager hurled his lance to catch it

behind the ear, but down it clattered making no dent in the beast. Acastus that had his horse swung about, rode alongside the monster and sought to heave his lance into its belly. No force could pierce it. Now Dryas and Lelex shot their arrows at its spine. The hog-back shrugged the feathered tufts away. The house now did the Boar attack. Leaping at the barrier, he cast apart its walls, then reared up with the roof upon his horns. Thrashing with this he stabbed a mounted farmer that joined the band, and here fell the first huntsman to his rage. Transfixed with the beam-splint, the man slid groaning into the tumbled vats, and human gore now ran amidst the wine.

'Why now,' said Acastus, 'this is a beast beyond the size of Nature! How can we kill it? Our weapons make no marks!'

'There's four of us struck it!' shouted Castor. 'Not one weapon has made a mark. His sides are invulnerable to our blades.'

'Let's four strike together,' then cried Meleager. 'See, where it turns about. Come! Ride!' He led his men with a shout.

The four horsemen spurred towards the monster, and hurling their second spears, hummed four pikes at its bunched-up neck.

With a roar the Boar shrugged the blades away. They clattered tamely to the ground. Then did the pig rage and thrust about with its tusks. Two other farmers it gored and ripped. From their hideaway it tossed them forth. One split with blood, the other lodged on its horns. The boar, now crimson, danced like a demon, thrashing in grapes and flesh, casting about vats, bones, hounds, spears and debris. Then snorting loud it ran at the hunters, burst through their flinching ranks, and rending the boughs ran off through the trees.

'Oh, this is a monster of the gods indeed!' then cried Ancaeus in anguish. 'We should not have ranged ourselves against it. Why, it is covered in gore and wine like a sacrifice! It will take us all if we have after it! Look, how the farmers lament their carnage. All here is destroyed! Let us home! It is not pious to hunt it! Let us home!'

'Stay on your horse and fight!' then cried Meleager, and lashed him with his whip over his back. 'No men will quit this havoc, I say, until the Boar is dead. We will after, and strike at him again! Acastus, do you take four men back down the valley-track, and where that brook joined the stream: go up into the hill, and set there your nets blocking the plain. Then drive up to meet us in the heights.'

Meleager led his men on again. 'We rest will pursue through the beech-wood.' So did he ride off with his men in fury.

But Caeneus stayed to lament. 'Alas,' he cried, 'what carnage! What poor souls have here been rent of their lives! See, how the poor countryman is torn and gored by the tusks of the beast! What mess and blood bring an end to this grieving harvest!' And he wept thus, until Acastus called to him to spur on, for now were they to ride into the valley. And so the last of the hunters rode away from the vineyard's slopes, and there was sudden silence alone left behind.

But the peasants stayed long to weep their carnage. Their life was a broken farm. With tears and sorrow they greeted now the wreck of the spilled vintage. Their year's work done, their neighbours lost, a sacrifice of blood: this was their offering to the killer. With their sad howls the feast of the wine was turned in the year's death to Dionysus' tragic dithyramb. But the others rode on, and following the hot trail of their monstrous quarry, to the beech-wood came and entered among the silent boughs.

Hushed was it in the woods where they rode on the tracks of the beast, sounding their horns when any had sight of the Boar. The day grew warm in the calling trees, with flutter of wings and snapping twigs, and the mystery of the forest hung thick about them. Then spoke Atalanta, 'The Boar is biding us now in his old home. He seeks his cave in the valley beyond. He is grim for fight.' So did they press on through the brakes and thickets, and sleepy noon befuddled the cries of hounds.

Here riding aslant Meleager and Rhexenor came now the two uncles. In the secret heat, where the moths and flies buzzed round, they stared at the pair with knowing eyes, fingering their spears. Rhexenor looked down, but Meleager gazed at them puzzled. 'Your favourite, we see, is a fair-faced youth,' then said Toxeus smiling. 'Such eyes and lips he has as would befit a woman. Take care he comes to no injury with the rage of the beast, for the Boar is surely a sacred beast of Artemis.' So did the pair glide away again, and were lost in the sun-dappled paths, while still the hunting-horns were mournfully braying.

By a lake they then rode where shafts of sunbeams fell into the brown water, and the idle frog was browsing by lily-pads. Here did the soft summer seem still suspended, where bulrushes burst with their down, and the red admirals were settled on elder-berries. Meleager looked at his riding-mate and said, 'We must watch two ways: before to the Boar and behind to the uncles. They boast and tell us. You are their quarry. Do not ride in front of their spears, and I will watch them ever as I can.'

Tall were the sandy rocks of the hazelled canyon where now the hunters came, and the valley led down through pine-trees to their left. Of resin smelt these sun-baked woods, and cicadas sang in the trunks, and from down the valley Acastus' men were heard calling. The tracks of the Boar were lost among rocks. Atalanta studied the pine-needles. Ancaeus pointed the way down the valley. But Atalanta shook her head, and showed the road upwards. 'He is gone to his lair,' she said, 'up in the heights.'

While Acastus drove from his nets in the valley, the others now set themselves to beat upwards in a half-moon through the canyon. They dallied while Lelex and Caeneus scaled the thistle-strewn cliff to peer for the Boar from the lonely summit. The scouts saw nothing. Acastus now arrived with his band. Sleepy and still were the autumn copses. So did they join in crescent ranks and thrash up the pebbly slope. So did they find a giant cave in the rocks.

With bones and skulls scattered about was that fly-blown place, while the sun struck from on high the cracking soil. In chilly breath the cavern loomed, echoing to their steeds' steps, and the stones that slipped from their uncertain hoofs. The horses whinnied. With roaming eyes they backed from the darkness within. Yet Dryas strode from his mount deep into the earth. But Atalanta shook her head. 'Here the Boar is not.' She peered about. 'Yet harken a while.'

There came a shriek of startled horses and a clatter of fleeing hoofs, as those tethered outside the cave broke free and bolted. The Boar rushed on them. With savaging tusks he gored the stallion of Dryas and flung the hounds yelping against the cliff. Now Caeneus did he hurl from his horse, goring his calf with his tusks. In blood the boy fell scrabbling up the slope. Now set he on Nestor, that with his spear was walking towards the cave. The man ran fast with the cloven hoofs fast after.

Now slung Acastus his second lance. It clanged down ineffectual. Nestor was but a pace from the gnashing Boar. Yet with fear quick-thinking, he used his tall spear to pole vault from his charge: he jumped in a pine-tree and clung on for his life. Now Dryas hurled forth. Now brawny Peleus. Polydeuces and his twin ran round by the heights and drove down with their spears. The missiles rained, but no man's weapon could pierce the skin of the beast: such was the magic power laid upon him. But Lelex and Atalanta now drew their bows tight to their chins and loosed their flighty arrows towards the beast. Lelex's glanced off, but Atalanta's struck the monster by his ear. The Boar roared furious. Meleager shouted in joy.

'The triumph is yours, my Atalanta! It needed a woman to strike!' But she frowned hard and hushed him with her hands.

'Why, there you salute her with truth at last!' then cried Plexippus in delight. 'Rash Meleager, you have delivered our prize! It may have needed a woman thus to make a wound upon the Boar, but now this woman is quarry for the goddess. She struck the first blow against Artemis, and now has she struck her last! Brother, leave the Boar: here is our sacrifice! Let us kill this woman, first to the city, in honour of our deity! Come! Attack! Now is our revenge!' And Plexippus ran with Toxeus hungrily ready to kill the girl. Yet Meleager flung at him his humming spear.

Plexippus thus was crossing with rash hand to seize the huntress, his other bearing unsheathed his fatal blade, but the spear of Meleager came winging famished, and thudded into his chest, piercing the rib-cage, sagging as it lodged. Plexippus gazed with dread and saw the lance set fast in him, the blood of his inwards over his belly gushing. With a gasp of despair he tottered forward, and all gazed at him appalled, while Toxeus shouted, and black-faced drew his sword.

Yet set the Boar raging. It turned in the glen, while Caeneus ran after, but he by a root stumbled and skidded to earth. Peleus to his help rushed with spears, while Lelex drew out his bow, and here he sunk another shaft into the beast. Toxeus, meanwhile, came down on Meleager to strike him with his sword. The hero drew his and parried him by the cave. Now pounced the Boar back. Meleager caught Toxeus' hair and held him, twisting his neck. Then did he slit his throat.

Spurning him in the dust then Meleager cast him towards his brother. Plexippus stared, transfixed on his knees. As one sunk down, the other also gasped into the darkness. The two brothers fell in blood at the feet of the Boar.

Now closed they about, the panting huntsmen, Peleus with javelin poised, Acastus with bow, the twins with hand-axes watching their time. The glen by the cave reeked of blood, and thudded to panting lungs, as the wild giant scattered the spume from his rowdy jaws.

Yet raged Ancaeus, 'Let me take the beast! A woman has struck the first blow. So she may have broken the spell upon it. But it will be a man, I swear to the gods, that fells this monster. In spite of Artemis thus will I do it!' And with these words he rushed forth, clasping a two-headed axe, threatening with the weapon in both hands. The Boar snorted at him, then charged low, aiming its tusks at his belly, and in spurting blood ripped him to the neck. So lurched Ancaeus, and his axe, and tossed by the Boar in the air, he thudded down on the crimson floor of death.

'Now fell this beast!' cried out Acastus. 'Ere any more of us fall. See where his cave is swimming in gore and blood! Castor, Polydeuces, aim for his skull! Set your javelin behind his ear, Peleus. Now Dryas, thrust under his belly from where you are. With this cast I curse him! Gods, aim my blow! Set on all for the kill! Now must we launch together!'

And when Peleus had called these orders, then did the band prepare. They drew back their arms, with the last of the lances aiming. Then did they strike. Acastus shouting hurled forth his cornel spear, which hummed through the air with its teeth of heavy bronze. Castor and Polydeuces crashed down with their axes from their vantage point, and into the skull of the beast set their blades hard. Now let loose Lelex his fiery points. Now Dryas span forth his spear. Now spearless Eurytion flung boulders on the foe.

And while Atalanta sped her arrows, shaft after shaft into the belly, there came Meleager, sad vengeance in his heart. With bitter mood he approached the beast, watching its head bedecked with foam. Then when it bellowed, ran under its tusks and neck. Thus did he jab his sword in deep, cutting under its jaw into the tongue. Then did he drive his lance thereafter to its brain. The beast shuddered rigid. Meleager pushed home. Curling up its throat, the bristling foe fell, lashing out amidst the carnage.

The heroes struck home again. Hosts of shafts dug into his shaggy flanks. The heaving hog-flanks lurched and twitched at their stabs. With foam-spewing breath the boar struggled yet to rouse and kill and live. The heroes dug hard and fetched his guts onto the ground. They carved,

210

each man, each clustering about, hacking his ribs and entrails, opening his veins, drenching themselves in blood.

All ebbed to stillness. The grunting heaves of the frothing lungs of the monster bellowed their last, and mournful was the sound. The Boar was dead. The panting heroes stood about their sacrifice. The sounds of the wood-doves came again in the trees.

Then spoke Meleager. 'The hunt is done. Friends, we have settled our task. The band of Kalydon have this day their triumph. In leafy Olympia we strove hard, and here our arts are graced with triumph over the hardships sent by the gods. Alas, yet this catch of mine is bitter! Much blood has been shed, and it was not alone of the Boar. These bodies of ours to the town of Kalydon, we must on lances bear home, and a true funeral give to each man.

'My friends, I have been your leader these months. Unworthy you have found me, yet loyal has each man been to my rash charge. It cannot be long that I speak to you as your task's commander. Wherefore let me thank each soul for his good heart. You saw, I think, you were witnesses all of my slaying of these priests, and assuredly have I stained my hands with my kinsmen's blood. Wherefore in defilement a type of exile or penance will be mine. And hence is it I must bid you soon adieu.

'Yet till that time, let me lead still. Come then, for we are victors. Carve the Boar hence. Let us have forest-lore. Lop off his tusks, and let Atalanta, who was the first to strike, bear them, as is tradition, in victory home. So let us hurry, for the noon has passed, and the sun begins to slacken. Dark is the triumph we have sought so long.'

Chapter Twenty-four

But in high-walled Kalydon at the palace, where the royal apartments looked out over woods at the onset of evening, there raged the angry Althaea against King Oeneus, her husband, and thus did she spin about and assail him. For thus she said, 'Why now you are a milksop to his pride! Is this the girl you would have chosen for a princess? What of the royal house of Akarnia, or Epirus of sturdy horses, and what of your long-serving Locrian allies? Them you insult for Arcady! What is this barbaric place? Its shepherds are backward and its land lost in the hills! She never, she never would suit either our kingdom or our son. Truly with your mildness you would ruin all! Oh, well is it I have two brothers who see the dangers of these things! Goddess Artemis, aid them in your rage!'

But then spoke King Oeneus sadly, 'Yet surely he must love this girl, and her has he brought to his home before he marries her. And what of the insult to Arcady, if we now send her back? Arcadia has powerful allies. Who would venture the wrath of Sparta? That would not I. Yet I would that you had told me earlier of this subterfuge. I might have noted her then at peace. But this boy you say is her: he seemed well spoken, he seemed good looking certainly.'

'Good-looking! Ay,' said the queen, 'a whore: she's that already! But she'll not prosper, long-legged beast of the woods! I saw them in his room together! Such deceit and lying and subterfuge! She has made him crafty as well as rash! But she'll not be long the siren of my son! Whatever comes to her now is deserved! She'll not be long the witch of Kalydon! Yet I would not have told you about her, were it not Plexippus and Toxeus guessed her cunning of their own observation. Why, those my brothers have sharp eyes!

212

Would you had half their wit! It is they should rule this kingdom, not yourself! Yet she will not endure my spite. The deed is perhaps done. Meleager will rage, but he can do nothing. Yet you are deceived when you say that for you Meleager has mellowed. No, my son burns yet with hatred of his mother! I will not trust his wrath today. You will see him mad. I'll have his brand, or he will seek my death!' But Queen Althaea ceased her fury, for now beyond the window she saw far off the dust of the hunt's return.

'Why now,' she breathed, 'the men approach, the hunters are home with their prize! Do I see them bear there the body of their quarry? Do I hear their horns braying in triumph that the gods have been appeased? Indeed, indeed fair is the sacrifice! Oh, see, my king, now. If my brothers are true, your realm will be safe! You will be purged of the goddess you insulted. Long rage has Artemis, but now with her sacrifice we shall dance in her honour, I and my maidens by the funeral pyre!' And Althaea went rushing then. Across the floors she hurried her steps, and black and fierce was the light in her eyes.

Now the pyre stood ready before the temple, festooned with leaves, of Artemis, and the maidens awaited the queen for the ritual. With urns and jars they stood scarfed about under veils and holy robes, ready to sprinkle the sacrificial fire. To them came Althaea. Laughing in madness, she danced with torches in her hands, waving the smoking brands through the descending dusk, and with gay steps she capered to the maidens and called, 'Ho, girls of the Ortygian, here am I come to set our fun ablaze! This will sparkle your eyes! A meat will we roast on this furious furnace that will feed our stomachs to contentment!'

And when the queen had spoken these words, she lit all the torches of pitch, so that they blazed with bitter-eyed smoke by the pyre. And angry tongues of flame licked out towards the funeral pyres, while the maidens stood back, fearfully guarding their jars of oil. Then did there approach the citizens, old men and wives of the town, coming to see what shrieks and madness was in the square, and with dread they watched, as the flush-cheeked queen, her robes falling from her shoulders, danced with dishevelled hair in the market-place. And the king came also gravely to watch. But the queen now ran through the streets, and panting with eagerness, rushed to look from the walls.

Through the evening fields the procession came, with horns blowing the hunt's return, and many countryfolk cheering the trophies of the Boar. With poles decked in vine-leaves, and swags of grapes, the carts were pranked for vintage, lumbering through the long shadows of the golden elms. Meanwhile, in glee the peasants pranced with waving pieces of the Boar. Here were his trotters, carried between four youths. Here was his tail, curly and snakelike, swirled about by Acastus. Here bobbed his ears by Lelex borne. The sad Meleager marched with boar-hair lodged in his travelling-cap, and Atalanta weighed down at his side, for the strapping huntress now bore on her breast the two huge tusks of the Boar, and they reached up like a canopy over her head.

But the queen called far off, 'Ho, homeward hunters! Hurry before night falls. I would see your triumph in the sun! You have slain the Boar! But I see moreover a bier borne among you! Shout to me: who, alas, has been killed! Could it be some youth of Sparta perhaps? Or a braving lad of Argos? Or Rhexenor of Arcady, pray that it is not he! Such a fair-faced youth! What would the great goddess do with his sacrifice? Come near! Come near! This do I long to behold!' And Althaea darted madly down, laughing and dancing with spite, and she hurried round to the gate where the huntsmen came.

But the first of the hunters were entering now, and cheers and jokes were abounding, as the people of the town rushed to welcome their saviours. For upon the walls and from the houses, they leaned and waved their garlands, and girls flung rose leaves red-lipped from the balconies. Meanwhile, the procession with ringing tubas marched swaggering into the streets, and the queen danced still, rioting at its side. But now she slackened, and looking about came to silence awhile, for dazed by the joy she could not see her brothers. Wherefore she went back and looked again at the tail of the procession, and began to comb the hunters with distrust.

Then King Oeneus greeted them, as they neared the flames of the torches, and he called, 'Now welcome in triumph, you men of victory! In Olympic spirit have you thus joined and reaped the triumph of the year, for your mighty band has slain the Boar that all dreaded. Hail then, O heroes! Great tripods are yours, bowls and victory cups. From the walls of Kalydon you will go loaded away, for our scourge is dead, the ravager of fields, the wreckers of my vines; this beast is gone, and Kalydon is again free. I salute your spirit, you men of Hellas. Meleager, my glorious son, I salute the fire and wisdom that brought you here.'

And Meleager answered and said, 'My father, I thank you for your good heart, and for all this triumph and all my men I thank you. Hard was this won, this hunt of ours, and long was the gathering for it. Vexed was the time wherein we formed the Kalydon band. Yet we have accomplished. The land is purged. The Boar has quit our vineyards. Alas, father, yet he has not gone without cost. Ancaeus of Arcady is no more. Caeneus and others are wounded. The countryfolk themselves have met with losses. And king, and countrymen, this must I tell you: the Princess of Arcady: she I brought home, trusting soon to marry. In her defence, for they set upon her, seeking to slaughter her, I have killed the priests, my kinsmen, Plexippus and Toxeus. Slain at the height of the Boar-Hunt were they, and here on biers are they brought, ready for Artemis' funeral flames. I am armed for whatever penance is set me. Yet this I would you remember: them I killed as they sought to kill my betrothed.'

A shriek then came from the anguished queen, and furious and rabid she rushed, and saw on the bier her brothers side by side, defiled in black blood, pallid in death, bemocked from the hunt. And the queen beat her breast, and loud was her lament. But then did she stop and stare at Meleager, and fixed him a ghastly gaze. And she looked to the torches burning their crackling brands. And she stood in the smoke beneath the sunset, and cold and hard was her stare. Into the palace she walked with no words more.

'What fearful news is this?' then said Oeneus. 'It is a blow of grief to hear such slaughter defiles your triumph. Penance indeed is yours, my son, for in the slaughter of kinsmen, a man is cursed by the very Furies. Harsh and blood-rimmed are the eyes, clotted the ghastly locks, savage and long the nails of these Eumenides. Flee them, my poor son, for they will drive you to madness, murderer of your kin. For there is no revenge for such a slaughterer! Alas, yet the monster is gone from us! What trouble has rained in its stead! Is there no end to Kalydon's lamentations? Ah, why do I in truth not now quit this weary world, that have stayed in it too long to see this slaughter?' And the king in bitter tears went also on his grieving way. But Meleager stayed and spoke thus to the people.

'Burn now the bodies of the fallen in the funeral pyre,' he called, 'though for others this burning was prepared. Let them and the grim recoils of Fate have hereupon their ceremony, for truly the pyre is built for its victim. Set on the bodies. Light the pyres. It may not be long ere others burn of the heroes of the hunt. The night sinks fast on Kalydon. Dashed is our merriment, men. Yet you have on! Rejoice at the hunt of the Boar. No better band has ever been in Hellas together gathered. I quit you now, saluting your victory.'

And Meleager then took a torch from the lines, and when the bodies were placed, he set the first of the flames of the funeral pyre, and he fired the branches that lay netted at the foot of the wood, and the glow went inwards seeking the luscious twigs. Then came smoke forth. Then roared the flames. The other heroes set to their brands. Now did red fires lick ravenously the sky. And Meleager turned now, and walked away, and entered the walls of the palace, and Atalanta in sadness hurried after.

But when they were in Meleager said, 'There is no hope for us now, but catching the queen and snatching from her the brand. For she is like to set her own son on the pyre this dusk. Nor have I indeed much spirit to prevent her. The Furies and a life of exile; these are my prizes promised. Bitter and short is the joy of winning. But truly the log she has locked away bears my life in it, and this day for sure she will sacrifice it.' And so they hurried through the palace, seeking for the queen. But nowhere did they find her among the galleries.

Yet within the palace, the king also was searching among the chambers, and he went quickly and asked after Althaea. And he said to his chamberlain, 'Stay the queen, if you should see her in her chamber, for she is like to fetch out Meleager's brand. Crazy for vengeance is the woman, and should she have his talisman, onto the fire she will cast it for good.' And together the two of them searched her room, found the chest and opened it. But therein they discovered no purple-wrapped wood.

Yet the queen was running, and from the secret spot she had lodged by the gate, she snatched up the scarf and log, and ran again to the square. Dancing she came, crazed with vengeance among the rejoicing crowds, and they parted to let her once more towards the funeral. Althaea laughed, and holding aloft from its purple veil the brand, she capered among the huntsmen who knew it not.

But then King Oeneus in ghastly haste came again to the steps and cried, 'Althaea, give back, give back that totem! How can you think to burn this outer soul of your own child? How can you think to set on the flames your son?'

But the crazy queen laughed, and into the fires she hurled both scarf and brand, and the fire dislodged and fell in roaring sparks.

Now the hero Meleager in the palace was seeking the

217

queen's chamber, when he felt inside him wracked with sudden pain. His inwards were mightily torn with fire, and the anguish made him slack, and he fell to the ground, catching Atalanta's hand. And he said to the princess, 'She has the brand. My heart is afire. She has put it in flames. There is no more to do.'

But the huntress left him, and ran instead full-pelt, swift-footed in the palace, and into the square, bursting on the fires and cries. And she leapt at the pyre and pulled it apart, scattering it with her hands, while Althaea in crazy spite danced laughing round.

Then came the king, and the queen he seized, dragged her back by her hair, and forced her to look where was the burning brand. Meanwhile, he called for water-buckets and the people to quench the flames, and the citizens ran to execute his orders.

Then shouted Atalanta, 'Meleager's life is tied to the brand she threw. Hunters, come seek to save the wood from burning.' Meanwhile the people hurrying up, threw the water from their little buckets, and fumes and steam brewed in the agora.

But grim with hoarse cries, in agony twisted, filling the palace with rage, there came Meleager, mad for the fire's pain. Aghast were they all, to watch his fever, for sweat stood on his brow, his veins bulged blue, and flaming his naked breast.

On the logs yet he fell, and the huntress beside him, and many of the band now, pulling forth flames, hissing, burning their hands, while to the square lamenting now with shrieks the palace-women came, and filled with wailing and weeping the garlanded city.

But above the twisted smoke of the town, rejoicing in the turmoil, the goddess Artemis laughed with her glittering weapons. With eager eyes she watched the riot, stirring the fumes with her spear, and clouds of black vengeance did she swirl about her.

'Now see,' she called, 'my implacable anger, people of Kalydon. Thus do I fan and whip the grief of sinners! Note

218

well, note well how into Hades go those I resent! All their hunting is come to this havoc!'

And she swirled again with her spiteful lance, brewing the smoke and flame, and the fire and the brands were thus all indistinguishable. Nor could the hunters or the huntress find Meleager's brand. And the hero cried aloud in pain of the fire.

Then did he race towards the air, and ran back in the palace, and seeking to breathe clambered gasping up the stairs. And the huntress ran after the dying hero, weeping to hear his groans, as apace he staggered to the terrace by his chamber. And when he came there, the air was cool, and the mists of twilight approached, and the hills and forest were grey in the dusk before him.

And Atalanta came to him, as he fell on the floor of the terrace, and the sun sunk down on the woods now purged of the Boar. And kneeling beside him, she took his head and held him in her lap, and she stroked his blackened brow and tangled hair.

But Meleager gasped, 'I die, Atalanta. Nor have I made you my wife. Wherefore, as I said, seek protection of Heracles. Have no more ado here, but haste away. Join Dryas or Acastus of the band, or lingering Lelex, for he returns to Olympia. Of hope is no more. Oh, my poor princess, what good have I done you now? In my rash days I led you from your safety. Farewell now for ever. We would have bred a race of strength, you and I. But one of us was tied to a fickle brand. Take watch. Keep safely. The sun is running. I shall catch him up. Westwards, westwards I go alone.'

'You go not alone,' said then Atalanta. 'Of your brand you spoke long ago. Of mine, being a woman, till now I kept silent. An apple of gold. See: how it gleams as the autumn sun declines. Long ago my life like yours was linked to this totem. I have kept it safe, for it holds my soul. To lose or misplace it is death. You see now why I stopped in the race at the Games? This I thought you had found where I hid it. It was for this I lost. But thus

219

I spurn it. With you I chase the sun.' And she took from her robes the shining sphere, and cast it over the mists, and flung the golden apple to the west.

But Artemis saw this from the clouds, and pity now wracked her heart, and sighing she spoke with tears at the virgin's death. 'Alas, Atalanta, my cruel maid, why cast you your life away, ending your days for the sake of this one man? Wherefore did you shake off − though sundered from me − all your fierce purity, for the sake of this prince, the man who dies beside you?' And sighing the goddess stared at the bodies, and altered was her heart, and tears of regret began to stain her cheeks.

But the bodies were changing, as the dead lovers lay in each other's arms, and golden their limbs were glittering with new glory. And beside the goddess, in the clouds of the sunset, the sun-god Apollo came, and naked he blazed over the smoking city.

And Phoebus said, 'Nay then, cruel sister, the ways of the gods are just, and heaven gives recompense for earthly suffering. By command of Zeus to Olympus' summit together shall these lovers be raised, and dying young, they shall be married in heaven.'

Appendix: The Homeric Epic and *Pangaia*

The Epic

The epic form is the most serious and grand in all literature. It has been a tradition among the Greeks, Romans, Mesopotamians, Hindus, Persians, Teutons and Modern Europeans to seek to enshrine the origins of their culture in epics. The classic example of genre is to be found in the epics of Homer. While his poems epitomise the heroic, grand and simple quality which is universal among epics, they have a strength, beauty and fire which singles them out as perfect models for the revival of the epic form.

Epic Structure

Homer's epics have a structure which is ideally dramatic, and unites all the work in a single span. In the very earliest section of the work they reveal a central and critical problem, which is the basic concern of the story. When this has been expounded, the epic turns to peripheral matters in an enrichening of interest. Around the halfway point, however, the epic returns to grappling with the central problem, advances steadily upon it thereafter, and reaches a climax of engagement just before the end of the work. This is the grid on which the famous epic actions such as battles, parades, journeys to Hell and prophecies are all ordered, and this has been the plan followed with some variations in the epics of *Pangaia*. In *Olympiad* there is a similarity of book-numbering, since the twenty-four chapters mirror those of *The Odyssey* in advancing in four-book movements.

Epic Style

Homer's epics have a style distinguished by objectivity, grandeur and universality. It is a poetic style that pictures everything at its maximum integrity and flavour, and concentrates on action unfolding in the light of timeless values. The narrative advances in clear and sizeable chunks. The scenes are conceived dramatically, the descriptions are dynamic, and the dialogue is structured by means of complete speeches. In the epic of *Krishna* the dignity of the style was played down for the sake of a folktale element. All the other epics attempt to maintain the style throughout.

Greek Metre

An innovation of *Olympiad* is the insertion of four poems, which use the ancient quantitative techniques of Greek metre. Homer's own metre, the quantitative hexameter, is used for two of the poems, and these are in the traditional genre of pastoral songs and utterances of the Delphic Oracle. Later metres: those of Sappho, who gave her name to the lyric metre, and Pindar the great composer of odes on the Olympics, are used for a lyric and an ode, the ode being composed in the metre of Pindar's *Second Olympian*. It has always been maintained by critics and writers of books on prosody that quantitative metres cannot be used in English. These four quantitative poems are the first ever published in the language, and could open up a new road for English poetry.

Celestial Machinery

In Homer's epics the principle of *celestial machinery* makes the action of the book take place on two levels. While the narrative action concerns men and is often tragic, the commentative action concerns the gods and is usually comic. The interaction of the two, with the gods influencing and directing human affairs, can be seen as a way of depicting human actions on a deep and universal level. This mythostorical method discovers a divine drama behind the scenes of human history.

Pangaia

The name *Pangaia* means the whole world from the Greek *pan* meaning *all*, and the Greek *Gaia* meaning *earth*. It has been well used, in a different spelling, as the name of the first supreme continent from which in geological terms all present continents broke away. Used here, it can be taken as the name of the current world-civilisation, and a suitable title for a series of works on the origins and nature of the modern world.

Pangaia: published works

Series	Sequence
Krishna	*Jormundgand* (AD 378)
Asgard	*Dragon* (AD 383)
Olympiad	